Ragnarok and Roll

Including:

Ragnarok and Roll
Undine the Boardwalk
I Believe I'm Sinkin' Down
Love Over and Over
Cayo Hueso – Part 1: A Farewell to Cats
Cayo Hueso – Part 2: The Buck Stops Here
Cayo Hueso – Part 3: Twisting Fate
God of Blunder
Bonus track: How *You* Can Prevent Forest Fires…

Ragnarok and Roll

Tales of Cassie Zukav,
Weirdness Magnet

Keith R.A. DeCandido

Plus One Press
San Francisco

Plus One Press

www.plusonepress.com

Book Design by Plus One Press

"Ragnarok and Roll" copyright © 2011
    (appeared in *Tales From the House Band Volume 1*, Plus One Press, 2011)
"I Believe I'm Sinkin' Down" copyright © 2012
    (appeared in *Tales From the House Band Volume 2*, Plus One Press, 2012)
"How You Can Prevent Forest Fires…" copyright © 1997
    (appeared in *Urban Nightmares*, Baen Books, 1997)

Song lyrics from "Just Came Down for the Weekend"
  Copyright © 1994 by Michael McCloud, used by permission

Bio photograph copyright © 2009 Tina Randleman, used by permission.

Cover photo of shield and axe copyright © 2010 by Maurits Knook, used under Creative Commons Attribution 2.0 Generic (CC BY 2.0)

ISBN: 978-0-9860085-6-6

2013936511

First Edition: August, 2013

10 9 8 7 6 5 4 3 2 1

Dedicated to the memory of Josepha Sherman, who edited the first-ever Cassie Zukav story in Urban Nightmares *way back in 1997. Rest in peace, old friend...*

Acknowledgments

Primary thanks to my editor and publisher Deborah Grabien, who bought "Ragnarok and Roll" and "I Believe I'm Sinkin' Down" for the first two *Tales from the House Band* anthologies, and is the one who said to me that what she really wanted to see was a collection of Cassie stories. Her editorial notes were magnificent and wonderful.

Secondary, and still pretty large, thanks have to go to the great Matt Gagnon at BOOM! Studios. I pitched a Cassie comic book to him, but while he wound up not buying it, he had an editorial note that really changed everything and brought the entire "Cassie-verse" into focus. In a lot of ways, this book owes its existence to Matt as much as it does Deb.

Thanks to my nifty galifty agent Lucienne Diver, production/art guru for Plus One Nic Grabien, and GraceAnne Andreassi De-Candido, Jacqueline Smay and Wrenn Simms for invaluable editorial aid. Also thanks to Danielle Ackley-McPhail, Jeff Lyman, L. Jagi Lamplighter, Lee Hillman, and Diane Raetz, who bought Cassie stories for their anthologies.

Additional thanks to the fine folks at the Key West branch of the Monroe County Public Library, who indulged me all those years ago when I wanted to learn more about Key West's history.

Gratitude as well to Jeremy Bottroff, Dale Mazur, Tina Randleman, Laura Anne Gilman, Michael McCloud, *Shihan* Paul and all the other fine folks at the dojo, and all the people I've met in Key West over my various trips there, especially the bands at Captain Tony's, the Hog's Breath, the Bull, and Sloppy Joe's.

If you ever find yourself in Key West, you should definitely see the bands at Captain Tony's Saloon, and you should consider staying at the Old Town Manor. It won't be exactly the same as going to Mayor Fred's or staying at the Bottroff House, but it's as close as you're likely to get. Also, make sure you get over to the Schooner Wharf Bar during the day and see Michael McCloud.

Finally, tremendous thanks to my ex-wife Dr. Marina Frants, without whom I a) wouldn't know a damn thing about scuba diving and b) would never have gone to Key West in the first place.

Ragnarok and Roll

Follow Cassie Zukav on Twitter:

@CassieZukav

Table of Contents

Just came down for the weekend,
But that was twenty-five years ago.
—*Michael McCloud*

Introduction

I first went to Key West, Florida as a compromise.

At the time, I was married to a woman who loved to scuba dive. I do not dive, so the problem was finding a place to go on vacation where she could dive and I could otherwise occupy myself. We found a couple places like that—Monterey, for example, where I spent all day at a great used bookstore—and a couple that didn't work—beaches bore the crap out of me, so there was nothing to do in the Caymans, since I am neither a banker nor a drug lord. Our biggest success was Key West.

I fell in love with this island pretty much the minute I set foot on it. I loved everything: the pastel architecture, the kitschy shops along Duval Street, the celebration of sunset every night, the casual friendly attitude, the history, and most of all the superb food and the excellent night life. The latter mostly manifested in a series of bars along Duval Street that feature live music. (And a few too many that do karaoke, but we won't mention that.)

We returned to Key West several times, and I went alone in

1999, while doing research for this book. Sort of. I'd come up with Cassie for a 1997 story in the *Urban Nightmares* anthology (reprinted at the end of this volume), but hit on the idea of doing more with her and transplanting her to Key West. I spent several days in the Key West branch of the Monroe County Public Library, perusing many a piece about wrecker captains and ghosts and the history of the region.

But it took until now for a Cassie book to happen for a variety of reasons. The novel series never came together, and then I tried pitching it as a comic book, and then I did a short story for the mighty Deborah Grabien, who then said she wanted to see a collection of short stories. I thought this odd, and I figured a novel series would be a better way to do the characters, but ultimately, while putting this collection together, I realized that Deb was right. Developing Cassie's world over a series of short stories has been a wonderful experience, giving me a chance to flesh out different aspects of it separately to make it better as a whole.

This volume includes three stories that were written for specific anthologies: the title story and "I Believe I'm Sinkin' Down" were for the first two volumes of Deb's *Tales from the House Band* anthologies (also from Plus One Press), and I wrote "Undine the Boardwalk" for the *Bad-Ass Faeries* anthology *It's Elemental* (which, thanks to the vicissitudes of small-press publishing, will actually come out after this tome). And we've added the original 1997 Cassie story "How *You* Can Prevent Forest Fires..." as a bonus track. The other five stories I wrote specifically for this book, deepening Cassie's Norse myth roots as well as fleshing out the various characters.

It's been a fun ride, and I hope it's only the beginning.

So sit back, have yourself a pint of your favorite brew, put some Michael McCloud or Black and Skabuddah or (if you must) Jimmy Buffett on your iTunes, and enjoy the nine stories of Cassie Zukav, Weirdness Magnet.

—*Keith R.A. DeCandido*
somewhere in New York City

4

Ragnarok and Roll

It was Thursday night in Key West. Thursday, Friday, Saturday, and Sunday nights always meant the same thing for me: head to Mayor Fred's Saloon, order a pint of beer, and sit down to watch 1812 play.

So I was kinda surprised to walk in and see a different band on stage tuning up.

"What the *fuck?*"

Mira, the Goth waitress (not to be confused with the mousy student waitress or the beach bunny waitress), was walking past me as I entered the open-air saloon and asked that very loud question. She stopped in mid-delivery of two glasses of some kind of froofy pink concoction—yes, I'm female, but I don't do girly drinks—to say, "Hey, Cassie. Yeah, 1812's kinda takin' a break."

I frowned. "Hey, Mira. What does that mean, exactly?"

Mira tilted her raven-haired head to the side in a manner she probably thought was meaningful. "Well, they *still* can't find a drummer after—you know."

I nodded. Zeke Bremlinger, their drummer, was killed by a

nixie in the Gulf of Mexico last month. "This island's *full* of musicians, they can't find a drummer?"

"Not a permanent one. C'mon, Cassie, you *know* what drummers are like." Mira shuddered.

"I *told* you that Terry was a bad idea," I said with a grin. Terry was a drummer Mira had dated for all of two weeks before he flaked out on her, which was a week-and-a-half longer than I thought it would take him.

"Yeah, yeah." She rolled her eyes. "I'm surprised Bobbi didn't tell you."

"She didn't dive this week." I worked part-time as a divemaster at Seaclipse, a dive shop on Stock Island, and 1812's guitarist Bobbi Milewski was one of my regulars. "In fact, she cancelled Tuesday. Now I know why, I guess."

"Uh huh. The usual pint?"

I nodded. "When you get a chance."

She moved on to serve her customers. I looked around for an empty table, of which there were many. When 1812 was playing, I usually sat to the left—as far away from the pool tables as possible, as that would only get me in trouble—but near the front. That gave me a nice view, but allowed other people to get closer. Or I'd sit by the big ficus tree that Mayor Fred's had been built around. (Back the nineteenth century, it was Key West's hanging tree.)

This time, though, I thought maybe it'd be best to take a table near the back, by the big glass table where they sold Mayor Fred's merchandise: T-shirts (I was wearing one tonight, as it happened), shot glasses, postcards, mouse pads, keychains, and so on, all with Mayor Fred's logo. The merch table was conveniently located near the exit, the ideal place to be in case this new band sucked.

Which, let's face it, they probably would.

All right, it was only fair that 1812 needed a break. Having your drummer get killed by a mythical creature really took the zing out of your motivation to play music four times a week. But dammit, they were *good*.

I made a mental note to give Bobbi a call tomorrow. Wasn't sure what more I could do—I already killed the damn nixie—but what're friends for, right?

Still, it was weird not seeing them on a Thursday night.

Upon achieving my hard-won Masters Degree in English Literature from the University of California-San Diego last spring, I'd decided to spend a few months driving across the bottom of the country in Rocinante, my battered old 1985 Ford F-150 pickup truck: Grand Canyon, Albuquerque, Austin, New Orleans, Biloxi, the Everglades, and finally Key West. I figured I'd stay for a week or so, spend my days scuba diving, my nights at the bars on Duval Street, and then head back home to start on my PhD.

After two nights of karaoke, mediocre cover bands, old farts with acoustic guitars, silly dance halls, and more covers of "Brown-Eyed Girl" than I ever expected to hear in a 48-hour time period in the places on Duval, I finally turned the corner onto Greene and found this open-air bar with a huge fish over the entrance, a big tree in the center, and a four-piece band on the stage that was plowing through "Sunshine of Your Love."

Two were up front: On left-handed guitar, a short blonde white woman in a white T-shirt and blue sweat pants; on bass, a tall black man with dreadlocks, wearing sunglasses, an open button-down T-shirt, and drawstring pants. Behind them were another short blonde on the keyboards—she came up front to play a second guitar or mandolin every once in a while—and a short, round white guy with a shaved head, and the world's longest chin-beard behind the drumkit. That last was the late Zeke Bremingler.

Bobbi's the lead guitarist, and she was like a buzzsaw on Clapton's riff. They followed that with "Love Reign O'er Me," where the keyboardist—Jane Anne Naharodney, who insisted on the stage name "Jana Naha"—made the piano sound like a waterfall. But what won me over was when they did Paul Simon's "You Can Call Me Al." Not only did Chet Smith nail the bass line, but Jana whipped out a tin whistle for that solo. Even Simon used a keyboard for that when he played it live.

Best of all, they didn't play "Brown-Eyed Girl" once. Or "Freebird," for that matter.

After my week-long trip entered its second month, I started talking to the band. By then I'd spent enough time at Seaclipse

7

that they were thinking about hiring me, especially since I was a certified dive-master *and* I knew how to steer a boat. Luring not only Zeke, Bobbi, and Jana, but all six of Bobbi's dive-nut brothers to take their business to Seaclipse did the trick. I'd become good friends with Bobbi, Jana, and Zeke, and Chet tolerated my being in his presence. (He's a bass player, what do you want?)

Nine months later, it was a rare 1812 gig I didn't show up for. Sometimes there were odd circumstances—I was sick, they needed me to run a night dive at Seaclipse, having to get that dragon out of the garden of the B&B I was living in—but I'd tried very hard never to miss a gig.

This was the first one *they'd* missed.

I looked at the new band. They were setting up, plugging in, tuning, and so on. Well, most of them were. There was this one guy, not too tall, with flowing blond hair, a red-blond goatée, ice-blue eyes, and one of those physiques that men probably thought impressed women, but which bitter experience has told me usually meant the guy was compensating for anatomical deficiencies elsewhere. He was standing off to the side, trying to look important while not actually doing anything.

He just *had* to be the lead singer.

Mira came over with my beer. "So who are these guys?" I asked as I grabbed it and gulped down a quarter of it at once.

"They're called Jötunheim."

Running the back of my wrist across my mouth, I asked, "Seriously?"

Nodding, Mira said, "Yeah, with those two dots over the O."

"An umlaut? Geez." I shook my head and looked over at the lead singer, who was now chatting with a woman in a tank top and shorts who'd just come out of the rest room. "How Nordic. And short, blond, and sinewy over there looks like a Viking who wandered into the wrong century anyhow, so the name kinda fits."

"Actually, he's kinda cute."

I whirled and stared at Mira. That drummer, Terry, that she dated? She went out with him because he was very tall, extremely skinny, and had dark hair, which put him in company with every other guy Mira had dated in the nine months I'd been

8

living in Key West. Jötunheim's lead singer was the exact opposite of her type.

She also had this goofy smile on her face. Mira had dark hair, pale skin, wore all-black even in the hot sun of Key West, had black nail and toe polish, and smoked like a chimney. I think I've seen her smile once, maybe.

So why the hell was she getting moony-eyed over *that* guy?

A signal from another table got her attention and she went off to help them, so I didn't get the chance to ask her about it. Reaching into the pocket of my shorts, I pulled out my smartphone and looked up Jötunheim. Unfortunately, none of the references I could find online were useful—it was all Norse mythology, Marvel Comics, or World of Warcraft, nothing about a band.

By the time my beer was down to almost nothing, the band was ready to start. Ihor, the bartender, grabbed the PA microphone and said, "Okay, everyone, let's have a big Mayor Fred's welcome for Jötunheim!"

The applause that followed was a mix of excited and reluctant. I went for a good old-fashioned golf-clap, myself—just enough to be polite.

"Good evening, Key West!" the singer said into the microphone up front. Next to him, the two guitarists—one acoustic, one electric—and the bass player were doing some last-minute tuning. I noticed a violin on a stand on the floor next to the acoustic guitarist, and I shuddered. A good fiddler was a noble thing, but a bad fiddler could absolutely and irrevocably destroy a band's entire sound forever.

"My name's Gunnar Rikardsen, and we are Jötunheim."

I shook my head and chuckled. With a name like that, he almost *had* to call the band Jötunheim, didn't he?

The electric guitar broke into the eleven-note riff from the Beatles' "Day Tripper." As openers went, it wasn't a bad choice. Everyone knew the song, and it bounced, so it might get a few feet onto the dance floor—which at Mayor Fred's was just the bit of floor between the stage and the bar.

Having said that, the rendition wasn't anything special. I mean, the notes matched what Lennon and McCartney did, but there wasn't any oomph.

So imagine my surprise when the song ended and the applause practically shook the beer glasses off the tables, it was so raucous.

I'd only heard applause like that in Mayor Fred's once before, about two months back. That night, 1812 was particularly *on*. It was Saturday, the place was packed, including about a dozen college students there for somebody's birthday, and they'd just *killed* with everything they did. The birthday boy asked for a Bob Dylan song, and they decided to do "Like a Rolling Stone." Jana's keyboards pierced the crowd, filling the room with the five-note organ bit during the chorus, Bobbi did a buzzsaw of a guitar solo, and Chet, Jana, and Bobbi all sang "How does it feel" in three-part harmony with so much energy that I got goosebumps just listening to them. I still get them, thinking about it.

The Thursday night crowd at Mayor Fred's, which was about half the size, responded with the same enthusiasm to this mediocre version of "Day Tripper" that Saturday night crowd two months ago to the most transcendent version of "Like a Rolling Stone" I've ever heard in my life.

And it only got worse. Don't get me wrong, they were a perfectly adequate cover band, but that just made them like everybody else on the island. None of the musicians screwed up anything—which actually put them one up on some of the guys on Duval Street—and Gunnar had a nice little tenor that he didn't strain too much.

But the crowd just ate it the hell up. It was like they'd gotten into a time machine to see the Rolling Stones in 1971 or something.

There was only one other person who didn't seem impressed: an older guy with a shock of white hair, sitting up front near the speakers. He nursed an amber drink of some kind—bourbon? Scotch?—and seemed to be very much not enjoying himself. I wondered why he didn't just leave.

I wondered the same thing about myself. After the crowd went batshit for the most uninteresting version of "House of the Rising Sun" ever, I noticed the second guitarist picking up the violin, at which point I finally gave up. No way was I subjecting myself to that.

I finished off my second pint of beer, got up, and headed out. I

10

didn't pay my tab before I left. Normally that wasn't an issue, especially on a Thursday, because I'd be back the next three nights. Now, though, I wasn't so sure.

Still, everyone who worked there knew where I lived and where I worked. Hell, Mira probably had my debit card number memorized...

I walked out onto Greene Street, the evening breeze blowing through the rat's nest of blond curls that I laughingly refer to as my hair. It wasn't even midnight yet, so there were plenty of folks on the street, and I found my mood—already soured by what just happened in Mayor Fred's—worsened by having to landshark through throngs of drunken tourists, drunken college students, and drunken locals.

(The way you told them apart, in case you were wondering, was simple. The tourists crashed into you and then apologized; the students crashed into you and *didn't* apologize; and the locals were able to avoid crashing into you.)

Luckily, after I made the right onto Duval, it was only a couple of blocks to Eaton Street. Cover bands, drunken shouting, and wretched karaoke all competed for my cars' attention. I was so used to closing Mayor Fred's down at four in the morning that I forgot what a zoo Duval turned into between the hours of ten p.m. and two a.m.

Just as I was about to cross Caroline Street, walking past the Bull and Whistle, a shit-faced white guy walked up to me, beer dripping from his five-o'clock shadow—which was getting into prime time at this point—and asked, "Where'za strip clubs at?" Then he squinted. "You're fuckin' tall, lady."

"I'm also tall when I'm celibate," I said with a smirk. At 5'11", I got that a lot. Then I gave him directions to the Mel Fisher Maritime Museum, which closed over six hours ago.

"Nicely done," came a voice from behind me. I turned to see Lio, the six-seven, no-necked bouncer for the Bull. "Shoulda known you could handle his drunken ass on your own, but I was here for backup just in case."

"'Preciate that, Lio," I said with a smile. I'd never actually encountered Lio anywhere but in the doorway to the Bull, but since that bar was a block from where I lived, and halfway between it and my primary night-time destination, we saw each other a lot. I was fairly certain I'd never told him my name, and I had no recollection of how I learned his.

With a nod to Lio, I continued to Eaton, turned left, and walked the two hundred feet to a white house with a big blue porch, on top of which was a sign that read BOTTROFF HOUSE BED & BREAKFAST. For the first month, this was where I'd stayed. After that, with my cash reserves starting to run out, I offered to update the B&B's web site. The owner, Debbie Dellamonica, had web skills that were probably cutting-edge in 1996 when she created the site, and as far as I could tell, she hadn't updated it since. I brought it into the twenty-first century, and she let me stay there *gratis* as long as I maintained the web site and did whatever other work around the B&B needed doing.

I walked around the main house, wandered through the garden's palm trees, past bushes and our parrot Harry S (who was asleep, thank goodness), before arriving at one of the two rear cottages. I trudged up the wooden stairs to my second-story place, using my key to open the sliding glass door.

"My goodness, are you ill?"

I sighed. Somehow, I just *knew* that the captain was gonna give me shit. "No, I'm not ill, I just decided to call it an early night."

"The only time in the past you have returned from your drunken perambulations before the witching hour was when you were suffering an illness."

I pulled off my cream-colored Mayor Fred's T-shirt, which I knew would get the old bastard's blood boiling.

Sure enough: "Must you do that?"

"It's my damn house, I can undress if I want to." I had on my one-piece bathing suit under the shirt and my shorts anyhow.

"In fact, it is *my* residence, bought and paid for by the fruits of my own labors, thank you very much."

"Cap, I'm really not in the mood for the usual banter tonight, so can we just skip to the part where I take my clothes off, you disappear in a huff, and I go to sleep?"

Now he sounded concerned. "You *are* ill."

"No, just cranky."

"Oh dear. It's not your moon time, is it?"

I stopped in mid-shorts-removal. "'Moon time'? Okay, now you're just making stuff up. They didn't really call it that in the nineteenth century, did they?"

"My wife did, on those rare occasions when she spoke of such things before me."

"Which was never?"

There was a brief, semi-awkward pause. The captain and I had those periodically.

Look, I don't know why no one else who stays at the Bottroff House can see or hear the ghost of Captain Jeremiah Bottroff, the wrecker captain who built this place in the 1840s, but I can. He's been my *de facto* roommate since I first started staying here, and he's also far from the weirdest thing that's happened to me. I didn't talk to Debbie about it—or anyone else, for that matter—but I'd kinda gotten used to being his Mrs. Muir over the past nine months.

There was a sudden breeze in the room, which meant he was gone and I could strip in peace. I'd long since stopped being self-conscious around the captain, but I didn't always want to fuck with his head, either. It wasn't his fault I was his first (and so far only) source of conversation the past 150 years.

Since it was still spring, I didn't need to turn on the AC. Keeping the windows open and the wooden ceiling fan over the bed going did the trick. So I just fell onto the bed without even bothering to pull the covers down. My head hit the pillow, and then I proceeded to stare at the ceiling fan for a very long time.

You ever try going to bed five hours earlier than usual? I know people who can do it, no problem. Me, I tend to settle into a rhythm, and it's a bitch to get out of it. In college, I got up every morning at the time of whatever my earliest class of the week was, even if I didn't have that class that day. Drove me nuts.

I tried everything, from trying to let the oscillations of the ceiling fan hypnotize me to getting up to check my e-mail to taking a quick shower to tossing and turning. For all that, I didn't actually fall asleep until almost five.

Like clockwork, I woke up at eleven, crawled out of bed, guzzled some of Debbie's amazing coffee—she always served Hawai'ian Kona and it was to die for—and hopped into Rocinante in plenty of time to drive down Route 1 to Seaclipse. As I inched along behind all the other cars on the only road that traversed the entirety of the Florida Keys, I wondered why that old man at Mayor Fred's stuck around so long to listen to Jötunheim when he obviously was as indifferent to them as I was. Was he related to someone in the band, maybe?

According to an e-mail this morning, I had four people for my one o'clock dive. I recognized three of the names: a couple who'd been diving every afternoon for the past week as part of their week-long vacation (I'd already warned them not to get sucked in the way I did), and Rany, a local who dove with me on Fridays a lot. The fourth was new, probably a tourist, named V.E. Bolverk.

Just before the bridge to Cow Key, I turned right and drove down to the coast, pulling into the large driveway that Seaclipse shared with the Waterfront. The latter was a restaurant that survived mainly because people were usually starving after a dive and would eat anything, no matter how wretched, a maxim they proved after every Seaclipse dive. I always swore I'd never eat at the Waterfront again after each time I did the Salmonella Shuffle there, but I kept going back anyhow. Bastards.

Anyhow, my couple was already there. So was the old man from the bar last night.

I nearly dropped my air tank.

This was my first good look at him—I only saw the right side of his head at Mayor Fred's—and I realized that he was missing his left eye. No eyepatch, no prosthetic, just an empty socket. Weirdly, it looked right on him. His white hair, which had been hanging loose at the bar, was now tied into a small ponytail, and he was already wearing the neoprene suit.

He and the couple were all looking at air tanks to rent. I had my own—why else do you think I drive around in a 25-year-old pickup? it's the best way to haul the tank around—but most people just rented when they dove. Especially travelers; you don't want to try and get a giant metal tube through airport security…

The female of the couple noticed me first. "Hey, Cassie!"

"Hey, Hannah—David. And you must be Mr. Bolverk. I'm Cassie Zukav, I'll be your dive-master."

14

Bolverk stepped forward and offered his hand. "A pleasure, Ms. Zukav. I'm sorry we didn't get to speak last evening at the saloon, but you departed before I had the opportunity to introduce myself."

I smiled. "That was going to be my line. Only, y'know, with fewer words. Why'd you stick around so long?"

"I am acquainted with the lead singer."

"Not even a relative, huh?" I chuckled. "Well, you're a better man than I am. We're just waiting on one more—"

From behind the desk, one of Seaclipse's owners, Cara Zimmerman, said, "Rany just called—he can't make it."

"Okay, then." Rany usually only made it to two-thirds of his appointed dives, anyhow. "Which one we got, Cara?"

"We've left *Harpo* for you."

"Great. Let's go, guys." Seaclipse had three dive boats, which Cara and her husband, Andy Wasserstein, had named *Groucho*, *Chico*, and *Harpo*. I usually preferred *Groucho*, but as a part-timer, I never got first pick. As we boarded the boat, I asked Bolverk, "Have you ever dived in the Gulf of Mexico before?" He had to be an experienced and certified diver, otherwise Cara and Andy wouldn't have signed him up for a dive.

"No, only in the northern Atlantic."

My eyes widened. "Really? Yowza." I cut my teeth in the Pacific, which was horribly frigid compared to what you got off the Florida coast, but the northern Atlantic was like diving in ice water. "Well, this should be nice and warm for you."

Because Hannah and David had already done the close-by dives, I went out a little further to where I knew there were some nice fish and beautiful coral reefs—David had purchased an underwater digital camera, so I went to where he'd get some good shots.

Since there were only three customers, I had to go underwater also, since you didn't dive without a buddy. Obviously, the happy couple stayed together, so I got to dive with Bolverk.

I anchored *Harpo* and put up the red flag with the diagonal white stripe that signified that we were a diving boat. We all checked each other's equipment one last time, and then we all went under.

15

It's so beautiful underwater. There's really nothing on land that can compare to it. There are so many different shapes, sizes, and colors, and the water embraces you and takes you in.

Bolverk and I went down by a beautiful coral reef. This one had so far remained undamaged by pollution or carelessness. Picture a cauliflower made of porcelain, and you'll have an idea what an unspoiled reef looks like.

There were critters all over the place, too, and I made sure to snap a few pictures. I got an especially nice shot of a blue angelfish. A moment later, something caught my eye. I swam over to the other side of the reef.

Something was poking out from under the sand at the bottom. It looked like something that had been deeply buried, and then unearthed by the current. The two ends of it looked to still be pretty well buried.

You found all sorts of garbage down here, but this one looked different than the usual detritus that collected. It actually looked like the tail of a lizard—but the scales were a deep, emerald green that was sharper than any amphibian I'd ever seen. And between the scales, it almost looked like a gold tinge...

Someone less scrupulous than I would have tried to unearth it, but there were several issues there. For one thing, it was just a small tube- or tail-like piece that was buried on either side, and there was no way to tell how deep it went. For another, I preferred to leave the ocean be. I saw myself as an observer, not a participant, in what was going on down there. And for a third, if that tail really did belong to a lizard, it might get pissed if I grabbed it.

After a while, Bolverk and I swam back to the boat, making a safety stop partway up. As we clambered back into *Harpo*, I saw that Hannah and David were already in the boat, the sun reflecting off the drops of water on their face and hair and on their neoprene suits.

"*There* you are," Hannah said with a grin. "We were starting to get worried."

I chuckled. "Sorry, found something weird." I turned the digital camera's display on and scrolled over to the picture of the weird lizard-tail thingie. "That look familiar to any of you?" I showed it to Hannah, David, and Bolverk in turn.

16

"Nope."

"Don't look like nothin' I ever saw, no."

Bolverk frowned. "It looks like nothing seen on Earth."

"So what," David said with a laugh, "you're sayin' it's alien? That's rich."

"I said no such thing," Bolverk said gravely.

There was a brief awkward pause. I started *Harpo* up and steered her back to Scaclipse.

Neither Cara nor Andy recognized the tail either. I sighed and wondered if I should've bothered getting prints of the pictures I took. Prints of my digital photography graced the walls of the Bottroff House. But I preferred ones I could identify.

Bolverk signed up for more dives for the next several days, which I took as a compliment. It was a relief, too, since I had no idea how he'd liked the dive, and I'm usually pretty good at reading people.

As I was loading up Rocinante, my phone beeped with a text message from Bobbi: "Going to Fred's to see new band. Coming?"

Oddly, I hadn't decided what I was doing tonight. I couldn't recall a Friday night where I didn't know what I was doing since I came down here. I didn't really want to go see Jötunheim again. But if Bobbi was going to be there, maybe I could get a straight answer about what was going on with 1812.

Bolverk passed me by in the parking lot. "Will I see you this evening at the tavern?"

That clinched it. I needed to know more about this guy, especially since he was the only other person who seemed unaffected by whatever mind-altering substance Jötunheim put in their amplifiers.

"You bet," I said, even as I texted a similar sentiment back to Bobbi.

Bolverk nodded, and walked off through the parking lot and continued in the general direction of Route 1. I wondered if he was going to walk all the way to Key West.

I climbed into Rocinante and pulled out onto the road, but I didn't see Bolverk anywhere. Maybe he just parked somewhere else.

That night, Mayor Fred's was *packed*. All the seats were taken, and people were jammed onto the dance floor. I procrastinated getting there, so the band was already on stage, and meandering through a lackluster version of Led Zeppelin's "Whole Lotta Love."

I found Bobbi and Jana both leaning against the merch table. Gratefully, I walked over to them.

Of Bolverk, I saw no sign. But the place was densely packed—way more than was normal, even on a Friday night—so he could've been almost anywhere in the bar, and I wouldn't see him.

They finished butchering Zeppelin and the room exploded in applause. Bobbi and Jana were among them, to my disgust.

"Hey, Cass," Bobbi said. "Aren't these guys *great?*"

"Fuckin' A," Jana added. "They fuckin' *rock.* Yeah!"

"Really?" I just stared at them. "They're *not* that hot. Certainly nothing on you guys. What the hell happened, anyhow?"

Bobbi and Jana exchanged glances. Then Jana said, "I need a cigarette."

The three of us went out onto Greene Street so Jana could suck on nicotine and we could talk in peace. Given that Jötunheim's next song was "Money for Nothing," which was a) one of my favorite songs, and b) eerily appropriate from my POV, I was just as happy to be farther away from it.

While Jana lit up, Bobbi said, "We just can't find a damn drummer, and hiring one's proving impossible. They either cost too much or they won't take the rehearsal time."

I couldn't help myself. "You guys rehearse?"

"Ha-fuckin'-ha, Zukav," Jana said. She had a thing for referring to people only by their last names. "We *gotta* get a drummer up to speed and in sync, and we can't do that with a new guy every damn weekend. Some of us have lives, y'know?"

"Since when?" I thought those words, but it was actually Bobbi who said it. "Anyhow," she continued to me, "we figured we should just take a break. Didn't realize they'd go and hire some-one so awesome."

"Okay, seriously?" I shook my head. "What is the big deal about Jötunheim? I mean, they're okay, but you guys are six times the band they are."

"That's sweet, Zukav," Jana said through a cloud of exhaled

18

cigarette smoke, "but you gotta say that 'cause you're our friend."

"No, really, I don't. If you guys sucked, I'd say so."

Bobbi regarded Jana with a smile. "She's got a point."

Jana shrugged and took another drag. "Still, these guys fuckin' rock. Pity they don't have keys."

"Yeah, I just hope we get the gig back when we finally do find a drummer. We're holding an audition in the garage Sunday afternoon." Bobbi looked at me. "Wanna come watch?"

My feeling on music has always been similar to what they say about sausages: love 'em, don't wanna see the behind-the-scenes stuff. Luckily, I had a good excuse. "Can't, I'm doing two dives on Sunday."

"Shit, Zukav, they got you doing the morning dive?" Jana was laughing at me.

"I can set the alarm."

"Yeah, and get Debbie to give you the coffee through an IV and you *might* manage to be awake before eleven." Bobbi chuckled. "C'mon, let's go back inside."

"Nah," I said with a sigh. "It's just not the same in there without you guys. I'm gonna head back."

We exchanged good-nights, Jana finished her cigarette, and they went in while I headed home. Briefly, I contemplated trying another bar for the evening, but I found my enthusiasm oddly waning. I just wanted to go home and curl up in a ball.

I arrived just as Debbie was locking the front door for the night. "Hiya, Cass," she said. "We got a new one in nine—big old guy with only one eye named—"

"Bolverk?" I asked in surprise. Room number nine was the downstairs of the cottage next to mine.

With similar surprise, Debbie said, "Yeah. You know him?"

"Uh, he was on my dive today."

"Well, thanks for telling him about us. G'night."

I hadn't told him about the Bottroff House—which was a failing on my part, since I made a habit of talking the B&B up to Seaclipse customers. For that matter, I always talked up Seaclipse to the B&B guests.

But now I was starting to feel seriously stalked by this guy.

This time I didn't even try to go to sleep, just spent the night downloading my pictures from the dives, catching up on e-mail, web surfing, and trading insults with Captain Bottroff.

The rest of the weekend got progressively weirder. Bolverk kept signing up for my afternoon dives. I didn't make it back to where that weird tail was again, as the other divers made specific requests for other spots, and the customer was always right.

And Jötunheim kept playing to bigger and bigger crowds at Mayor Fred's. In fact, their biggest crowd was Sunday night, which was usually the second-deadest night of the week after Tuesday.

To make matters worse, the three surviving members of 1812 were there both nights, and they were all bopping to the music. Even Chet, who doesn't bop to *anything*.

I stuck around both nights, partly because I wanted to keep an eye on Bolverk—who was sitting there nursing what Mira told me was bourbon every night—and partly to see if maybe I was just missing something. Whatever it was, though, I couldn't find it.

Sunday night, between sets, I was standing in line for the women's room—something I'd never had to do on a Sunday night before—and Gunnar noticed me. Wasn't sure why— beyond the fact that, at 5'11" with a mess of blond curls, I tend to stand out—but he peeled off from these two brunettes who were hitting all over him to say, "I have been noticing you."

I stared down at him—he was half a head shorter than me. "Oh yeah?" I tried to put on my best Southern California "what-*ever*" voice.

"Yes. You are the only woman in this entire place who is not having a good time. Yet you keep coming back."

I smirked. "Maybe I'm a glutton for punishment."

"I am simply surprised." He showed perfect teeth when he smiled, and I swear to God, his eyes glinted. "Do you not find it odd that no one else in this establishment feels as you do?"

"Yeah, well, I can't stand *American Idol* or Steven Spielberg movies, either, so I guess I'm used to it." Thankfully, the line moved forward, and I was able to enter the inside of the women's room, the one place where Gunnar dared not follow. As the door closed behind me, I saw two more women glom onto him like moths dive-bombing a candle.

Okay, so the guy was the lead singer of a band that had been packing the house like no one had packed it before, but even taking that into account, ego much? He's got half of Key West falling at his feet, but he's gotta know why it's not half plus one?

I sat fuming during the second set, made worse by how much Bobbi, Jana, and Chet were enjoying themselves. First off, Chet enjoying himself was just *weird*. Though in some ways, it was worth hanging out listening to Jötunheim's drivel just to see this sight, if for no other reason than it was bound to provide blackmail material down the line.

But more importantly, these guys were totally eclipsing 1812. Every other band in the universe would be ripshit over what these guys were pulling off, but there they were, just bopping along.

After the final song—an appallingly uninspired version of "Join Together," about which the nicest thing I could say was that Gunnar played a decent harmonica—I left without even saying goodbye to anyone.

It was around three, but since it was Sunday night (Monday morning, whatever), the streets were pretty sparsely populated. Some of the bars closed early on Sundays, and the ones that were open weren't all that crowded.

So I was all alone at the corner of Duval and Caroline when the giant jumped me.

We're talking an *actual* giant here. He was at least eight feet tall, and that's *not* an exaggeration. He had a thick beard, a huge nose, and breath that came straight from Satan's ass. His arms were also the size of my entire torso, and one of them was grabbing right for me.

"Hey! Leave her alone!"

The voice came from my left, and was oddly familiar. Sure enough, it was the guy who'd asked me for directions to a strip club and commented on my height Thursday night. He was running up to the giant, screaming at him.

At least, he was running until the giant backhanded him across the face, sending blood flying out his nose and his entire body skidding across the street. A woman screamed.

I just kept staring at the giant. I'd seen some weird shit in my time, from the nixie that killed Zeke (and a bunch of others) to the dragon in the garden to Captain Bottroff—and that was just here on Key West. You don't even want to *know* about that thing I stumbled across in San Diego…

Now that I was over the initial shock, and since my drunken admirer had been kind enough to distract the giant at the cost of some serious pain, the least I could do was take advantage.

I kneed him in the groin.

Like any male, the giant screamed in agony at that, right in my face (since he bent over after I damaged the family jewels), at which point I realized that his breath didn't come from anywhere as nice as Satan's ass.

"Step away from the lady nice and slow, chuckles."

I turned to see Lio pointing a gun at the giant. The giant snarled at Lio.

Lio pulled the trigger.

I'd never heard a gun fired in my life up until that point. My parents were crunchy-granola Southern California types, and I honestly thought everyone in Key West—beyond, y'know, law-enforcement—was too laid back to pack heat. For the record, it doesn't sound *anything* like a firecracker or a car backfiring or anything else I've ever heard. It's also incredibly fucking loud, especially when it was fired less than fifteen feet from you. If I didn't spend four nights a week listening to loud music, it might have messed up my hearing, but mine came pre-damaged.

Another scream from the giant, and then he turned and ran around the corner.

Shaking my head, I chased him, but as soon as I turned onto Caroline, there was no sign of him.

Lio ran up right behind me, holding the gun with both hands. "How the hell'd a ten-foot dude disappear like that?" he asked.

"Dunno—but thanks, Lio."

"No problem."

I shook my head. "My name's Cas—"

"Cassie Zukav, I know. Debbie told me." He grinned. "Figured you'd let me know in your own time. C'mon, let's see if any'a these fools called 911 on their cell phones."

Two of them had, as it turned out. I went over to my admirer, who was sitting up on the pavement of Duval Street, his head leaning back while a brunette woman cared for him. "I can't believe you did that," she was saying.

"You okay?"

"Yeah." The woman was holding a tissue to his nose as he leaned his head back. As I got closer, I saw that his nose was still bleeding. He was talking in a nasal voice from the nasal blockage. "I guess now we're even."

I frowned. "Huh?"

"I was *really* drunk Thursday night, and if you'd given me the right directions, I'd have wound up at an actual strip club instead of a closed museum, and Tanya here'd have killed me."

The brunette shot him a disgusted look. "You were going to a *strip club?*"

"I didn't, though! And it's 'cause'a this lady."

"So you got your nose broken for her? Jesus, Billy."

Leaving Billy and Tanya to their domestic bliss, I hung out until the cops and the ambulance arrived. Wasn't sure what to tell them, but—well, one of my closest friends is a federal agent, and I'd never hear the end of it from him if I didn't make a proper report.

That particular ordeal took a couple of hours, and I finally stumbled back to the Bottroff House at five. The captain actually sounded relieved when I showed up. "Thank God. I was beginning to grow concerned. First your uncharacteristic early returns, and now tardiness."

"I've been late before," I muttered as I took my T-shirt off.

The captain didn't even make a fuss, which told me a lot right there. "Tonight is far from a standard night."

I wasn't really in the mood for riddles. "What's that supposed to mean?"

"I mean that the occupant of the ground floor of the next cottage over attempted to gain ingress into this dwelling. However, I was able to drive him away."

It took me a moment to parse Bottroff's words. "Hang on, Bolverk was here?"

"Indeed."

"And he *saw* you?"

"Yes. Had he been a less belligerent sort, I might have welcomed another to share words with, but he seemed intent upon seeing you. He used a phrase I've heard you utter from time to time: 'low key'?"

I snorted as I climbed out of my bathing suit and crawled into bed. "Yeah, low key isn't exactly this guy's style. And he's the least of my problems tonight." As my head sunk into my pillow, I gave the captain the brief version of the night's events.

"That settles it, then. I will brook no argument, Miss Zukav—I will remain vigilant tonight, to guard against any further assaults upon you."

It was a testament to how incredibly tired I was, that it never occurred to me that the captain's notion was at all creepy until long after I fell asleep.

The next few days were shockingly normal. I did my afternoon and occasional evening dives at Seaclipse, I helped Debbie out around the B&B, I saw very little of Bolverk, and no giants leapt out at me on Duval Strreet. Apparently Bolverk did a couple of dives with Andy during the week. I tried not to be insulted.

I was almost starting to believe things were getting back to normal until I was greeted by a text from Bobbi when I woke up Thursday morning: "Jana quit 1812. Drinks after diving?"

I stared at my phone in disbelief. Bobbi and Jana had been best friends since kindergarten. 1812 was their baby. How could Jana quit?

I texted back a simple, "sure," then got ready to head to Seaclipse.

Bobbi wouldn't even talk about it during the dive. Afterward, we went straight to the Waterfront and sat at the long wooden bar. "Two beers, Jack," Bobbi said to the bartender as soon as her ass hit the stool.

Grinning, I added, "And I'll have two beers, too."

"Very funny," Jack said with a sour face, and he went and got us each just the one beer.

"I cannot *believe* her," Bobbi said after Jack handed her a full pint. "The whole week, all she's talked about is Jötunheim and how good they are, and how if they just had keyboards they'd be perfect. We're trying to audition drummers, and she's talking about this other band! So when we finally get someone, she quits on us."

That surprised me. "You got a drummer?"

"Yeah." She smiled. "Another girl, believe it or not. Poor Chet's gonna be the only guy now."

I rolled my eyes. "Yeah, he must *hate* that."

"Well, you never know with Chet." Bobbi sighed and gulped down more beer. "Anyway, it's not *just* that Jana quit. I mean, bands don't last forever, and teaching takes up a lot of her time, and it was always kinda in the back of my head that the band could fall apart, y'know?" She sipped some more beer. "But to go another band? I mean, 1812 was *us*. It's like she's not even my best friend anymore!"

Frowning, I asked, "What other band?"

"Didn't I tell you?"

"Uh, no."

"Oh, sorry. Yeah, she quit to join up with Jötunheim."

I thoughtfully sipped some more beer before making my next statement. "How do you plan to kill her and how much help do you need from me to dispose of the body?"

"Don't tempt me." Bobbi shook her head. "What especially sucks is, I got us a gig at the Hog's Breath tomorrow night." That was a completely open-air bar on Duval, about half a block from Mayor Fred's. "Looks like now we're gonna have to do it as a trio."

"Well, the Hog's Breath has a tiny stage, anyhow. Jana would've had to use the Casio, and you know how much she hates that."

"Yeah." Bobbi finished off her beer. "You wanna meet the new drummer? She's meeting me and Chet at Fred's tonight."

I stared at Bobbi as if she'd grown another head. "Excuse me? Why're you going to Fred's?"

Bobbi shrugged. "Jana's first night on the keys. When we were eight, we were both already singing and playing music a lot, and we pinky-swore to each other that we'd never miss the other one performing. There've been a few we've missed because of other commitments—and I won't be able to see her tomorrow—but I've got no excuse tonight."

25

"How about, 'Sorry, but you just pissed all over our friendship, so I think I'll skip it'?"

"Tempting, but it *was* a pinky-swear."

"When you were eight," I said slowly. "Seriously, you're gonna torture yourself for this?"

Bobbi grinned. "Do not mock the sanctity of the pinky-swear." Then the grin fell. "Besides, there's two other things. One is: she'll make Jötunheim sound even more awesome. And also? I want to remind her that *I* still think our friendship means something."

That drew me up short. Holding up my pint, I said, "I'll drink to that."

We risked actually eating the food at the Waterfront, and then headed back to Key West. After I changed clothes, I wandered up to Greene Street. Lio nodded hello as I passed by the Bull, and I nodded back.

"You hear if they caught the guy?" I asked.

He shook his head. "Nah, I ain't heard shit about it."

"Figures."

When I got to Greene Street, there were already people spilling out on the sidewalk, as Mayor Fred's was packed to the gills. The show hadn't even *started* yet. I didn't even want to think about what the waitstaff was going through inside.

I saw Bobbi and Chet standing with a short redhead. Bobbi waved when she saw me coming toward them. "Hey, Cass! Can you believe this?"

"No. In fact, I'm pretty well convinced this is a mirage."

"Good thing the PA pipes the music out here, too." Bobbi looked over at the redhead. "Ginny Blake, this is Cassie Zukav, our biggest fan."

I winced. "Seriously? *That's* how you introduce me? Not 'my friend Cassie,' or 'my dive-master at Seaclipse Cassie,' but 'our biggest fan'?"

Chet stared at the crowds all around us. "This rate, you gonna be the only fan we got *left*."

Ginny held out her hand. "It's a pleasure to meet you, Cassie. I've heard a lot about you."

Returning the handshake, I said, "Well don't believe any of it, I'm actually pretty damned awesome."

"Good to know."

Ihor's voice came over the PA. "Ladies and gentlemen, put your hands together tonight and now *every single night* for Mayor Fred's new house band, Jötunheim!"

Everybody around us cheered wildly and clapped. My jaw fell. I leaned over to Bobbi. "*Every* night? What about Fiona and those two guys with the beards?"

Bobbi shrugged. "Guess they'll have to play somewhere else."

So the Monday and Wednesday acoustic acts got screwed along with 1812, not to mention losing the Tuesday open mic. I mean, all right, you can't argue with crowds like this, but it still wasn't fair.

The piano opening of "I'm Still Standing" came over the PA, and 1812 had covered this often enough for me to know that it was Jana's fingers tickling the ivories. Obviously they were taking advantage of their new band member right off.

Sure enough, the next three songs were all keyboard-heavy. Jana was a virtuoso, and Bobbi was right—she improved Jötunheim's sound tremendously. But she also showed up how mediocre the rest of the band was.

At least, to me. Everyone else was eating it up, with one exception: Ginny seemed unmoved by all of this, too.

I leaned over to her after she golf-clapped while everyone was having orgasms over a blah version of "Kashmir." "It's about time someone *else* was unmoved by these guys."

Ginny just smiled.

I added, "It's like someone cast a spell over the whole damn island."

She raised her eyebrows. "Maybe someone has."

Just after she said that, I felt something brush across my nose. Looking up, I saw white flakes start to fall from the sky.

Okay, I'm from Southern California, and I live on Key West. It took me few minutes to recognize snow. Ditto most of the folks around me, since snow is just about the last thing anyone expected to find in South Florida in springtime.

Within a few minutes, the snow was really starting to pour down. And it was getting *cold*.

"I gotta go," I said. Besides the fact that listening to Jötunheim suck while standing on a street being snowed on was pretty low on my list of ways I wanted to spend my Thursday night, I had a feeling that things were gonna be bad at the B&B.

After navigating the throngs of very confused people on Duval, I got to the Bottroff House. I arrived just in time for Debbie to beg me to drive to the storage unit down on Virginia Street, since I was the only person she knew who owned a vehicle that could handle snowy roads.

Two and a half hours later, and after using the heat in Rocinante for the first time since I left San Diego, I stumbled into the snow-covered garden, my feet like ice cubes from walking through snow on flip-flops. Just getting to the storage unit and back, all of a mile from the B&B, took ninety of those minutes. The rest of the time was spent distributing heaters, extra blankets, and other stuff I liberated from the unit and tossed into the back of Rocinante.

By the time I got to my cottage, the final space heater in hand for my own room, my bones were cold. I'd never been this chilled in my life.

Bolverk was sitting on the steps.

"Shouldn't you be in your room hiding from the weather?" I asked tiredly.

He rose to his feet. "I was waiting for you, Castor Lisbeth Zukav. We must speak."

I winced at his use of my full name. My twin brother was named Pollux. Yes, really. Talk to my parents. We went by "Cassie" and "Paul" for a reason.

"Can't it wait till morning?" I asked plaintively. "I have a bed that desperately needs to have me sleeping in it." After all this running around, I doubted I'd have trouble sleeping this much before my bedtime.

"No, it cannot. Fimbulvetr is upon us, which means that Loki's plan to bring about Ragnarok has started to come to fruition."

I blinked. "Okay, basically *none* of that made any kind of sense."

"The man you know as Gunnar Rikardsen is, in fact, the trickster Loki. He is my blood-brother. I am Odin, the Allfather of the Aesir. And we do not have much time."

I remembered some of what I saw online when I was doing my search on Jötunheim's name. "Hang on—Loki, Odin—you're a Norse god?"

"Of course."

"Right, because that's the most natural thing in the world." I sighed. "Says the woman being snowed on in April while on her way to the room she shares with a ghost. All right, fine, let's get in out of the cold and you can tell me *all* about Loki and his evil plan."

Pulling my keys out, I walked past Odin up the stairs while he started to explain himself. "Fimbulvetr is the eternal winter, and is the first stage of Ragnarok. Soon Loki will be powerful enough to sunder Yggdrasil, the World Tree that binds the Nine Worlds together."

I unlocked and slid open the door only to be greeted by Captain Bottroff. "You should heed what this—this person says, Miss Zukav."

At that, I *almost* dropped the space heater onto my foot. I *did* drop my keys onto the white-carpeted floor. "You're kidding, right? The guy whose favorite epithet is 'Mary, Mother of God' is telling me to listen to the pagan deity?"

"I still believe in the Lord God and His Savior, Jesus Christ, as I did in life. But the *after*life has taught me that there is more to this world than I could have imagined. I have learned that there are other gods, and they cannot be labelled 'false' as the vicars of my youth insisted. Therefore, yes, I do believe that you should listen to what this person has to say."

"Your friend's shade speaks truth," Odin said as he took a seat in my white wicker chair.

"Jesus fuck, it's cold." I plugged in the space heater and turned it on, standing as close to it as I could while rubbing my goose-bump-covered arms. "Fine, so Gunnar is really Loki. How'd he get to this point?"

Odin had a sonorous voice that was well suited to storytelling, and I found myself almost mesmerized by his story. "Loki tricked Hoder into killing Balder in an attempt to bring about Ragnarok—the end of all that is. But he failed, and he was punished. Loki was trapped in a cave with a serpent dripping poison onto his face forevermore. However, Loki's wife Sigyn remained loyal to him, and held a bowl to catch the poison before it struck him. Unfortunately, she had to periodically empty the bowl, and when she did so, the poison struck Loki's face, and his convulsions shook the very earth."

"Uhm—okay," I said, "why didn't she just have two bowls?"

That brought Odin up short. "I do not know. You would have to ask her that." He shook his head. "Regardless, Loki managed to free himself from his prison. But gods are only as powerful as their worshippers. When the peoples of the Scandanavian region believed in us, our power was at its zenith—but in time the Aesir were forgotten, given over for other gods. Today, we are little more than an academic curiosity, or fodder for popular fiction. Our end was prophesied to come about via Ragnarok, but instead we simply faded."

"Not with a bang but a whimper, huh?" I shook my head, the space heater having managed to get my blood actually circulating again. "Okay, fine, so you all faded away."

"Save for a few of us. I still live, obviously, as does one of the frost giants, Geirrod, who is loyal to Loki. I believe you had an encounter with him."

"What, the lunatic outside the Bull? He's a frost giant?"

"Indeed."

"So why the hell did he want to kill *me*?"

Odin stared at me with his one eye. "Loki sent Geirrod to kill you because he sees you as a potential threat. As one of the Dísir, you are immune to his glamour—and one of the few who can stop him."

My eyes widened. "Excuse me? I'm one of the *what*, now?"

"The Dísir. The fate goddesses. The Norns are Dísir, and periodically a set of triplets is born on Midgard who are also Dísir. You are one of three, are you not?"

Now my heart was pounding against my ribcage. Yes, Mom had triplets, but Paul's and my never-named brother was stillborn.

I found myself with the need to sit down. The heater had only just started to warm up the room, but I no longer felt the cold—or, really, much of anything. I planted myself on the edge of the bed, since Odin was in my only chair. In a very quiet voice, I said, "Yes, I'm a triplet."

"Just so. Why do you think you are able to speak with the shade or survive an encounter with a frost giant?"

Before I could elaborate on the role that two other people played in my driving Geirrod off, Bottroff finally spoke up again. "If such is the reason behind our ability to communicate, Miss Zukav, then I, for one, am filled with gratitude."

I stared at the captain. In nine months, that was the nicest thing he'd said to me.

Unable to entirely parse this, I forced myself to focus on the point at hand. "Okay, hold it—the band's using magic?"

Odin nodded. "Loki is using a glamour, yes, to make his music more appealing. It is a minor glamour, not strong enough to affect me as the Allfather, nor you as a Dís. He was unable to revive worshipful interest in the Aesir—our time has passed. The Christians were little more than conquering fodder for Vikings in our heyday, but now you are everywhere."

I held up my hands. "Don't look at me, I'm Jewish." I sighed. "All right, so he formed a rock band. Figures—fan dedication's probably stronger than a church would be anyhow. So why here? Why Key West?"

"Because, as I said, the next step is to sunder Yggdrasil. And one of the roots of the World-Tree is the ficus around which the saloon on Greene Street is built."

I put my head in my hands. "Of course it is. So, fine, how do we stop him?"

"There is a counterspell that may be cast while Loki casts the spell to sunder the World-Tree. He will cast it tomorrow night—Fimbulvetr must last for at least a day before he may attempt it. You must cast this counterspell."

"Whoa, whoa, whoa!" I stood up. "You're the Allfather, the big badass of Norse myth. I'm just a tall chick with bad hair. Why aren't *you* casting the spell?"

"Loki is my blood-brother, and we swore never to harm each other. You, however, have made no such vow, and as a Dís, you can easily cast the spell."

"Oh, I can, can I?" This was getting insane. Insaner.

"Yes." He rose to his feet. "I must depart. I will return in the morning with the components you will need to cast the spell and instructions on how to cast it."

"Uh, okay, but I've never cast a spell before."

Odin slid the door open. "You are a Dís. You will be able to." With that, he left.

"Okay, then," I told the closed door. I turned to the captain. "You really believe this?"

"I believe that it is snowing heavily, a phenomenon I have never encountered in a century and a half. I believe that these musicians you have described are enchanting the good people of this island. I believe you were attacked by a vicious monster. I believe that the gentleman who just departed has a notion as to the reason for these occurrences and also the method by which they may be rectified."

"So you're saying I should see this through?"

"Yes. Yes, I do."

I collapsed on the bed. "Yeah, me, too."

My dreams that night were filled with random images of Bobbi and Jana in a catfight, Gunnar giving Bolverk the finger while standing on Mayor Fred's stage, the Gulf of Mexico totally frozen over but Cara and Andy still trying to dive in it, Geirrod shooting Lio in the chest with a big shotgun, Ginny, Chet, and the rest of the crowd at Mayor Fred's giving Jötunheim a standing ovation, and a bunch more.

When I woke up, I frowned. Ginny *wasn't* into Jötunheim. How was she unaffected?

I put on the sneakers I hadn't worn since December and the long pants I hadn't worn since I arrived on the island and put them on. The snow was still coming down and piling up in the garden. Seriously, this was the first time my legs weren't exposed to the open air in nine months.

"What a fucking nightmare," I muttered. "This is gonna cripple the island. We don't have salt, we don't have plows—hell, most of the people who live here don't own *socks*."

I trudged through the snow to the main house in order to get some of Debbie's killer coffee. Several guests were in the dining room, scared and subdued. Nobody knew what to do, and probably the whole island was shutting down. I had a text on my phone from Cara saying that Seaclipse was closed, to my lack of surprise. I doubted that any business was going to be open. Plus, how were deliveries supposed to get here on unpassable roads?

Then again, the world was going to end tonight, anyhow....

I trudged through the frozen tundra back to my cottage with an entire pot of coffee and then fired up my laptop to do a litle online research before Odin came back. Sure enough, Norse mythology tracked frighteningly well with everything Odin said and the whole eternal-winter thing.

When Odin arrived, he had the spell components: a bunch of really stinky herbs, a mortar and pestle, a electric mini-stove, and a familiar-looking lizard scale.

"You took that from the tail-thingie we found last week!"

"Indeed. It is from the Midgard Serpent, the creature that surrounds your world. That it has allowed itself to be seen is another omen of Ragnarok's imminence."

"Joy."

I spent the entire day in my room with Odin and Captain Bottrott going over how to cast the spell. Apparently, I had to get the mix of herbs *just* right, say the incantation *precisely* (in a language I totally didn't know or recognize), and time it exactly to when Loki cast his spell, which would be him singing a song with a set of lyrics in the same weird language as my spell.

But no pressure...

Debbie managed to provide enough food for me and Odin, as well as the other guests, though she wasn't sure what she was going to do Saturday, since there weren't going to be any deliveries.

That night, I drove to Mayor Fred's. Duval Street was eerily not crowded. A bunch of hearty souls were trudging through the snow drifts to the few bars that decided to open up—which was maybe a quarter of them.

Rocinante was able to slowly plow its way through the snow, and when we turned the corner onto Greene, I just parked right across the street. I couldn't park right in front, because it was packed with people. Even though snow was still coming down, *hundreds* of people were trying to cram into Mayor Fred's.

But this time, unlike last night, there was a clear path from one part of the entryway, past the ficus, to the stage. That meant I had a clear line of sight, although I'm pretty sure it was so *Loki* had that same line of sight…

Ginny Blake was in with the crowd outside, and when she saw me and Odin climb out of the truck, she walked right over.

I was about to ask her what she was doing here, but she wasn't paying any attention to me. She stared at my companion. "Hello, Odin."

"Greetings, Sigyn."

Son of a bitch. "*You're* Loki's wife? The one not bright enough to have two bowls?"

Ginny frowned. "Excuse me?"

"Never mind—no wonder you're immune to his glamour."

She smiled. "What wife can't see through her husband? In any event, after spending eternity protecting him from that serpent, he repaid my loyalty by abandoning me when the cave collapsed and he was freed. So I have followed him in the hopes of watching him fail." She turned to Odin. "I assume you are here to expedite that failure, Allfather?"

"Not I. I swore an oath not to harm my blood-brother, and I will not go back on it."

Ginny's eyes widened. "You mean there's a chance he'll *succeed?*"

I sighed. "Hope not. I'm casting the spell."

Staring at Odin, Ginny asked, "Are you out of your mind? She is a novice."

"She is a Dís. She can cast the spell." Odin's voice was absolutely flat.

"I don't care if she's one of the Norns, she's never done this before. The fate of all the Nine Worlds is at stake, and you're risking it on a promise you made to *him?*"

Odin stared down at her with his one eye. "Yes."

Ihor's voice sounded over the PA. "Welcome to snowpocalypse, ladies and gentlemen!"

"You don't know the half of it," I muttered.

"Tonight and every night, it's Jötunheim!"

The crowd cheered like crazy. This time I could see them—

same short blond muscular guy up front, same other three, plus Jana on stage right behind her usual keyboard setup of a standup piano and two sets of electronic keyboards. They opened with an old Jethro Tull song called "Hunting Girl" that used to be an 1812 standard.

While they played the song, and I wondered why Jana was going around throwing her old band's music for these guys to play, I started putting together what I needed for the spell. As the song spiralled to a finish, Loki held up a hand. "All right, I need some quiet for this next one."

As he spoke, Jana started playing a quiet, dirge-like melody very low on the keys, set to "organ" mode.

Slowly, the crowd started to quiet down, until there was total silence—something, I gotta say, I'd never heard in this part of Key West before, not even at four after the bars closed—save for Jana's organ playing.

Then Loki began to sing a song in a language I didn't recognize.

Except I *did* recognize it. Odin had been giving me the words all day. I lit the mixture in the pestle, dropped the scale from the Midgard Serpent into the flames that licked up from it, and then started a chant of my own.

I had no idea what the words *meant*, but I'd been practicing them all day until Odin was ready to kill me (and I him, believe me), and dammit I was gonna say them *right*.

Even as I said the words, I could feel—well, *something* pulling at my chest.

Loki saw me standing at the entryway. Everyone else in the bar was mesmerized by the music and didn't even notice me standing there with a flaming pestle in my hand. He finished what sounded like a verse of his chant, then looked at me with obvious annoyance. "I was wondering where Geirrod got off to. Couldn't even kill a Dís. Can't find good help these days, it seems."

I just kept chanting. Maybe he could afford to do his spell piecemeal, but I wasn't risking it. The pull on my chest got weaker as I went, which I hoped was a good sign.

"But there's nothing you can do, little Dís. Oh, if Allfather was doing what you're doing, I'd be doomed, but he won't harm me.

His insistence on keeping his word is so charmingly old-fashioned, isn't it?"

Then he sang another verse, and the pulling on my chest grew worse.

Sweat beaded on my brow even though it was so fucking cold. I had come here wishing I had something thicker than a denim jacket, and now I was wishing I'd thought to throw it off before I started casting the spell.

The pull grew stronger, like someone had reached into my rib-cage and was trying to yank my heart out through it.

I kept chanting. I wasn't about to miss anything.

"Haven't you learned *anything*, Loki?"

That was Ginny, who my peripheral version told me was standing just behind me and to my left.

"Sigyn!" This time Loki cut off in mid-verse. The pull on my chest disappeared, and I kept the chant up, louder this time.

"Yes, Loki, I'm still alive. And you are about to fail to bring about Ragnarok *again*, just as you did last time. Oh, and you can rest assured that I will *not* be there to stay the poison from your brow again."

"I won't need it, *dear* wife of mine," Loki snapped angrily. He sang the next verse, and the pull grew even worse.

Thanks a lot, Ginny. If you were trying to distract him, that *totally* didn't work.

Suddenly, just as a hand touched my shoulder the pull stopped. The words, which were a bitch and a half to pronounce right even after a day's practice, were now coming easily, as if it was a language I'd spoken all my life.

And Loki stumbled on the stage.

"You're going against your word, old man?" Loki asked with a sneer.

Only then did I realize who was touching my shoulder.

"Yes," was all Odin said in response.

"We are blood-brothers! You swore an oath, Allfather!"

"And now I am breaking it. As you broke yours, many times. What good is my word, if existence ends because I held it?"

"What good is existence if your word while living in it means nothing?"

When I finally got to the end of the chant, I decided to answer Loki's question before taking the final step. "Words ain't no good if the music sucks."

I threw the pestle at the ficus. It sparked and shattered, yellow flame shooting out in all directions. The pull on my chest increased, and I fell to the floor.

Loki collapsed on the stage.

Wind whipped through Mayor Fred's, a cold, bitter wind that the body heat of hundreds of people couldn't warm. It blew out the flames caused by my shattered pestle. Then the entire world went white, as if we were all suddenly buried in a snowdrift.

I heard voices: Loki's, Odin's, Sigyn's. I had no idea what they were saying, but I heard them as I lay there on Mayor Fred's floor, unable to move. I struggled to get up, but whatever force had been pulling on my chest all this time was keeping me from moving.

After several seconds of struggle, I closed my eyes, shivering from the bitter cold.

When I opened them, I was in my bed.

Captain Bottroff's ghost was standing over me. "At last, you awaken. Even one with your prodigious ability to slumber should not be in such a state for so many days."

I swallowed. "Days?" I sat up, realized I was still in the outfit I wore to Mayor Fred's on Friday night, minus the denim jacket, which was hanging on the back of the wicker chair.

"Yes. It is now Sunday. I will fetch the gentleman—he wanted to know when you awakened."

A breeze, and the captain was gone. I sat up slowly, stomach growling. Looking out the window, I saw that the sun was shining and there was no sign of snow. I could see the garden clearly, though some flowers seemed to be missing. I guess they got frosted to death or something.

First thing I did was get out of bed. That took longer than it should have, as pins and needles shot through my legs, and I had to stand at the side of the bed, hand braced on the mattress, for several seconds before I felt confident enough to actually walk.

My arms and legs felt like they were made of jello, as I shakily pulled my shirt over my head. Removing my bra proved an act of dexterity almost beyond my means, and I sat back down on the bed, not trusting myself to remove my pants while upright.

By the time Odin showed at the sliding door, I'd managed to get into a bathrobe. I cursed the fact that my bathroom only had a shower stall, since what I really needed was a long bath. For one thing, I wasn't sure I'd be able to stand in the shower for more than a minute or two without collapsing.

He slid the door open. "It is good to see you well."

"'Well' is a relative term, but I'm alive. I guess it worked?"

"Yes." Odin nodded. "I have accepted responsibility for Loki and Geirrod."

I frowned. "What does that mean, exactly?"

"No Midgard jail may hold either of them, and your enforcement officials cannot arrest someone who does not actually exist."

Nodding, I said, "Yeah, okay, good point."

"I must take my leave of you, Castor Lisbeth Zukav."

I winced again. "Will you stop that, please? It's 'Cassie.'"

For the first time since I met him, Odin smiled. "Very well, Cassie. I hope you continue to use your gifts as a Dís wisely."

"I didn't even know I had gifts."

Bottroff spoke up, then. "Yes, you did. And rest assured, sir, that I will endeavor to keep Miss Zukav on the proper path."

"You have *got* to be kidding me." I put my hands on my hips and stared at the captain. But I was smiling.

"Be well, Cassie." And with that, Odin departed.

My cell phone had been in my pants pocket, and had long since lost its charge. I plugged it in to find it had a dozen messages.

Half were from Bobbi. I called her back, and we filled each other in on what had been going on. Well, as much of it as I was willing to talk about in a phone call. Bobbi had become a dear friend in the past nine months, and if there was anyone I could talk to about being a Dís, it was her. But not now.

Eventually, we got around to talking about 1812. "Mayor Fred's actually asked us back. Without Gunnar, Jötunheim has just sucked. We're starting tonight."

"As a trio or a quartet?"

38

Bobbi hesitated for several seconds. "Dunno yet. Jana and I—" She sighed. "We got some stuff to work out."

I didn't know what to say. Jana's quitting wasn't entirely her fault, thanks to Loki's glamour. On the other hand, nobody *else* in 1812 quit and joined Jötunheim. That was something those two were gonna have to figure out.

We promised to have lunch the next day to catch up in more detail, and I promised to tell her everything. Then I called Seaclipse, and worked out my schedule going forward. I told Andy that I wasn't up to working today, but I'd be okay tomorrow.

That night, after a not-nearly-long-enough shower in which I did *not* fall down and a huge meal provided by Debbie, I went to Mayor Fred's. Jana wasn't on the stage, but Chet, Bobbi, and Ginny were. I took a seat near the ficus tree. I suddenly felt protective of it. I ordered a pint of beer, and Ihor came over the PA.

"Ladies and gentlemen, back after a brief absence, Mayor Fred's favorites, 1812!"

Bobbi walked up to her mic. "Good evening, Key West! This one's for our biggest fan."

And then Chet walked up to his mic. He wore sunglasses, like usual, so I couldn't tell where, exactly, he was looking. But I chose to believe he was staring right at me when he started singing their first song: "I Put a Spell on You."

Undine the Boardwalk

"It's an open-air bar—can someone please explain to me, in words of two syllables, why the *hell* we can't smoke in there?"

I barked a laugh as I heard that complaint from the circle of people huddled outside the entrance to Mayor Fred's Saloon on Greene Street, puffing away on their cigarettes. I was approaching that entrance, and the gathering of the smokers' union told me two things: 1) I wasn't late for the start of 1812's set because their keyboardist, Jana, was one of the nicotine hounds, and 2) Larry was in one of his moods again.

Larry was short—and not just the way lots of people look short to me because I'm a 5'11" woman, I mean his-head-came-up-to-my-boobs short—with a thick white beard and an unruly shock of white hair, which was barely held in check by a Tampa Bay Rays ballcap and a sloppily tied ponytail. Replace the Rays cap with a cowboy hat, and he could play the lead in the bio-pic of the life of Walter Brennan.

"I understand why they don't want people smoking in enclosed spaces, second-hand smoke makes everything smell like a chimney something died in, and so on. I understand that. I really do. But this place doesn't have a *roof*. Yes, the pool tables are enclosed, so don't let people smoke *there*. Jesus, Mary, and Joseph." He puffed on one of his Menthols and caught my eye. "Hi, Cassie."

"Hey, Larry. I'd ask how you're doing, but your rant covered most of it."

Next to Larry was Paolo Jiminez, who kept the cigarette between the fingers of his prosthetic hand, the acquisition of which signalled the end to his career as a local bar musician. He ran the sound board at Mayor Fred's these days. "This way is *so* much better. I always hated coming home after a gig with all my clothes smelling like smoke."

"C'mon, Jiminez." Jana exhaled smoke into the humid Key West air. "You smoke like a fucking chimney. Your clothes smell like smoke when you come home *now*."

Paolo shook his head. "I don't take up smoking till I stop making music."

The last of the four was Mira, the Goth waitress, who pulled her cell phone out of her apron and hit the button to activate the screen. "I gotta get back inside. Cassie, you want your pint?"

I nodded. "Please."

She looked at Larry. "You ready for your coffee, or is it still Coke?"

Larry considered it while puffing down the last of his cigarette. "Nah, keep it on Coke. I'll go hot a little later."

I shook my head. Larry was the textbook definition of "regular." I'd never gone to Mayor Fred's when Larry wasn't either at his usual spot at the back corner of the bar, at a pool table hustling tourists (he called it "educating"), in the bathroom, or out here smoking.

But he never drank alcohol. It was always either a soda or coffee, the latter with a metric ton of sugar added. I often wondered how he ever slept.

"I still got my mojito," Paolo said.

Mira just rolled her eyes and went in through the entrance that had a giant fish hanging over it. She didn't ask Jana for her drink order, since she was part of the band, and they were taken care of directly by Ihor, the bartender.

"I should probably head in, too." I started toward the fish.

Jana dropped one cigarette onto the ground and stepped on it while simultaneously taking out another to light. "Oh, hey, Zukav, couldja do me a favor?"

I stopped and turned to look at Jana. "I guess."

"My guy's coming to see us tonight." Jana's voice lowered, and she actually sounded shy. You have to understand that *shy* is pretty much the last word anyone would use to describe Jana. "Couldja keep an eye on him, make sure he has a good time while we're on stage?"

"Uh, okay," I said, more confused by Jana's tone than her request. "Who is this guy, anyhow?"

"I'm tellin' ya, Zukav, this guy's the *one*. His name's Russ, and he's just…"

Paolo rolled his eyes. "Here we go again."

Larry adjusted the bill of his cap. "We'd just got her to *stop* talking about this fella."

Jana snorted. "Yeah, by listening to your sorry ass piss and moan about indoor smoking."

"It *isn't* indoor smoking! There's no *roof!*"

"*Anyway*," Jana said with a glare at Larry, "Russ is just awesome. I really think he's the *one*."

"Like Alfredo?" I asked. The previous "the *one*," Alfredo had lasted all of a week.

Paolo put in, "Or Christian?"

I added, "Or Jelani?"

"Or that funny-looking one with the bad hair," Larry said.

I grinned. "Isn't that all of them?"

"Fuck you *all*." Jana shook her head. "Look, I know I ain't got the best track record ever, but this guy's seriously awesome."

Larry looked up at Paolo. "What's the difference between 'awesome' and 'seriously awesome'?"

Paolo shrugged. "For me, it means he puts out on the first date."

"Jesus, Mary, and Joseph." Larry made a face. Key West had as many gay people per capita as San Francisco, so I never understood how an island lifer like Larry could have such a problem

43

with homosexuality. It was the mention of actual sex between same-gendered folks that squicked him, not gay people themselves, given that he was friends with Paolo and Ihor and Adina, one of the other waitresses.

Regarding Jana with amusement, I asked, "So when do we meet this hunka hunka burnin' love?"

Jana looked past my shoulder and broke into a huge grin. "Right now! Russ!" She started waving with both hands, her lit cigarette gadding dangerously about.

I turned to see someone who, I swear, was tall, dark, and handsome approaching. He had perfectly combed dark hair that was barely affected by the Key West winds, yet had no evidence of product. (As the owner of a rat's nest of blonde curls that usually needed garden shears to untangle, I was jealous.) He had lovely hazel eyes, a solid jawline, cheekbones you could cut glass with, and perfect teeth when he smiled.

Something about him made me feel more than a little nauseated—what my uncle Harry used to call a queasy feeling in his gizzard.

"Hey, baby," he said as he leaned down to give Jana a very long, very deep kiss.

"Get a room," I said when the kiss threatened to go on into the night. I also had to resist the urge to punch him, and I wasn't entirely sure why.

"Oh, sorry," Jana said sheepishly when she came up for air. *Sheepish* is another word I had never used as an adjective to modify Jana. "Russ, this is Cassie Zukav—she's 1812's biggest groupie."

I supposed I deserved that. "Hi."

He offered his hand, and I returned the shake, noticing a smooth, firm grip and uncalloused hands—and a sudden urge to grab his wrist and break his arm. I swallowed, quickly letting go of the handshake, but *damn*. I am most assuredly *not* a violent person—I wouldn't even know *how* to break someone's arm on purpose—but something was just *off* about this guy, and not just because he made Jana turn goofy.

"Is that something you can make a living at, being a groupie?" he asked with a lovely voice.

I considered and rejected several retorts, but decided to tamp down the revulsion and play nice. "Sadly, no. I work at a local B&B and also at Seaclipse, one of the local dive shops."

"Same place Bobbi and I go to dive," Jana added, referring to her bandmate and oldest friend, 1812's guitarist Bobbi Ann Milewski.

"I'm a bit of a diver, too," Russ said. "Maybe I'll check your place out."

After introducing Larry and Paolo, Jana practically dragged Russ into the entrance under the fish. "C'mon, you need to meet the rest of the band."

"Okay, baby. Nice meeting you all," Russ called back as he let Jana guide him in.

The three of us stared after them for a second or two.

Paolo broke the silence. "I would *totally* hit that."

Larry winced again. "What do *you* think, Cass?"

"I totally *wouldn't* hit that," I said honestly. "Or maybe I would, but with my fist." And there's the violence again. Sheesh.

"Of course not." Larry smiled. "Your young man's already in there."

I assumed that meant that Rance Demitrijian was in the bar.

Before I could reply to that, Paolo got a wolfish grin. "Fine by me, I ain't needin' the competition."

Larry stared at him. "You *do* remember what happened with Mickey and Perla, right?"

"Hey, I saved her a lot of grief—ain't like *he* was gonna tell her he pitched for the other team too."

"What do you think, Cassie?" Larry asked me.

"Well, the last person who used 'awesome' in her presence got a ten-minute tirade about how stupid and overused that word is, and the last person to call her 'baby' got kneed in the groin, so I'd say it's true love." I shook my head. "But I don't like him."

"I don't know," Larry said, "I kind of like the cut of his jib."

Both Paolo and I stared at him. "You know," I said, "I don't think I've ever heard anyone use that phrase in real life."

"Let's go inside." Paolo dragged on the last of his cigarette and stomped it out. "I need to see more of him."

I felt I needed to see less, but didn't say anything.

Thing is, this wasn't just me not liking the guy Jana was dating. I've always been kind of a weirdness magnet, finding strange-ass shit, and knowing things I shouldn't know about, and so on. Recently, I learned I'm one of the Dísir—a fate goddess. I found this out from, of all people, the king of the Norse gods. Yes, really. This means I notice things that other people can't even see.

Looking over at the table near the ficus tree that Mayor Fred's was built around, I saw Rance Demitrijian sitting there nursing a pint. I hadn't been sure that Rance was going to make it. He's a special agent with the Monroe County Field Office of the FBI, and his ability to make it to Mayor Fred's depended on his caseload. Rance was also a diver; we'd actually met at Seaclipse, and started hanging out at Mayor Fred's together.

Larry liked calling him my "young man" because he was weird like that, but the truth was, I had no idea what we were to each other. Yeah, we hung out at Mayor Fred's and went diving together, and yeah, we could talk for hours about pretty much anything, but we'd never actually kissed or been on a date. Though I had seen him naked, when he was almost killed by a nixie. I mean, I'm at the same table at Mayor Fred's from Thursday to Sunday night regardless of whether or not he is—and he's not always, since work keeps him busy—and as for Seaclipse, that's him hiring me to dive with him. That's not a date.

The evening rolled merrily on, 1812 playing their usual three sets, an impressive range of rock-and-roll cover songs, some famous, some obscure, all hard-rockin'. While they played, Russ sat at the bar, not far from Larry's seat, charming the shit out of everyone. At one point, when it was particularly crowded, Rance went up to get fresh beers for both of us, since Mira was a little too crazed dealing with a group of needy drunken tourists. Rance stood near Russ and Larry, and it took about a year for him to get back to the table, as he was talking to Russ.

Now, to be fair, Rance can babble, but Jesus.

"I thought I was gonna die of thirst," I said when he came back with the two fresh pints.

"Alcohol dehydrrates you, so it's not like this is gonna help all that much. You probably should've asked me to get some water from Ihor, too, though that probably would've meant I'd have to take two trips, since I think we all remember the last time I tried to carry three drinks."

"It's a figure of speech, Pedantic Boy." I chuckled and sipped my beer. "So what were you and Jana's new beau talking about?"

Rance shrugged. "Just talking about how much he liked it here. Said he's been all up and down the Florida coast, but this is the place he likes best. He and Larry are getting along remarkably well, too. Usually it takes Larry a week or so to get to liking someone."

"Tell me about it—he wouldn't even talk to me for the first week."

"Well, that's because he thought you were a tourist. And to be fair, you were one, then."

I nodded while sipping more beer. My plan had been to visit Key West for a week or two before going back home to San Diego. That was almost a year ago now.

"You okay, Cassie?" Rance sounded concerned.

Shaking my head, I said, "I don't know. There's something about Russ I don't like."

"Is this a Dís thing?" Rance and Bobbi both knew about my unexpected second life as a fate goddess. It wasn't something I told everyone, but they were the two living people I was closest to these days.

"I don't know—I think so. Any chance you can check him out?"

"I'll stop by the office in the morning and run him, sure."

As soon as he said that so casually, I got nervous. "This won't get you in trouble, will it?"

"If I get caught, yeah. And if anyone else had asked, I wouldn't do it without it being part of an investigation, but your instincts tend to be pretty good on these things, so we'd better check him out and be sure. Besides, we don't have any big cases pending, so a Saturday morning will be pretty quiet. It'll be fine. If I find anything, I'll tell you about it at the dive."

I smiled. I was running an afternoon dive at Seaclipse tomorrow that Rance had signed up for. So had Bobbi, actually. "Thanks, Rance."

By the time 1812's third set started, Russ had made friends with pretty much the entire bar. Even Chet, 1812's bassist, said a whole sentence to him. Hell, it took me four months to get a second word in sequence from Chet.

Which just kicked up the queasy gizzard again. Rance wasn't just being flattering when he talked about my instincts. After all, the last time I didn't like someone that everyone else adored, he tried to destroy the world.

When the final set ended, Rance had already gone home. Jana and Russ had left before teardown, which earned a grumble from Bobbi. Then again, Bobbi and Jana hadn't been on the best of terms lately, after Jana temporarily left the group for another band. They'd probably get over it—they'd been friends since they were little kids—but it made things a mite awkward.

After the happy couple left, I went over to say goodnight to Bobbi.

"Can you believe this shit?" she said without preamble as she latched her battered black guitar case shut. "This *better* not be the start of a new trend."

The drummer, Ginny Blake, chuckled. "C'mon, Bobbi, she's in love. Cut her some slack."

I added, "Yeah, tall, dark, and perfect probably wanted to get her home for the post-concert booty call."

"Nah, it's Jana's fault, not Russ. He's a good guy."

How much of this stemmed from my bad feeling about Russ and how much was Bobbi's still being pissed at Jana, I couldn't tell, but it annoyed me that even Bobbi had fallen under this guy's spell.

And I was genuinely worried that it was an actual spell.

Changing the subject, I made an offer. "I can help haul stuff if you need it." Years of carrying air tanks around had given me upper-body strength that was greater than that of the average 5'11" amazon.

"Nah, we got it. See you at Seaclipse tomorrow?"

"You bet."

As I left, Larry was, of course, the only one still sitting at the bar, with only the remnants of 1812, Ihor, Paolo, and the two waitresses left besides him.

I headed to the Bottroff House, the bed-and-breakfast where I not only worked, but also lived. I got a good night's sleep, woke up at eleven, and managed to pull myself together enough to get to Seaclipse on Stock Island—the next island in from Key West—in plenty of time for the afternoon dive.

Bobbi and Rance were both already there and suited up by the time I pulled into the driveway in Rocinante, my ancient Ford F-150 pickup truck. It was just the two of them for the dive, so we hopped onto *Chico*, one of Seaclipse's three boats, and hit the Gulf of Mexico.

Once we were far away from the coast, and any prying ears, Rance said, "So I ran Russell A.L. Kamen."

"Two middle initials?" I only didn't roll my eyes because I was steering a boat. "How pretentious is *that?*"

Bobbi put in before Rance could continue, "You ran Jana's boyfriend?"

"I asked him to," I said. "There's something about him I don't like."

After pausing for a second, Bobbi said, "Okay."

Now I hesitated. "You okay with this, Bobbi?"

"Jana's still my best friend, even if I totally want to rip her face off right now, and if *you* don't like him, he needs to be checked out."

And this was *why* I told Rance and Bobbi about being a Dís. "So what kind of horrible person is he?"

Rance shrugged. "Born in Florida to Anne O. Kamen, no father listed on the birth certificate, though Anne was married to someone named Lawrence St. Joseph, but they split up nine months before Russ was born. Even money he's the father and may not even know it. Anyhow, they live on a boat that's been docked all up and down Florida, which tracks with what he was telling me last night about how he's, well, lived all up and down Florida." He smiled.

I didn't. "So that's it?"

Another shrug. "No criminal record, nothing stands out. He and his mother hire the boat out for tours and things, and their tax records indicate that's their source of income. Not that it's much of a living, based on those records, but I wouldn't be surprised if a lot of their clients pay cash and it doesn't get reported."

I pounced on that. "You can investigate them for that, right?"

Rance just stared at me. "Seriously? Every tour boat in the

state takes money under the table. It's really not that big a deal and not worth the paperwork an investigation would generate, especially once I got to the part about my probable cause."

I knew that, of course, but I was grasping at straws.

"Maybe he's just a jerk you don't like," Bobbi said.

"But he isn't a jerk. Hell, even Larry and Chet like him, and they don't like anybody. *That's* what worries me."

We got to the spot where we were going to dive—or, rather, they were. Since it was an odd number of people on the boat, I didn't have to go down, since no certified diver would go down without a buddy. And I suddenly didn't feel like it anyhow, preferring to stay up top and brood about Russ.

Unfortunately, brooding was all I could do. There was nothing legitimate on him, and I couldn't go to Jana with, "I don't like him." For one thing, that was what I had said about all her *other* nine hundred boyfriends over the past year. For another, she *didn't* know that I was a Dís, and I wasn't about to tell her now. Discretion had never been Jana's strong suit.

This went on for two weeks. I went to Mayor Fred's and brooded, Russ had a grand old time chatting everyone up, 1812 rocked the house, and Jana got more and more attached.

That last part was *really* creepy. Every second she wasn't on stage, she had her arms around him. She didn't go outside to smoke, she didn't help with set-up or teardown—which was making Bobbi crazy—and she giggled.

Okay, I've only known Jana for a year, but giggling? Not in her lexicon. This is a chick who pretty much defined cynical Goth, complete with the stringy hair, black nail polish, cigarettes, and "bitch, *please*" attitude. She not only didn't giggle, she routinely mocked people who did.

Finally, one Sunday night between sets, Bobbi came up to me and said, "We have *got* to do something about this."

"What did you have in mind?"

Flailing her arms, Bobbi cried, "I dunno! Do whatever Dís thing you do!"

I flailed my arms right back, mocking her a little. "I don't even know what that is! Seriously, this didn't come with an instruction manual."

Shaking her head, Bobbi looked over at where Jana, Russ, and Larry were chatting away like they'd known each other forever instead of less than a month. "C'mon, Cassie, you stopped a dragon, a nixie, and the end of the world—you can't stop this?"

I opened my mouth, and closed it, helpless. I had no idea what to do. Each of the occasions Bobbi mentioned, I was either being given explicit instructions or it was easy to figure out what to do. Bobbi didn't even know about the thing Rance and I found in the Gulf of Mexico, not to mention that sea monster back in San Diego...

Russ and Jana wandered off, and Bobbi and I went up to the bar to refresh our beverages. While Ihor poured my pint and prepared her screwdriver, Larry said, "Cassie, where's your young man tonight?"

I rolled my eyes at the phrase. "Off on a case. It sucks, but at least he gets overtime."

"Maybe you two can take more dives together." Bobbi waggled her eyebrows.

"Oh, please. It's not like those are dates."

Bobbi looked at Larry. "When it's me, Rance, Cassie, and someone else, she *always* buddies up with him. *Always.*"

I glared at her as Ihor handed me my pint. "Right, because the conversation is so scintillating when we're underwater."

"Well, I think it's high time you two started having a proper courtship," Larry said. "I mean, look at those two."

He was pointing at Jana and Russ, who both had big smiles on their faces as they approached the bar. Jana was holding up her arm and waving her hand back and forth. "*Look* at this!"

"Stop moving your hand so fast, and maybe we can," I said with a smirk.

She held her hand right in front of my face, and I saw a diamond ring. This on a woman who'd never owned a piece of jewelry that didn't have a skull on it.

"We're gettin' married!" Jana squealed, a verb that also had never applied to her.

Based on the look on Bobbi's face, she wouldn't have applied it, either, and she'd known Jana since they were six. "Seriously?"

"Ain't it *great*?"

51

"That's wonderful." Larry had a big grin on his face. He raised his coffee mug. "To the happy couple!"

"Screw that." Russ walked up to the bar and slapped a credit card down on the bar. "Everyone gets champagne on me, Ihor."

That got a rousing cheer from everyone in the bar—well, except for me and Bobbi. We exchanged worried looks.

Ihor whipped out two bottles of champagne, the popping corks echoing off the walls, and started pouring into the plastic cups he kept around for occasions like this when he didn't want to create three dozen dirty glasses at once.

Everyone took a cup with the exception of a couple of tourists who chose that moment to walk out, another tourist who'd been there all weekend and had been prominently displaying his one-year chip from AA the whole time, and Larry.

Russ didn't even pay attention to the AA tourist, instead looking at Larry. "C'mon, man, how often does a guy get engaged?"

"Happened to me twice. And alcohol puts me *right* to sleep."

Ihor laughed. "Dude, we got a cot right in the back."

"Look, just take my word for it, all right?" Larry was angry now. "I don't drink, and I won't drink—not for you, not for anybody. Ain't worth the risk."

Russ glared at Larry for a second before turning his back on him. "Fine. Everyone *else* raise their glass! I'm marrying the most beautiful woman in the world, and I hope everyone except this asshole is happy for me!"

Everyone in the bar cheered loudly with three notable exceptions: me, Bobbi, and Larry.

I will give Jana this much: being stupid in love didn't do anything to diminish her musical ability. The last set of the evening was some of 1812's best. Jana was a music teacher for kids during daylight hours, and she was damn good at it. For the band, she played keyboards, guitars, mandolin, and accordion, all of them incredibly well, plus she sang lead on about a third of the songs. Tonight her playing was just superb, and her junkyard growl on vocals was amazing. It was enough to make me cry.

Unfortunately, her attitude was making Bobbi cry. After teardown, she just looked at me and said, "Em's."

Em's was an all-night eatery on Duval that catered to people who were kicked out of the bars at three a.m. and wanted to nosh on something before bed. I actually was desperate for sleep—I'd had two dives that afternoon, and they'd been rough—but the look on Bobbi's face indicated that she needed to have words.

We ordered a large basket of conch fritters with fries—Em's made the best fries in the Keys—and two coffees, and sat across from each other.

"We gotta do *something*, Cass. I mean, Christ, *married?*"

I nodded. "Okay, maybe we talk to his mom."

"How're we supposed to do *that?*"

While popping a fritter into my mouth after dipping it in Em's special sauce, I said, "Rance knows where their boat's docked. We just go in and say hi."

"Okay, and what do we ask her? Why's your son a weirdo?"

I pretended to think about it. "Maybe we should be more subtle."

"How?"

"Call it a hunch, but I don't think we'll come up with a good gameplan at three in the morning after ten beers and one glass of shitty champagne."

"I only had four, but yeah, I see your point. Fine, we'll talk tomorrow at Seaclipse."

The next day at Seaclipse, I walked in to see both Rance and Bobbi all in their neoprene outfits. Bobbi stood with hands on hips, looking frighteningly resolute. "After the dive, we go to the boat."

I frowned. "What boat?"

Rance turned to look at Bobbi. "You told me that this was entirely her idea—that was how you sold me on this."

"It *was* her idea." Then she stared at me. "Right?"

I shook my head. "Bobbi, *what* are you talking about?"

"I'm talking about going to see Russ's mother on their boat."

The previous night's conversation burbled forward from a haze of beer. "Yeah, okay, that was my idea, but I thought we weren't going to do anything until we figured out a gameplan."

Primly, Bobbi said, "I have a gameplan. We go in and ask her what's wrong with her son."

I put my head in my hands. "No, that was the plan we came up with while drunk, and we both agreed we'd need something more subtle."

"We *will* be subtle. Her son is marrying my best friend, and I'm gonna be the maid of honor, which means I need to consult with the mother of the bride to plan shit."

I frowned. "Jana asked you to be maid of honor?"

Bobbi looked down at the floor guiltily. "Well, no—and if she did ask, I'm not sure I'd say yes. Jana quit the band—again—because, and I quote the voicemail message she left this morning at 8am, 'I want to devote all my spare time to my sweetie-pie.'"

"She called him her 'sweetie-pie'?"

Bobbi nodded.

I blinked. "Wait, she called you at 8am?"

Again, Bobbi nodded.

"She was *conscious* at 8am?"

"I know, right?"

"Yeah, this is dire."

Rance raised his hand. "Okay, I haven't been following this with any kind of comprehension, but I agree that Jana's behavior could charitably be described as odd. There's something extremely peculiar going on here, and we need to get to the bottom of it. Talking to his mother seems like the proper next move."

As usual, Rance summed up in fifty words what anyone else could say in ten. "Let's do it."

We had a fourth for the dive—a tourist whose name I never got—and I pointedly went with Bobbi as my dive buddy just to shut her up about how I always dived with Rance. Afterward, the tourist thanked me profusely and said he'd definitely come back to Seaclipse the next time he came to the Keys. I kinda brushed him off, which wasn't my usual style, but now that we had a gameplan, dammit, we were going to execute it!

We decided that taking three vehicles was silly, so after we changed out of wet neoprene into dry T-shirts, shorts, and flip-flops, we hopped into Rance's FBI-issued Prius. Rocinante and Bobbi's Corolla would be safe in Seaclipse's parking lot. Rance took us up Route 1 to Sugarloaf Key, where Russ's boat was currently docked.

When we arrived at a dock on the southern end of the island, Rance pointed at a battered houseboat that had seen better decades, with the word RUSALKA etched on the prow.

But then he said, "It's that really nice one in the middle that we want to go to."

I frowned. "Next to the dumpy one?"

Bobbi asked, "What dumpy one?"

There went my gizzard again. "The one called 'Rusalka.'"

"Y'know, someone with a truck that looks like yours really shouldn't go casting aspersions—that's a great boat!"

I didn't respond because I saw someone come out onto the deck—though "someone" may not have been the right word. She didn't so much walk as flow out of the boat's interior. Her pruney skin was a kind of puke green, halfway between the prettiness of teal and the dullness of chartreuse, and that skin was covered in seaweed, jellyfish, and sand, with shells all throughout her long, stringy brown hair. She wasn't actually wearing any clothes, though the crap all over her body covered her up some. Her face was wrinkled and she had just an awful sour expression. Dark green, water-soaked wings grew out of her back and drooped down to her knees. They didn't look like they'd help anyone get airborne, but maybe they helped with swimming.

"Look at that," Bobbi said, staring in amazement. "Now I know where Russ gets his good looks."

I shot Bobbi a glance. "What?"

"I'm finding myself in total agreement with Bobbi," Rance said. "She's amazing looking, even without accounting for her advanced age."

Rance, of course, had seen Russ's birth certificate, which would have included the mother's age. But now the queasy gizzard was on overdrive. "Okay, Bobbi, describe her right now." I'd get a better description from Rance, but it would also take half the afternoon.

"Tall, blonde, beautiful, perfect skin, *great* smile, and if I had that figure, I'd wear a string bikini, too. Plus—"

"It's a glamour," I said before she went on. "I'm guessing she's some kind of water elemental or something, and uses the glamour to make herself look like Anne Kamen."

55

Bobbi winced. "Shit. It's Loki all over again, isn't it?"

I nodded. Loki had used a glamour to get people to like his rock band enough to give him the power to cast a spell that would destroy the world. This was a more traditional glamour, making someone—and something in the case of the boat—look good.

Luckily, one of the cool side effects of being a Dís was that glamours don't work on me.

The creature finally noticed us and called out. "Can I help you?" Her voice was actually quite mellifluous, with just a hint of an accent, enough to sound exotic without being incomprehensible. Since that was what I heard, it had to be natural. Add the visual Bobbi described, and she could probably charm the pants off anyone.

I saw Rance reach into the back pocket of his shorts to pull out his badge, which was sweet, but probably wasn't going to get the job done. People responded better to badges, at least sometimes, but this wasn't a person.

"You can start by dropping your glamour so my friends can see you for what you really are, and then you can tell us what your kid's up to."

She just stared at me for a second. "Interesting. My glamours are strong enough to even affect documents and electronic records, yet you are immune."

"I'm one of the Dísir." I had no idea if that would mean anything to her—hell, I'd never even heard of them until Odin came 'round—but I figured she should have some kind of explanation.

"Holy *shit!*" That was Bobbi, and I gathered from that, and the look of sheer revulsion on her and Rance's faces, that she had, in fact, dropped the glamour.

"I assume, Dís, that my son has seduced a friend of yours, and you wish to release her from his spell?"

I blinked. That was a little too easy. "Uh, yeah. And my name is Cassie."

"That *idiot.*" The wings started to quiver, and her hands clenched into fists. "He'd promised me he'd stopped seducing humans. Where is he?"

56

Rance glanced at both of us. "This boat is listed as his place of residence. It's possible that he's with his new fiancée, but we needed to ascertain whether or not he was—"

The elemental—or Anne, I guess—strode off the deck and past Rance. "We must go to him. I wreaked enough havoc in my time, I will not allow him to carry on my legacy!"

I shook my head. "Okay, then."

"I assume, Cassie," she said as she walked past me, "that you have a ground conveyance of some sort. You will take me to where my son is."

Bobbi looked at me. I looked at Rance. Rance looked at me. I shrugged. "I guess we're going to Jana's place."

"Hang on, let me call her," Bobbi said, pulling her phone out of the front pocket of her shorts. After a few moments of touch-screen fondling, she put the phone to her ear. "Hey, Jana, where you at? ... Really? I thought you'd quit— ... Okay. ... I'm with Rance and Cassie, we just finished our dive. We'll meet you there. ... Great, bye!" She tapped her phone's screen and pocketed it. "She's at Mayor Fred's. Russ called an impromptu engagement party."

"Engagement? That *fool.*" Anne shook her slime-encrusted head. "Take me there."

Bobbi and Rance suddenly stopped looking like they were going to throw up. Rance said, "Don't you think you should put something else on that's a bit more appropriate to the setting?"

Snorting, Bobbi said, "She wouldn't be the first MILF in a bikini to wander into Mayor Fred's."

"We are wasting time," Anne snapped. "If you care about your friend, you will make haste. And even if you don't, I care about my son. I will not see him subjected to what I endured."

We piled into the Prius and headed back down Route 1 toward Key West. After a few minutes of what could charitably be called tense silence, I asked, "What, exactly, did you endure?"

She hesitated for long enough that I was on the verge of asking the question again when she finally answered it. "The curse of our kind is that any relationship between us and a human dooms both us *and* the human. I did not learn that lesson until after I became with child, sadly."

That didn't bode well for Jana. "So Russ's father is human?"

"Yes."

"I'm guessing he takes after his old man in the looks department." If he'd been using a glamour the way his mother did, I'd have seen through it, but—queasy gizzard notwithstanding—Russ *looked* human.

Late-afternoon traffic in Key West is never fun, and Route 1 was down to a crawl by the time we crossed onto the island. At my suggestion, Rance cut over Palm Avenue to Eaton Street to park the Prius at the Bottroff House. Mayor Fred's was only a short walk from there, anyhow. Even then, going on foot meant we had to weave our way through the college students and tourists who choked the sidewalk—many of whom gaped openly at Anne—but it was still faster than the stop-and-go traffic the cars were stuck in on Duval Street.

At Greene, we turned left. I had the longest legs of anyone present, so I pulled ahead, and walked in to see a bunch of people gathered around the bar: Jana, Chet, Paolo, Adina (the only waitress working this afternoon), a few others I didn't recognize, and Ihor behind the bar.

At the center of it all, though, were Russ and Larry, and they were staring each other down. Larry's ponytail had come loose, and his Rays cap was on the floor next to his stool. Russ was holding a plastic glass in front of Larry's face and screaming so much he was spitting. It reminded me of the way my father and my twin brother Paul got when Paul fell off the wagon.

"What is *wrong* with you?" Russ cried. "Just have one damn drink!"

Okay, maybe not *exactly* like the way Dad and Paul were.

As soon as she saw me, Jana ran over. "Zukav, you gotta help me, something's *really* fucked up with Russ!"

Before I could explain that she didn't know the half of it, Anne strode in behind me. "Russell, stop this right— Lawrence?"

Russ stared at Anne. "Mother?"

"Anne?" Larry was also staring, with a look on his face I'd never seen before. I'd been coming to Mayor Fred's four times a week (mostly) for almost a year, so I honestly thought I'd seen everything that Larry's face could do.

Until now—he looked like the happiest guy in the world and the saddest all at the same time. Which was when it all clicked in my head.

"I don't believe it," Larry whispered. "I never thought I'd see you again."

"Nor I." Anne's voice had gotten even more imperious, amazingly enough. "I did not expect you to survive this long."

"I ain't gonna if this jackass has his way."

"He's not a jackass," I said. "Well, okay, he *is* a jackass, but he's also your son."

Almost everyone looked at me funny at that point.

I figured I should explain. "Russ's birth certificate didn't list a father, but his mother was married to Lawrence St. Joseph. That's you, right, Larry?"

He didn't answer me, instead just looking at Russ. "Jesus, Mary, and Joseph. It's true, isn't it?"

Russ sneered. "Yeah, well, don't start expecting Father's Day cards, asshole."

"I'm not." Larry turned to Anne. "Why didn't you tell me?"

"You had already left me, and your fate was sealed, before I realized I was with child."

I frowned. "What do you mean, his fate was sealed?"

"It's our curse," Russ said. "If a human leaves one of us, then that human dies the minute he falls asleep. And when I found out that my dear old Dad wasn't dead yet, I had to make sure that he finally got what was coming to him."

And then the rest of it clicked into place: Larry's sugar-and-caffeine obsession, his alcohol avoidance, and why he didn't seem to have a life.

Except for one problem. I regarded Larry. "How the hell are you still alive?"

"Oh, I'm immortal until I fall asleep. That's the fun part. Been sittin' at this damn bar since Hemingway was a regular, tryin' to keep awake."

"Shit." That was Jana, and with that one syllable, sounded like herself for the first time in ages. "So, what, if I don't marry you, I'm gonna die when I go to sleep?"

"No, baby, no." Russ's voice got gentler, and he walked over to her, cupping her face in his hand, a gesture that suddenly was a lot creepier. "No, it's only if you leave me. But you'll never leave me, right?"

"I—" Jana seemed helpless—the latest in a series of emotions that didn't really fit on her.

"What's the problem, baby?"

I put myself between the two of them. "Maybe she doesn't find patricide a turn-on."

"She will not leave my son," Anne said. I was about to object strenuously—if futilely, since I didn't really have any way of stopping her—but then she went on: "My son will leave her."

"No, Mother, I have to finish what I started!"

Anne walked up to her son and put both hands on his shoulders. It looked ridiculous to me, since she was all seaweed-covered and smelling of muck—and it probably looked just as ridiculous to everyone else seeing her in a string bikini and looking hot as hell. "Lawrence knew his fate. And if he has found a way to postpone it, then he deserves to continue to live."

Larry snorted. "If you call this livin'." He'd retrieved his Rays cap and was putting it back on top of his unruly white hair.

"If he wishes to end it, all he need do is lie down and close his eyes, and the curse will run its course. It is not for us to determine when that will happen. Plus this poor girl." She glanced at Jana, who looked confused, angry, and sad all at the same time. "She will be as miserable with you as Lawrence was with me, and she will eventually leave you as he did—and as all humans who have made the mistake of falling in love with our kind do sooner or later. You must release her, or condemn her to the same fate as your father."

Russ stared at his slime-caked mother for several seconds, then looked at Jana. "I guess I should take the ring back."

"You must ask her for it," Anne said before Jana could respond. "If she gives it back to you of her own volition—"

Shrugging her arms off, Russ said, "All right, all right! Jana, give me the ring back—I don't want to marry you."

Jana stood with her mouth open for a second or two. "God-fucking-dammit." She practically ripped the ring off her finger. "If that's what you want, fine. Take your fucking ring back."

He said nothing, but accepted the ring.

Anne turned to Jana. "You will not emerge from this un-scathed, young woman. Never again will you have a love as strong as this, and forevermore will you long for my son—but he can never be yours."

Jana pulled out a cigarette and stuck it in her mouth. "Yeah, well, sounds like what my love life was like before anyhow."

She turned her back on the Kamens and walked outside to light up for the first time in a week and a half. No, she didn't walk out, she stomped. And Jana had possibly the worst posture in the history of the world, but instead of her usual slump-shouldered shuffle, she walked stiffly, her shoulders rigid. Bobbi, tears welling up in her blue eyes, went after her. She moved to put an arm around Jana, but she shrugged it off.

I was about to join them when Anne stopped me.

"Thank you, Cassie. Were it not for your ability to see through my son's lesser glamour, this might have had a bad ending."

She led Russ out of the bar. Russ cast one last pissed-off glance at Larry as they exited, turning left toward the boardwalk. They were probably going to swim home.

I looked at Jana, who puffed angrily on a cigarette, her life having been turned upside down half a dozen times in the past two weeks, and whose already ridiculous love life had just gotten worse. I looked at Larry, who was just miserable, seeming very much like a person coming around to the notion of going to sleep and never waking up. I looked at everyone else in the bar, who were utterly confused by what they had just seen.

"Yeah, 'cause this was just *such* a happy ending."

I Believe I'm Sinkin' Down

My first thought upon entering Mayor Fred's Saloon was that the crowd was fairly subdued for a Thursday night.

Then I remembered that it was Saturday night.

My confusion as to what day it was could, I think, be forgiven. See, I generally spent my Thursday through Sunday nights at Mayor Fred's, my favorite bar in Key West. Those are the four nights when 1812 plays. Like most bands on the island, they're a rock-and-roll cover band, but a particularly talented one, and they have become good friends of mine, as well.

Mayor Fred's—just off the main drag of Duval Street, and a short walk from the Bottroff House Bed and Breakfast where I worked part-time and also lived—was an open-air bar with a big ficus tree in the middle of it. Tourist web sites will tell you that it was Key West's hanging tree in the nineteenth century; they will not tell you that it's also a root of Yggdrasil, the world-tree of Norse myth, a bit of trivia which I had learned the hard way when I had to stop a Norse god from destroying the world by sundering the ficus. The crowd was usually about two-thirds tourists, one-third regulars, but on Saturdays it was more eighty-twenty in favor of the tourists.

I was later than usual because I'd been putting in a lot of extra time at my *other* job, as part-time dive-master at Seaclipse, a dive shop on Stock Island. Lately, it had been more like full-time, since the two owners, Cara Zimmerman and Andy Wasserstein, were badly hurt when a UFO crashed into Dry Tortugas. Andy was still in the hospital and Cara's arm was still broken, so Noah, the other part-timer, and I were running all the dives. It was the only way to keep the business going, and since they were responsible for the only actual income I made—the work at the Bottroff House was in exchange for room and board—it was the least I could do. Besides, they'd have had to close down otherwise.

As a result, this was my first chance this week to make it to Mayor Fred's, and I was late. My usual table by the ficus was taken, so I just sidled up to the bar near the sound board while the guitarist, Bobbi Milewski, said, "We've got a request for this next one, then we're gonna take a little break."

Chet started up a bass line, then the rest of the band came in. I realized the song was "Crossroads," the Eric Clapton song.

Paolo Jiminez was running sound like usual. "Wussup, Cassie?"

"Why's it so quiet in here?"

"Ain't you heard?" He glanced back down at the board, adjusting one of the levels. I didn't notice a difference, but he nodded as if the whole thing sounded infinitely more appealing now. "See that funny-lookin' dude over there?"

Paolo had an artificial right hand, and he pointed with the prosthetic toward the corner near one of the speakers. I saw an African-American man wearing a ballcap with the Miami Dolphins logo on it. He also wore huge mirrorshades, and sported an impressive set of sideburns.

"What, the seventies reject over there?"

"Mhm." As usual, Paolo made that into a four-syllable sound. "He was here last night, too, and we *think* it's J.R."

I blinked. "Huh?"

Paolo stared at me like I had grown a second head. "*You* know. J.R."

"Still not—"

"John Robertson, girl, don't you—"

I threw up my hands. "Christ, Paolo, why didn't you just *say* that?" When people referred to Michael Jackson as "M.J.," I never knew who they meant then, either.

Looking back over at the corner, I saw that the guy definitely could have passed for Robertson, or Robertson thirty years ago, anyhow. "C'mon, he's been around since the sixties. That guy's too young."

But Paolo was shaking his head. "Me and Gavin—y'know, back when we were a thing—we saw him at the Seminole Hard Rock up in Lauderdale. He was lookin' *fine* for a man his age. Shit, he was lookin' *fine* for a man *half* his age."

Thinking about it, I remembered one time when he joined the Rolling Stones on stage a year or two ago. When I watched the clip on YouTube, Keith Richards and Mick Jagger both looked practically desiccated, while Robertson, who was supposed to be a couple years older than them, looked great.

"All right, so what's he doing here?"

The answer to that question had to wait, as 1812 hit the final note of "Crossroads." Over the applause—which, despite the subdued nature of the crowd, was pretty enthusiastic—Bobbi set her left-handed guitar onto its stand and walked up to her mic, saying, "We're gonna take a break. Be back in twenty, so don't go away!"

Chet Smith put his bass on a stand next to Bobbi's, Jana Naha and Ginny Blake stepped out from behind the keyboards and drumkit, respectively, and Paolo hit several buttons that muted the outputs on all the instruments.

Jana, fishing a cigarette out of the pack in her pocket, headed straight outside. Chet went for the bathroom, but Ginny and Bobbi came over to me at the bar.

"Hey there, stranger," Bobbi said. "Was wondering if you were gonna make it."

"You know what it's been like at Seaclipse," I said. Bobbi was one of our regular customers, after all.

"Yeah. So Paolo fill you in about tall, dark, and mysterious over there?"

"You think it's John Robertson."

"I'm sure it's John Robertson," Ginny said emphatically. "I met him once. It was a few decades ago, but I could never forget those cheekbones."

Since Ginny was also a Norse god—the wife of the one that tried to destroy the world—I figured I'd take her word for it.

Ihor, the bartender, finally materialized at that point. Bobbi and I both ordered beers, and Ginny ordered her usual between-sets bourbon. Bobbi looked at me intently.

"Okay, Cass, maybe you can break the tie. Jana and I think we should approach the guy, find out what he thinks of us. I mean, it's John fucking Robertson, and he's been here to see us twice now."

Ginny rolled her eyes. "I think we should leave well enough alone. If he wishes to speak to us, he's had ample opportunity."

"And Chet's on your side?" I asked Ginny.

She shrugged. "More or less. He said, 'Yeah, fuck it, what she said,' after I explained my position."

I couldn't help but grin. "So the woman who spent centuries catching poison in a bowl to keep her husband alive is preaching patience. Big surprise."

Ginny just glowered at me. Her husband, Loki, had been so grateful for her assistance that he'd abandoned her as soon as he escaped the trap, and then tried to destroy the world. He was the one who had gone after the ficus, until I stopped him, with some help from Odin. Yeah, *that* Odin.

"So, what do *you* think, Cass?" Bobbi asked. She was staring at me intently with her sea-blue eyes, hoping to cash in on our friendship to have me go her way. Thing was, I was more on Ginny and Chet's side on this one.

Luckily, I didn't have to choose. I noticed movement behind them that made me smile. "Doesn't matter. Turn around."

The man in question was approaching. He'd removed the ball-cap and mirrorshades, and now there was no doubt who he was. The wide nose, the flat smile—not that it wasn't broad or pleasant, but his mouth had no curve to it at all, which was weird—and those intense, soulful brown eyes couldn't possibly have been anyone else.

"'Scuse me, but I was wondering if I could speak with y'all for a spell."

"Uhm—" That was all Bobbi could muster, as she openly gaped at the man.

Ginny came to her rescue, holding out a hand. "Hello. I doubt you remember me, Mr. Robertson, but we met at the Fillmore a while back. I'm Ginny Blake."

"I do not recall, I'm afraid, Miss Blake, and that is surely my loss. You are one fine-lookin' woman." He then actually kissed her hand. "And please, y'all can call me Jack."

While Ginny just smiled, Bobbi gaped, making a few gurgling noises, before finally managing to get out, "Bobbi! I'm Bobbi Milewski."

He kissed her hand, too. "You play an out-of-*sight* guitar, Miss Milewski."

"Thank you! Coming from you, that—that means a great deal."

Ihor brought the drinks over at that point, and Bobbi grabbed her beer, gulping about half of it down in one shot.

If he was bothered by this sudden display of alcoholism, Robertson didn't show it. He just said, "After y'all are through, maybe you can meet up with me at my hotel? I've got me a business proposition."

"For *us*?" Bobbi was still gaping.

"Well, it's past time I did me a followup to *Diamonds in the Rough*, and I parted ways with my last backup band. The songs I've been writin' for the new one need a sound, and I think these last two nights, I found it."

"Really? Where?" Bobbi asked.

I tried not to snarf my beer. I almost succeeded. Bobbi, to her credit, realized right away how ridiculous she sounded. "I'm sorry. You meant us, didn't you?"

"I did indeed." He gave her that flat smile again, just as Chet came out of the men's room and Jana came in from her cigarette break.

"Uhm—" Jana started.

Robertson grabbed her hand and kissed it, too. "Miss Naha, listening to your piano playing on 'Love Reign O'er Me,' I was transfixed. And you pick yourself a mean mandolin."

67

He looked at Chet, who held up both hands. "You ain't kissin' my hand, yo."

"Too right I ain't," he laughed. "I was really diggin' that bass line before 'Crossroad Blues.'"

I frowned. "I thought it was called 'Crossroads.'"

Jana stared at me derisively. "Yeah, when *Clapton* did it. The *original* was a great old blues song called 'Crossroad Blues.'"

"I like a girl who knows her music," Robertson said, admiringly. "Anyhow, I gotta split, but y'all come by the Hilton after your set's done. Ask the front desk for Mr. Brown, they'll send you right up to me."

He headed toward the exit, and Jana stared around at all of us. "What the *fuck* just happened?"

I called out after Robertson, "I'm Cassie, by the way! You can ignore me, I'm just some tall chick at the bar!"

Bobbi winced. "Sorry 'bout that, Cass, I just—"

I waved her off. "It's okay—I really *am* just some tall chick at the bar. *You* guys are the ones that are having a four-a.m. meeting with John Robertson."

"Okay," Jana said slowly, "so that *did* just happen. I need another fucking cigarette. That was really *him*?"

Now Bobbi was practically bouncing. "Yes, and he *really* wants to talk to us about being the backup band on his next CD."

"Waitasec, thought he *had* a band," Chet said.

I shook my head. "He's like Dylan, he goes through bands like underwear. In fact, he toured with the Grateful Dead as his backup band before Dylan did. I saw them together in San Diego when I was a kid."

Ginny just stared at me. "You must've been only four years old."

I laughed. "Blame the same post-hippie parents who named me 'Castor' and my twin brother 'Pollux.' They never passed up a chance to see the Dead, even carting along a little kid, and getting John Robertson was just icing for them. As it turns out, the show sucked rocks, and I don't think that tour lasted more than a couple months."

"But yeah." Bobbi gulped down the rest of her pint of beer. "He goes with a different band all the time. I think it's usually just session guys, but I'm not sure, honestly."

"This is fucking *huge*," Jana said. "Shit, this could be the break we've been *waitin'* for."

Chet stared at the others, though it was muted by the plastic sunglasses he always wore. Seriously, after a year, I still had no idea what color his eyes were. "We been waitin' for somethin'?"

Bobbi shook her head. "Not we, 1812, we, me and Jana."

At that, Chet just nodded. Jana and Bobbi had been best friends since they were six, and had dreamt of musical stardom pretty much for that entire two-decade period.

Ihor brought over another beer for Bobbi, which she hadn't asked for, but grabbed nonetheless. He also had a tequila for Jana and a bottle of Corona for Chet.

Bobbi raised her glass. "To fame and fortune!"

We all clinked our glasses. After I gulped down some of my amber beer, I added, "And hey, don't forget the little people when you get all rich and famous and stuff."

Jana grinned. "No worries, Zukav. We're gonna need groupies, am I right?"

I slapped her playfully on the arm. "You're not my type."

"Speakin'a which, where *is* Demitrijian?"

I rolled my eyes. Special Agent Rance Demitrijian of the FBI and I were *not* dating. Exactly. Sure, he always sat with me when he was able to make it down from Miami to see 1812, and he always dove with me when he came to Seaclipse, and there was that one time I rescued him from being killed by a nixie where I got to see him naked and gave him mouth-to-mouth on the boardwalk.

But we weren't dating. Really.

"I got a text from him earlier," I said. "He's stuck late at work, but he should be here tomorrow night."

"Good." Jana grinned. "This may be our last weekend here."

The next night, I walked in during the middle of the band's first set. Once again, the table by the ficus had an occupant, but this time it was Rance.

I sat down next to him and smiled—we weren't even going to try talking, especially since the band was plowing through a particularly loud rendition of "Smoke on the Water"—and signaled Adina, one of the waitresses, for my usual beer.

Once 1812 was done with their cover of Deep Purple, Rance spoke up. "A rumor has been moving throughout the bar that 1812 was approached by a very famous musician about the possibility of their performing on his long-awaited next CD."

That's our Special Agent Demitrijian—tall, dark, handsome (he does have the cutest cleft chin), and never uses two words when ten will do.

"Yup. Got to meet him. Well, for small values of 'meet'—I was standing next to the four of them when *they* met him, and even talked to him for a second, but we were never formally introduced."

The band was introducing themselves, which gave us a bit of time to talk, followed by Jana doing the piano intro to Jethro Tull's "Locomotive Breath." Once the song kicked in properly, though, it was back to nodding, smiling, and sipping our drinks.

They ended the set with Marvin Gaye's "Don't Do It," and afterward they came off the stage. Just like last night, Jana ducked outside to smoke, Chet headed to the bathroom, and Bobbi and Ginny came over to me.

As the two of them grabbed two other chairs from other tables and put them at our little round table, I asked, "So tell us, how'd it go last night?"

Bobbi closed her eyes and sighed. "We can't tell you."

"What!?"

"We signed an NDA," she added quickly.

Before I could respond to that, Rance held up a hand. "Say no more, please. The last thing I would do is ask you to violate a non-disclosure agreement. In fact, as a federal agent, it's my responsibility to ensure that you *don't*."

"We do need one thing from you, though," Bobbi said, "and you gotta tell us before Jana and Chet get back."

I gulped some of my beer. I was getting a very bad feeling about this.

Leaning forward and staring at me intently, Bobbi asked, "Did you—well, *feel* anything from Jack?"

I rolled my eyes. "Jesus, Bobbi."

Ginny regarded Bobbi with an expression that almost looked like pity. "I warned you that she would not necessarily—"

Waving a hand back and forth, Bobbi said, "Yeah, yeah, I know, but I had to ask. After Russ…"

I gulped more beer.

Recently, during that whole mess that served as my introduction to Loki, Ginny, Odin, and the mystical nature of Mayor Fred's ficus, I had also found out that I'm a Norse fate goddess— a Dís. If nothing else, it explained why I've always been such a damned weirdness magnet.

It was also something that Bobbi knew because I told her, and Ginny knew because she was already a Norse goddess her own damn self. I didn't think Chet would get it, and I didn't think Jana would keep her mouth shut about it, so I didn't tell them.

"Put it this way," I said after swallowing the beer, "he looks that young some way *other* than a glamour." That much I knew. I wasn't all together clear as to what, exactly, being a fate goddess entailed, but one thing I did know I could do was see through glamours. It was how I discovered that Russ, Jana's ex-fiancé, was actually a water elemental. "And I'm not getting any weird-ass vibes off him."

"Okay, good." Bobbi sounded a lot more relieved than she probably should have, but I couldn't pursue it, since Chet came ambling over.

"Anyhow," Ginny said quickly, "we shall be taking a pause from our performances here starting next weekend."

"Y'know," I said with a smirk, "the last time you guys took a break from playing Mayor Fred's, the replacement band almost destroyed the world."

Bobbi grinned. "Yeah, but what're the odds of that happening twice? Besides, that was 'cause we couldn't nail down a drummer. This time? We'll be livin' the high life in—" She stopped herself.

Again, I rolled my eyes. "You can't even tell me *where* you're recording this CD?"

Rance put a hand on mine. "You really should go easy on all of them, Cassie, NDAs these days have a tendency to be *extremely* thorough."

"It's some *bull*shit," Chet said. "Can't even say that we're recordin' nothin'."

"Chet, I was standing *right here* when he made the offer." I shrugged and pointed at the bar. "Well, okay, over there. But you know what I mean."

Jana had come back from sucking nicotine and was grinning from ear to ear. "What it *means*, Zukav, is that we are *going places*. We just can't tell you what those places *are*."

I had to admit, I was glad to see a smile on Jana's face. She'd been pretty down since the business with Russ, during which she almost became cursed to fall in love with him so badly that it'd kill her. After a succession of brief, stupid relationships, Jana had really found true love, even if it was helped along by magic, and then had it yanked away from her. She'd been even more sullen than usual.

So maybe 1812 going somewhere beyond Key West clubs would get her groove back.

The next few weeks could charitably be considered crazy. Noah had a family reunion he had to go to, which meant I was pretty much running every dive at Seaclipse for a week. Plus, it was the August busy season, with vacationers, students getting in their last dives before the school year started, and so on. I pretty much woke up, went to Seaclipse, lead as many dives as I could stand, and went back to the Bottroff House and collapsed. I didn't even get *near* Mayor Fred's for three weeks.

Finally, Labor Day weekend rolled by, and on Thursday night it was raining. Normally, this wouldn't be enough to cancel the night dives, but of the seven people who'd signed up, five cancelled. I gotta say, I never got that. I mean, if the rain was heavy with nasty winds then *we* cancelled the dive. But light rain, the type we got every third day in Florida anyhow? What's the big deal? I mean, c'mon, are these people who are about to go scuba diving worried that they're going to get *wet*?

So I convinced Noah to take the two who were willing to brave the drizzle, and I went to Mayor Fred's, figuring, it had been almost a month, they *had* to be done recording, right?

Apparently not, since I walked into Mayor Fred's—with the tarp on top to keep the rain off the bar—to see three guys on the stage. One had an acoustic guitar, one had an electric bass, one sat at a minimal drumkit. All three were wearing white t-shirts with pictures of sea anemones on them, black shorts, and (I swear I am not making this up) hot pink flip-flops.

That was strike one. Strike two was the fact that I walked in on them covering Jimmy Buffett's "Margaritaville." I know some tourists like it, but they can always go to one of the damn karaoke places and sing that crap themselves.

And then strike three: "Good evening, Mayor Fred's, we're Friends Anemones, and this next one is a request from Martha!"

Okay, that was actually a pretty clever pun, so I gave them a pass on their name, but then the *next* song was *also* Jimmy fucking Buffett ("A Pirate Looks at Forty"), at which point I ran screaming from the bar before Adina could even catch sight of me to get me my beer.

I bumped into Ginny as she was striding down Greene Street toward the bar, her red hair covered by a big floppy hat to protect her from the rain. "Ginny! Oh, thank Christ. Please tell me you guys are coming back soon. Mayor Fred's is turning into a Parrothead bar."

Ginny frowned. "I'm sorry?"

Shaking my head, I said, "The guys in there seem like a Jimmy Buffett cover band. I had to get out of there before 'It's Five O'Clock Somewhere' started and I'd have to kill someone."

"Well, actually, I was coming here because that lovely woman at the inn where you live said you were here. I need your help."

My turn to frown. "With what?"

"The rest of the band. Since we got back from Mississippi, they've been—*wrong*."

I stared at her for a moment. "C'mon, let's go somewhere to talk out of the rain."

We headed down Greene Street to Duval Street. "You recorded in Mississippi?"

She nodded. "In a town called Hazlehurst. Mr. Robertson— Jack—has a private studio there."

We landsharked our way through the tourists on Duval until we reached Em's, an eatery with the best fries on the island. As we walked, I said, "I haven't heard from Bobbi at *all*. I figured I'd get texts or something."

"There was no time to communicate outside the studio except to order food deliveries." Ginny sounded more than a little grumpy. "Jack worked us very hard the first week, making sure we rehearsed all through the days and evenings in order to learn the songs."

We arrived at Em's and walked up the stairs. The place was crowded, but the tables on the balcony were free. The rain was letting up, and the chairs out there had umbrellas over them, so we took one of them. I was already damp from both seawater and sweat, and Ginny never seemed affected by weather. We sat down, hunched under the umbrellas, and ordered conch fritters and fries and a beer each. Once we were settled, Ginny went on.

"The second week, we laid down the tracks. Chet and I put down the bass and drums first, and then we added everything else later." She shook her head. "He seemed fine with my drumming, but he kept making Chet do things over, and that was as nothing compared to what he put Bobbi and Jana through. *Constant* re-takes. He finally freed us on Monday, and he said he would be doing post-production work for a fortnight."

The beers came, and Ginny practically drank hers all in one swallow. I openly gaped. Usually, she's a sipper.

"We agreed to all go home and sleep for a day, just to be away from each other, but to meet at Mayor Fred's on Wednesday to discuss restarting our weekend gig. Nobody showed but me." She sighed. "I went to Bobbi's house, to Chet's boat, and to Jana's apartment, and they were all *exactly the same*."

"Exactly the same, how?"

"Lethargic. Unwilling to move from their chairs. From Chet, I almost expected that, possibly even Jana. But Bobbi?"

I nodded. Bobbi Milewski was a bundle of energy, and even when she was exhausted after a dive or a gig, she was back to bouncing around an hour later.

"That's not the worst part, though," Ginny said gravely. "When I mentioned that we had to meet at Mayor Fred's to discuss returning, they all said the same thing: that they did not wish to."

I choked on my beer. "Say *what?*"

"None of them wish to play music anymore. At all. Not at

Mayor Fred's, not with 1812, not again."

"That's crazy! Chet—well, who the hell knows what goes through Chet's head at any given time, but Bobbi and Jana have been playing music together since they were kids. Jana's quit 1812 twice in the last four months, and Bobbi was apoplectic both times."

"I know. Jana even said she was not returning from her leave of absence at her teaching position."

My eyes widened. While the four members of 1812 made decent money playing Mayor Fred's, it wasn't enough to live on, generally. Bobbi worked at her parents' store, Chet gave tours on his boat, and Jana was a music teacher for kids. I had no idea what Ginny did for food and shelter, and was kind of afraid to ask. But Jana *loved* teaching kids—and she was also a virtuoso musician. I couldn't believe she'd give that up.

I decided I needed to see this for myself. Jana lived closest—she was the only one who lived on Key West itself, in an apartment on Ely Street—so after dinner, we went to the Bottroff House and retrieved Rocinante, my beat-up 1985 Ford F-150 pickup truck. It was only a five-minute drive to Ely Street, and the building had parking spaces in front. Of course, they belonged to the people who lived there, but half of them were empty, and I doubted we were staying all that long.

Jana answered the door looking half asleep. She was wearing a black Sex Pistols T-shirt and black shorts, a cigarette dangling from her mouth. "Hey, Zukav. Hey, Blake. C'mon in, I guess."

We followed her into her apartment, which had a single path through the piles of clothes, empty cigarette boxes, papers, CDs, jewel cases, half-empty glasses, and other *stuff* on the floor that led to a desk that had her laptop on it. She sat down at the computer chair and rested her cigarette in a Conch Republic ashtray.

"I been checkin' out s'm jobs online."

Playing dumb, I said, "I thought you had a job."

"Just not int'the music thing no more, y'know? Need t'try somethin' different." Then she yawned. "May go take 'nother nap, first."

Music had been Jana's everything for her entire life. Bobbi once uploaded a video to YouTube of Jana playing the Beatles'

"Blackbird" on an acoustic guitar at the age of seven. "So—what? You're quitting 1812 again?"

"More like breakin' up." She shrugged. "Happens. I guess. Had a good run, now s'over."

We stayed for a bit longer, making stupid chitchat, but Jana was falling asleep before our very eyes, so we excused ourselves.

Ginny hit me with a "see? *see?*" look.

"Yeah," I muttered. "Let's go to Cow Key."

Bobbi still lived at home with her folks and some of her brothers. One of those brothers—they all dived at Seaclipse, but I honestly couldn't tell them apart, as they were all blond-haired and blue-eyed like their sister, and they all overused the words "dude" and "whoa"—answered the door.

"Hey, Cass. Wussup?"

"Is Bobbi around?"

Grinning stupidly, he said, "Dude, you guys gettin' a whiffle-ball game goin'? I'll see if she can come out to play."

He probably thought he was funny. He was alone in this. We waited outside while he fetched her.

Bobbi was even more bleary-eyed than Jana had been. She was wearing her usual outfit of plain white T-shirt and blue shorts. Seriously, it was all she wore. I think she had an infinite supply of them in her closet. "'Sup?"

"Just wanted to see how you were doin'," I said slowly. "You okay?"

"Been sleepin' all day. Need t'go back t'bed."

"So, uh," I started, playing dumb again, "when's 1812 gonna be back at Mayor Fred's? I mean, me and Rance have to have *something* to do on the weekends, right?" I grinned gamely.

"Nah, done with 'at. Don' wanna do music no more. Gotta get t'sleep."

She wandered off, shuffling like a zombie toward the interior of the house.

The brother came back to the door, the stupid grin replaced with a scared frown. "Dude, I dunno what's wrong with her, but it's *bad*. I ain't *never* seen her like this. Only time she woke up was to put her guitar on eBay."

I actually did a double take at that. "What?"

"For real, dude. I put a bid on it just so's it'll stay in the house, y'know? For when she changes her mind? But, dude, she's *seriously* got me worried."

"We'll see what we can do," I said lamely, considering I had no bloody clue what *to* do. We headed back to the truck. I whipped out my smartphone.

"Who are you telephoning?" Ginny asked.

"Rance. Hope he's still in his office."

After I hit his work number on my "frequently dialed" menu, I put the phone to my ear. He hadn't been at Mayor Fred's, so I was hoping it was because he was stuck in Miami working late.

"Special Agent Demi— Oh, hi there, Cassie, good to hear from you. How are you doing?" That last was probably added when he finally looked at the caller ID.

"Not so hot." I gave him a brief précis of 1812's travails. "I assume you're sitting at your desk with its computer on it?"

"Yes, of course I am. Do you need me to look something up online?"

"Yeah." I took a breath. "First, I need you to find out who the musicians are who played on John Robertson's recent CDs and find out where they are now."

"You think he did something to 1812? Is this something you're sensing as a Dís?"

I shook my head, even though the gesture was meaningless over the phone. "No, but do I really need it? I mean, Jana's talking career change, and Bobbi's selling her Les Paul. Whatever's going on here, it is *not* natural."

"Actually, it's completely natural for people to undergo traumatic experiences and change their lives entirely. I've seen it plenty of times with families of murder victims."

"All right, fine, maybe it is that, but why didn't it affect Ginny the same way?"

Ginny just stared at me.

"Okay, dumb question, but still—I don't like it. Just—just look into it, okay?"

"Fine. I've got tomorrow off, so I signed up for the afternoon dive. I'll meet you tomorrow at Seaclipse."

The next morning, I woke up to a text message from Rance: "This is bigger than we thought am driving down to meet you at b&b at 11:15 know you're not conscious before then."

Rance knew me way too well. I woke up at eleven pretty much every day, and the first thing I needed after a shower was a cup of coffee, usually in the garden in the midst of the Bottroff House. Every morning, Hawai'ian Kona was served, a.k.a. the nectar of the gods.

By the time a quarter after eleven rolled around, I had showered, climbed into my bathing suit, and stumbled down the stairs from my cottage on the B&B's grounds and walked toward the table where breakfast was laid out. I'd also received and replied to a second text, this one from Cara. It turned out her cast was off, and she was ready to run dives again. That meant I had my life back.

Rance was sitting in one of the white wrought-iron chairs that was off to the side, away from the guests who were congregated around the picnic table. I poured some of the blessed coffee into a mug, clutched it for dear life, and went over to sit on the stool nearest him.

Rance had a look on his face that I just did *not* like. "Okay, look, I found some things out, but it wasn't anything I could transfer to a tablet or print out or anything. I mean, I could have, but I wasn't entirely sure I wanted to, because I didn't like where any of it was going, and I didn't have probable cause for the searches I was doing within our databases, so I kind of need there not to be a trail of what I was—"

I tried to hang in, I really did, but I'd only had two sips of coffee. "Rance!" I snapped. "The point? Some time this decade?"

"Right." He took a deep breath. "I checked into everyone who played on *Diamonds in the Rough*, which came out two years ago. None of them have any music credits on any albums since, except for the bass player, but that was a live CD of a concert from 2002. Turns out, they were all in a Chicago-based band called Uptight Garage, but all of the band's live performances in Chicago-area clubs predate the recording sessions for *Diamonds*, and they haven't performed anywhere since. In fact, the last time they updated their web site was the day before the *Diamonds* sessions started, and they used to update it daily prior to that. One of them committed suicide last year, and another checked herself into a mental hospital and is still there. Now, Robertson's previous album was *Immoral Mortals*, and that time he used another local band, this one from New York, called Waldorf Salad Astoria. Same deal with them, they didn't play any gigs after the recording sessions of the CD they played on. Their lead singer and guitarist both committed suicide—they were lovers, and NYPD chalked it up to some kind of suicide pact, especially since their families didn't know they were gay. Can't find any records on the other three bandmembers, which isn't exactly encouraging, either."

Despite having only had two sips of coffee, I was now completely wide awake. "How did nobody notice this?"

"All I can say is he's being very careful. The last two bands he chose were in cities that have hundreds of bands playing in clubs every night. No one outside of a few hardcore devotees would even notice if a particular band stopped playing in New York or Chicago. As for here, there's fewer bands, but the turnover of the customer base is massive. It's the perfect cover for..."

Then he trailed off and just stared at me. "What?" I prompted.

"See, this is the problem. I've got a pattern of criminal behavior, but no *actual* criminal behavior. This is why I covered my tracks and didn't save anything or print anything or leave any evidence that I did any of these searches. There's no crime here, just a pattern that I wouldn't even think twice about, except—" He shook his head. "Except I know you. I've seen what you've done and..."

I reached under the strap of my bathing suit, where I kept my smartphone pressed against my left boob. (What? I don't have pockets in the bathing suit.) I called Ginny.

"Hello, Cassie."

"Ginny, is Robertson doing post-production on the CD in that same studio in Mississippi?"

"Yes, he is. Why?"

"You think if we go up there, you can get us in to see him?"

There was a long silence on the other end of the phone before Ginny finally replied. "It's an eighteen-hour drive, Cassie. Jack flew us out, I doubt he'll fly me back."

"Then we'll drive it. You with me, or not?"

A pause. "I, ah, guess I'm with you."

"Good. Meet me at the Bottroff House in an hour. Pack light."

I ended the call and hit Seaclipse on the autodialer. It was a good thing Cara was back on dive duty, because I was gonna need a couple of days off.

Rance was squinting at me. "What do you have in mind?"

I blew out a breath. "No fucking clue. But this guy's already driven at least three musicians he's worked with to suicide, and I'm *damned* if I'm going to let him pull that shit on my two best friends."

I first came to Key West after getting my Master's from the University of Calfornia-San Diego. I then drove across the bottom of the country, what I jokingly called my "I-10 tour." Using that interstate highway, I hit a bunch of places, before going south on I-75 to the Florida Turnpike to Route 1 to Key West.

A year later, I was finally going back the way I came, and I had to say that the Florida panhandle was even more boring this time. It didn't help that I was worried about my friends.

It didn't occur to me until we went through Gainesville to ask if Ginny even knew how to drive—you never knew what she knew and didn't know, being a Norse goddess and all. Luckily she did, and she took over part of the drive through northern Florida. I spent that time on my smartphone, trying to find out what I could about John Robertson.

I was surprised at how little there was in terms of actual substantial information. Everything was press release hype or canned stories or bland interviews with cliché answers to everything.

And then one bit from an old *Rolling Stone* interview that had been archived on Robertson's own web site caught my eye. He was asked why, when he listed so many blues players as influences, he never covered any blues songs, and said in reply: "I did my time playin' the blues for a long time. I'm playin' other stuff now. Movin' on, you dig?"

Except Robertson had never played the blues. I checked his entire playlist, from his debut album, where he kind of came out of nowhere in 1966 with the single, "Saving My Soul," then opening for the Dead and for Hendrix before touring on his own. All his stuff was straight-up rock-and-roll. Sure, some blues influence—every rocker had blues influence—but he said he'd played the blues for a long time. Yet there was no record of it.

That got me bopping around to look up old blues players from the 1920s to the 1960s—John Lee Hooker, Leadbelly, Sonny Boy Williamson, Muddy Waters, Howlin' Wolf, Etta James...

"Holy fuck!"

Sounding almost panicky, Ginny asked, "What?"

"Pull over, right now."

Obligingly, Ginny hit the right turn signal, and slowly decelerated onto the shoulder of I-10. Once Rocinante had come to a full stop, I shoved the display of my smartphone in her face. It currently showed a picture, with a caption identifying the subject.

"That's—" She shook her head. "That can't be."

"Add the sideburns. Looks *just* like him."

We drove the rest of the way to Hazlehurst, Mississippi in nervous silence. I gotta say, I've got no kind of recollection of what the drive through Alabama and Mississippi was like. I was focused entirely on the picture I found, and the stories that were told about him—stories I never would have believed if I hadn't spent the last year killing dragons, driving off nixies, casting counterspells against gods, chasing down UFOs, and spending large chunks of my days with ghosts and immortals.

I also have no recollection of how we got into Robertson's Soul Saving Studios—a name that I was coming to realize had a lot behind it besides relating to the title of his first hit—but there we were, standing in the engineering booth of a recording studio, Robertson and his sideburns sitting at a laptop that was hooked up to a big sound board. The far wall had LPs, 45 RPM singles, CDs, and cassette tapes all framed. Every physical version of all his recordings was enshrined on that wall.

Over the speakers, a song was playing that I didn't recognize, though I instantly placed the guitar lick as being Bobbi's. It was probably something from the new CD, whatever it might be.

"Uh, Virginia, I don't know what you and your friend here need, but I'm a little busy trying to—"

"My name is not Virginia—as I told you several times during

the recording. It's Sigyn. And Cassie and I are here to tell you that we know your secret, Jack."

"Or," I added, "should we say Robert. Or do you prefer Mr. Johnson?"

He just stared at us with those incredible eyes of his. "Say what? You two been hittin' the reefer?"

"Look, I know the stories—that Robert Johnson sold his soul to the devil to become the greatest musician in the world. And if you did that, more power to you—your soul, you can do whatever the fuck you want with it. But now? You're hurting other people, including my friends."

"I ain't never hurt *nobody*, little girl," he said tightly. I noticed he did not deny being Robert Johnson.

"Really? Tell that to the bassist for Uptight Garage. He committed suicide. So did two people from Waldorf Salad Astoria. Someone else from Uptight Garage is in a loony bin in St. Charles, Illinois. She checked herself in. And I'm betting they all did it because you stole their music from them—same way you did from Bobbi, Jana, and Chet."

Now he just stared at me. "Tommy committed suicide?" His voice was much more subdued.

I nodded. "Last year."

"And two people from Waldorf?"

"The lead singer and guitarist."

He looked away, shaking his head. "Aldo and Swoop. They were such a nice couple, those two. I was hopin' they'd be able to jump the broom, now that New York made it all legal—didn't know they'd killed themselves." To my shock, I saw him wipe a tear from one of his soulful eyes. Then he turned to look at us. "I swear to you both, I had no idea that happened."

"Right, you'd already used them up and spit them out."

"I didn't use 'em up!" Now he was back to being the bombastic rocker. "I gave them a *voice*! They was all fine musicians, but they was toilin' for shit clubs to a dozen people a night. Or they were your friends, just some tourist-town wage slaves. Without me, nobody woulda ever heard 'em."

"People heard them all the time before you came along! So, yeah, it was just in some little club in New York or Chicago or

Key West—they still had audiences! And those audiences *never* get to hear them again."

Pointing to his wall of fame, he said, "They could hear them any time and every time! I *recorded* them, so the whole world could know them! And all I took—"

He cut himself off.

"Their souls?" Ginny said quietly.

"Not exactly." He took a breath. "Yeah, I sold my soul down at the Dockery Plantation, like they say I did, and then they tried to take me away in '38." He shook his head. "Stayed one step ahead'a them demons for decades, but they finally caught up to me in '64. Said I owed 'em more music. See, when they call it soul music, they ain't just whistlin' Dixie. Music has *power*, and my music gave it to 'em. So I made 'em a deal. I stay alive, but I give 'em more power."

I shook my head. "That's why you used so many different backup musicians. And why they were always people nobody ever heard of."

"But it didn't work on me," Ginny said.

"Yeah, I still don't get that. It's like you ain't human."

She smiled. "I'm not. Like you, I'm immortal, though I came by my eternal life more honestly, having been born to it. Whatever demons you did your deal with have no dominion over the souls of the Aesir."

"I got no idea what that means," Johnson said, "but I guess the cat's outta the bag, huh?"

"We know the truth," I told him. "And we will share that truth with whoever'll listen. Sure, most people will think it's bogus, but there's a trail. It's not the easiest one to see at first, but once Ginny and I expose it, you're screwed." He opened his mouth, but I interrupted. "And before you try to threaten us? We also confided in a federal agent in Miami. If we disappear, he'll look into it, and he already knows what you did."

"I wasn't gonna threaten you, little girl." He barked a mirthless laugh. "I don't even know your name."

"Cassie Zukav. I'm a dive instructor, a B&B manager, an 1812 groupie, and one of the Dísir."

"What's a dee-seer?"

"A Norse fate goddess."

"Yeah, okay." He blew out a long breath and looked to the ceiling. "Look, Miss Zukav—or Miss Fate Goddess, or whatever the hell you are—I ain't never meant to hurt nobody. I figured it was just a piece'a their soul. Wouldn't nobody miss it."

I found myself starting to feel sorry for him, for some reason. "Some of them didn't. They didn't *all* commit suicide, and I'm sure a lot of them went on to have productive lives. Bands burn out and break up all the time. But they should do it on their own schedule, don't you think?"

"Yeah. And Tommy, Aldo, and Swoop—they was good people. They didn't deserve that. Ditto your friends."

"Jana teaches music to kids. What happens to her students? How many more musicians'll be lost because she can't guide them?" It was twisting the knife a bit, but I was annoyed at myself for feeling sorry for this selfish asshole.

"Yeah." He stared at me, and I could see why so many people were mesmerized by him over the years. Including me. It wasn't a glamour, it was just plain old charisma. "I can't give back what I already paid. But they ain't come for the delivery of your friends yet. I can give *that* back."

"Then what happens?" Ginny asked the question simply, but she knew better than most about the consequences of actions taken by powerful beings.

"Probably best not to find out," said a deep, resonant voice from behind me.

I turned around to see—well, *something*. For a moment, it looked like a young, African-American man. Then a second later, it was a white woman wearing too much makeup. Then a Latin guy with a smirk. And on and on and on—but those were just flickers. Between them, though, I kept seeing a formless, smoky mass.

The voice seemed to echo off everything in the room. "You *know* the consequences, Mr. Johnson. If you do not provide me with the soul shards I require, we will have to revert to the original contract."

"You again," Johnson said. "Funny, you don't look no different."

84

"Neither do you." At this point, all I saw was the formless smoke.

"What do you see him as?" I asked.

Johnson frowned at me. "Same little man I met back at Dockery."

Ginny added, "I see a young woman. What do you see?"

I shuddered. "I'm guessing his true form. Glamours don't work on me, chuckles."

"This is not your concern, creatures of the Norse. Your days are in the past."

Smiling, Ginny said, "My days, perhaps, but Cassie was born of Midgard."

"Besides, it became my concern when this jackass fucked with my friends." I took a step toward the demon.

"Regardless, it is, ultimately, Mr. Johnson's decision." The demon started to—float, I guess?—closer to Johnson. "Whether to continue to enjoy a long and fruitful life while giving obscure musicians an exposure they would never have otherwise had, or to die a painful death followed by eternal suffering."

I stepped between the demon and Johnson, and thrust out a hand. "Back off, asshole. You've done enough—"

The smoke brushed my hand, and suddenly the room lit up like a Christmas tree, while the demon screamed so loud it made my ribcage vibrate. Wincing, I bent over, hands on my ears, trying to block the demon's cries.

Then the room dimmed again to normal. The demon was gone.

"What the fuck was *that*?" I asked, my heart pounding in my chest.

Ginny, though, was grinning. "What I suspected would happen. That demon was vulnerable to you because he alters people's fate. As a fate goddess, you may banish him with but a touch."

"Oh." I shook my head. "Someone really needs to give me a fucking instruction manual for this."

"That was—outta sight." Johnson was staring at the space where the demon was. "That's some powerful mojo you got there, little girl."

"Yes, it is." I stared hard at him. "So how badly do you want to piss me off?"

"What I *want*—" Johnson blew out a breath. "Shit, what I want is to live a nice long life. But I done *lived* a nice long life, and 'cause'a that, three people are dead who shouldn't be. 'Sides, if I do what I want, you two'll make sure nobody works with me again, and that little man'll come back and take what's due." He gave me his flat smile. "And if I do what you want, same thing. So I guess I ain't got no choice, do I?"

The following Thursday, I walked into Mayor Fred's and saw a beautiful sight: 1812, back onstage.

They were just tuning up as I sat down next to Rance at the table by the ficus. After I ordered my usual pint, Rance said, "We got an alert just before I left the office tonight, and I made sure to read it over. John Robertson was found dead in his studio this morning. No COD yet, obviously, but everyone's assuming a drug overdose, since he's an old rock-and-roll musician, and he's not one that has much of a history with rehabilitation centers and the like. Apparently, he'd just sent the masters of his latest recording off to his record company so the CDs could be pressed. Looks like it'll be released posthumously now, which is kind of too bad. Though I guess him still being alive would've been a good deal worse?"

I shuddered. "That's an understatement. You were right, Rance, it was a pattern of criminal behavior. Just not something that'd be all that easy to prove in a court of law, since I can't imagine a U.S. Attorney being able to prosecute someone for stealing souls."

Rance smirked. "I can safely say that not a single one of the AUSAs I work with would be willing to touch such a prosecution with a proverbial ten-foot pole."

Adina brought my pint and I held it up for a toast. "To stopping the soul-sucking Robert Johnson—or John Robertson, or whatever the hell he called himself."

I clinked my full pint glass against Rance's half-empty one, and we both gulped down our beers. Then he stared at me with those nice green eyes of his. "So how *did* you stop him? Some kind of spell? Or something else?"

I shrugged. "I'm a fate goddess. I just reminded him of his fate."

Bobbi stepped up to the microphone, then. "We've got a couple songs we'd like to start the set with, dedicated to a dear friend of ours. Probably the best friend 1812 has ever had." She looked right at me, then slammed into a series of chords—three long, followed by two short that blended right into the next set of three.

Chet leaned into the mic and started sing, "Woke up this mornin', I was feelin' around for my shoes."

They followed "Walkin' Blues" with another Robert Johnson song, this time with Bobbi on vocals: "Hellhound on My Trail." They followed that with a rousing rendition of "Crossroad Blues," with Jana again singing it as she had that fateful night when a famous old rocker approached them to be on his CD. I belatedly realized that he was probably the one who requested that they do "Crossroad" that night.

"Now," Bobbi said after the applause died down, "we'd like to do something a little different. I don't know if you all saw the news today, but John Robertson passed away this morning. We had the privilege to be his backup band for what turned out to be his final CD, which is gonna be called *Old Man's Blues in a Young Man's Body*. This is the title track."

Jana started a lovely blues piano riff, and then Bobbi sang in a soulful soprano about a man trying to recapture the blues and failing. When the guitar solo started, I realized it was the same tune that had been playing when Ginny and I walked into Soul Saving Studios.

When the song ended, I held up my pint again. "Rest in peace, J.R."

Rance lifted his glass. Around us, the crowd was grooving to 1812's sound as they played a rare original song rather than a tune they'd heard many times before. "Amen," he said quietly. "Amen."

Love Over and Over

I really should never check my e-mail before I've had coffee.

Since settling in Key West, I've fallen into a pretty consistent pattern of going to bed at five a.m., and getting up at eleven. During those six hours of slumber, the e-mail tends to pile up a bit: digests from scuba-diving related mailing lists I'm on, e-mail from various family and friends, the newsletter from that awful guitarist who's been hitting on me since I got here, the daily e-mail from Mom sent before she goes to work in San Diego, and a metric fuckton of spam. (No, I don't have a spam filter. I used to, but I didn't check it often enough, and that almost got a friend of mine killed by a nixie.) Plus, I usually have e-mail from either Cara Zimmerman or Andy Wasserstein, my bosses at the Seaclipse dive shop, telling me who's signed up for the afternoon dive.

On those mornings when I remembered to charge my smartphone overnight, I check my e-mail when I get up. This particular Friday morning, I had charged it, so the e-mail from Cara informed me that my afternoon dive included Rany (one of my regulars), a trio of college students who'd been diving with me all week, and V.E. Bolverk.

I nearly dropped the phone.

After my shower, I squeezed myself into my neoprene dive suit and stumbled down the wooden stairs that led down from my second-floor hotel room in the Bottroff House Bed & Breakfast. I knew better than to try to talk to anyone before coffee, so it wasn't until after I guzzled down some of the B&B's excellent Hawai'ian Kona that I dialed Seaclipse.

"Hey, Cass," said Andy on the other end.

"Please tell me your wife is playing a joke on me."

"Whaddaya mean?"

"Bolverk?"

"No joke, he's back. In fact, he's here now—gave me a chance to catch up, since I haven't seen him since April. I figured the snow scared him off."

I briefly considered telling Andy the truth—that "V.E. Bolverk" was really Odin, the Allfather of the Aesir, and the snowstorm in April was actually Fimbulvetr, the beginning of the end of the world, being brought about by Odin's blood-brother Loki, until Odin and I stopped him, and oh, by the way, Odin also told me that I'm a Dís, a Norse fate goddess—but he'd probably fire me for being a crazy person.

Or not. I totally saved his business after the UFO crash on Dry Tortugas.

Andy was still talking: "I offered to take him out sooner, but he insisted on going on your dive. And hey, customer's always right, right?"

"Right." I shook my head and poured another mug of coffee before heading back up to my cottage. "See you soon, then."

"You seem distressed," said the captain as I came in. As usual, the ghost of Captain Jeremiah Bottroff had avoided being there when I woke up. Nineteenth century wrecker captains got all squirrelly when they had to look at naked female flesh, and this particular one tried to avoid dealing with the owner of that flesh being as cranky as I am first thing, but he was waiting for me upon my return from the coffee run.

"That's one word for it. Odin's back."

90

"Really? That is unexpected."

I grabbed my dive bag from the closet. "'Unexpected'? That the best you can do? Last time he showed up, the world nearly ended."

"True, but the gentleman was also the only person with whom I have had any intellectual congress besides yourself since my demise."

I hadn't thought of it that way. I'd been the captain's first conversation in a hundred and fifty years when I showed up at the Bottroff House last year. Odin was his second.

With a sigh, I went back outside and tossed the bag into the back of Rocinante, my 1985 Ford F-150 pickup truck. The drive to Stock Island seemed to take forever. I mean, yeah, there was traffic on Route 1—there's *always* traffic on Route 1—but the anticipation of wondering why the fuck Odin was back after six months just dragged it out.

When I got there, the three students were standing at the counter debating the merits of buying a dive knife with Andy. Rany had actually deigned to show up—he generally missed, like, a third of his dives—and was looking at the regulators. And off in one of the corners of the shop, behind the magazine rack, was a big guy with a bald crown, shock of white hair around the temple, tied back into a ponytail, and a missing left eye—no eyepatch or anything, just a blank socket, but Odin made it work.

I honestly wasn't sure how I was going to react to seeing him again, considering how much he turned my life inside out. Okay, that's not fair, my life was *already* inside out, he just was the one who explained to me why.

But when he turned to say, "Hello, Cassie" in that deep, authoritative voice of his, I actually smiled and realized I was glad to see him.

"What," I said with a cheeky grin, "you can't just come visit, you have to set up an appointment at my job and surprise me?"

Solemnly, Odin said, "I'm afraid that it was the only way I would be able to speak to you directly."

"Actually, they have these fabulous new inventions called 'telephones.'"

Odin mouth twitched a bit, and for a second, I thought he might actually smile. "So I've been lead to understand. However,

I felt it was best for this conversation to take place in person, and it needed to be here rather than your home or the tavern."

"Why's that?"

"Because the other two locales are on Key West, and I am unable to set foot on that island."

"How'd that happen?"

Shaking his head, Odin rubbed his bearded chin. "A spell so prevents me. Ah, Cassie, I have grown old and careless to allow this to happen."

"Allowed what to happen? Who cast the spell?"

"Loki did, after he escaped."

I blinked. "Loki *escaped?*"

"Yes."

Throwing my hands in the air, I asked, "Why the fuck didn't you *lead* with that? God-fucking-dammit, we've got to—"

Odin put what he probably thought was a comforting hand on my shoulder. Last time he did that, he used his own mojo to boost mine so I could cast a counterspell that would keep Loki from destroying the world. This time, I felt a jolt of—something. Encouragement, maybe? In any case, I was suddenly less pissed off.

"Loki has a fraction of the power he had when last you met. Indeed, he only has as much as he has due to the continued fascination with the comic book versions of the Aesir that have propagated for the past several decades."

I snorted. Prior to actually meeting the remnants of the Norse pantheon, what little knowledge I had of the Aesir were from my twin brother Paul's comic book collection. And man did they get it wrong, from Stan Lee and Jack Kirby, all the way through to Kenneth Branagh and Joss Whedon and beyond …

"That power is what enables him to keep me from Key West—but he can do little else at present. So the threat is not imminent, nor is it likely that he will again try to bring about Ragnarok."

"Yeah, but there *is* a threat. Right?"

"Perhaps," Odin said slowly.

I frowned. "What does 'perhaps' mean in this context, exactly?"

"There are always many possibilities where my blood-brother is concerned."

"Okay, for the record? When I ask you to clarify one of the

cryptic-ass things you always say, don't respond with something even *more* cryptic."

Before Odin could respond, though, Rany walked over, asking if we were going to be heading out to dive soon. Looking over at the counter, the students had decided not to buy knives and were standing around waiting impatiently. Being teenagers, this meant they were fondling their smartphones.

I gotta admit, I have no memory of the dive itself. You have to dive with a buddy, so I went with one of the students—the other two making up another pair—while Rany dived with Odin. I'd forgotten to charge the batteries for my underwater camera, so I couldn't even get any pictures.

Two hours later, I pulled the boat back into the dock and turned to Odin. "Wanna get a bite?"

"Very well. Where?"

"I'm starving, let's just go to the Waterfront." That was the bar/restaurant that shared a parking lot with Seaclipse. Diving was hard work, and afterwards, one tended to be so hungry as to be willing to eat whatever crap was thrown in front of you. The Waterfront catered to this by offering quite the variety of crap to so throw.

We walked across the parking lot and took a booth. I ordered a pint of beer, and gulped half of it down once it arrived.

Odin raised a bushy white eyebrow. "Is it wise to imbibe so much following an underwater sojourn?"

"Says the Norse god famous for feasting and getting drunk who's holding a bourbon in his hand. Besides, the only thing this place has going for it is its halfway decent beer selection, and if you drink enough of it, you won't notice how dire the food is." I let out the belch that had building since I guzzled the beer. "'Scuse me. So, if Loki isn't trying to destroy the world again, what do you think he's got up his sleeve?"

"I suspect, given that he's used all his magickal resources to keep me away from him, that his concerns are a bit more mundane. Most likely, he wishes to win Sigyn back."

I snarfed my beer. "Seriously? He'd be better off trying to take Ragnarok out for another stroll. Ginny made it pretty clear that she doesn't want anything to do with him."

Odin hesitated before replying to that. "This would not be the first occasion wherein Sigyn swore off Loki only to take him back. Nor even the second or third."

I frowned. "Say what?"

"Loki and Sigyn have had quite a tempestuous relationship…"

Sigyn smiled as the earth nymphs brought her a plate filled with vegetables, as well as a mug filled with water taken from the nearby river. The nymphs always moved quickly to fulfill her desires.

"Thank you for these gifts," she said to her subjects.

The nymphs tittered and giggled, as they did. "You are a goddess, my lady," one said.

Another added, "We live to do your bidding."

"Perhaps, but I still am grateful, and see no reason not to express it."

Hearing chuckling from behind her, Sigyn whirled around to see a man standing behind a nearby tree. The nymphs scattered, for they refused to be seen by any of the Aesir or the Jötunn—and the man behind the tree was both.

The man stepped forward. "Only a fool would thank such creatures as they—and it is an even bigger fool who thanks them for that."

Sigyn smiled. "Does the trickster only eat the meats of animals he has slain?"

"You know who I am?"

"Of course. You are Loki, Laufey's son, and the Allfather's blood-brother. I am surprised that you are not partaking of Aegir's feast."

Loki sat down on the ground next to Sigyn and grabbed a carrot from her plate. "I was partaking of it. Aegir had me removed, the pompous windbag. I never liked him, you know. He criticized my table manners, can you believe that?"

"Yes." Sigyn stared at the carrot in his hand.

Throwing his head back and laughing, Loki said, "I like you, commander of the earth nymphs. Why have I not seen you before?"

"No doubt because Loki pays attention to no one who does not benefit his own desires and ambitions."

Another laugh. "No doubt."

"I am Sigyn."

Loki took her hand and kissed it. "A pleasure, my dear."

"Mine or yours?"

Grinning, Loki replied, "Can it not be both?"

They both laughed at that. Sigyn took a bite of a radish, and then asked, "Why did you leave the feast?"

"I told you, Aegir had me removed."

"So Aegir's wishes are to be fulfilled, but mine are not?"

"Excuse me?" Loki stood up now, staring angrily down at her.

"I desired privacy and to have my meal alone here in the woods. Yet you ignored my desires and took my carrot and invaded my privacy. Aegir desired that you depart his hall, and you acceded to his wishes. So you treat Aegir, whom you just told me you never liked, with respect. Yet you treat me, whom you claim it is a pleasure to meet, with none. Why is that?"

For several moments, Loki stared at her some more, but soon his face softened, and for the second time, he leaned back and chortled to the sky. "You pose a most excellent argument, Sigyn! I shall return to Aegir's hall and demand a seat at the table!" He bowed low. "I thank you, my dear, and hope to see you again."

I finished my burger at the same time that Odin finished the story. "That's how they met?"

Odin nodded.

I shook my head, finally placing the story in my head. "Wait, wasn't that the story from the *Lokasenna*? I don't remember Sigyn being in that." After averting Ragnarok in April, I'd done an in-depth study of Norse myth. By Memorial Day, I'd read more Snorri Sturluson than I had Lord Byron, and I did my Master's thesis on Byron. "Hell, I didn't even realize she was the goddess of the earth nymphs. Makes you wonder what she's doing living on an island."

"You mortals told many tales of the Aesir," Odin said dryly, "and many details were lost in the retellings."

"Didn't Aegir kick Loki out because he killed one of Aegir's servants?"

"It does not matter," Odin said, "the point—"

I wasn't letting that go, however. "It probably mattered a helluva lot to the servant."

"Regardless, that was how they met." Odin was sounding a bit exasperated. "They eventually married, and had two children, Nari and Vali. When Loki tricked Hoder into killing Balder—"

"Yeah, yeah." I waved my hand in a get-on-with-it gesture. "He failed to bring about Ragnarok and you trapped him in a cave with Sigyn."

Odin stared into his glass of bourbon. "In fact, I did nothing. It was Skaldi who imprisoned him, though everyone assumed it was with my consent."

"Wasn't it?" I asked.

Pointedly, Odin didn't answer that one, the fucker. "Also, it was only to be Loki's prison. But, as Skaldi chose to trap him beneath the ground, Sigyn was able to instruct her nymphs to find him, and so she joined him, sparing him from the snake's poison."

I ordered another beer, then asked Odin a question I never was able to bring myself to ask Sigyn, not even when we took a massive road trip from Key West to Hazlehurst, Mississippi and back: "How *did* they get out of that, anyhow?"

"The cave was located under a city that has gone by many names over the centuries—the descendants of our worshippers called it Viiburi. Currently, it is known as Vyborg, and during a conflict some seven decades past known as 'the Winter War,' the city was devastated by fire from the sky."

I nodded. "Yeah, I bet you didn't anticipate air strikes when you stuck Loki down there."

"Indeed. One of those strikes exposed the cave, and allowed Loki to escape." Odin finished his bourbon. "The incident at the tavern in April was far from the first time Loki attempted to gather worshippers to provide him with the power to bring about Ragnarok…"

"And remember, when you fail to plan, you plan to fail. You must reach down into your heart and tell yourself that you are the master of your own fate. You don't need to be scared of what may come, because you're the man in charge. Be a man, and you can be the man." Smiling, he added, "I'm Stu R. Lurson, and I thank you all for being here."

There was a smattering of applause and the men in the room all got up from their chairs. Many headed for the exits, but a few went up to talk to the man in front. His short blond hair carefully Brylcreemed into place, his clean-shaven face displaying a bright smile, his dark suit exuding confidence and authority, he stayed to shake hands with the men *who came up to him after the talk.*

"I gotta say, Mr. Lurson, I think these talks are really swell."

"Thank you, but I can assure you that I'm just here to bring out what you've already got inside you."

After the stragglers left, only one remained in the room with "Mr. Lurson," and that was an older man with a monk's fringe of white hair and an eyepatch over his left eye.

"Well, well, well—you found me, Allfather."

Odin stepped forward, tugging on the tie he wore. "Your choice of alias proved impossible to resist, blood-brother," he said with a wry smile. "You believe that this—this cult you've formed will grant you what you desire?"

"Sigyn left me, Allfather. After Viiburg, she tracked me down to Toronto, wanting to know why I abandoned her." He snorted. "Silly cow, as if I would wish to spend any more time with her after eight centuries of torture. But she soon reminded me of why I loved her, and after the mortals' tiresome war ended, we lived together in London for a time—until she refused to help me steal the Gosforth Cross, can you believe that?"

"Yes," Odin said with a small smile. "The cross is guarded and in a public place, Loki."

Loki rolled his eyes. "Sigyn's precious little earth nymphs could have easily pulled it underground and brought it to her—all she need to is ask, and they fall all over themselves to do her bidding. She refused, accused me of using her, and left me." He sighed. "So I came here to St. Louis."

Odin shook his head. "You believe the devotion of a few annoyed young men will provide you with the power to bring about Ragnarok?"

"It's worth a try." He grinned. "Especially since I've been denied the Gosforth Cross."

"I swore an oath not to harm you, blood-brother, and so I shall not."

"Good," Loki said emphatically.

"But you will not succeed. Your message is not one that will inspire the devotion you require."

I rolled my eyes as I gulped down my third beer. "A cult? Really?"

"It is no stranger than forming a musical troupe."

"Fair point. Obviously, it didn't work, seeing as how the world's still here and all."

"Indeed. He was unable to garner sufficient devotion from this cult, nor any of the others that he attempted over the years. Indeed, his endeavor on Key West would also have failed, but for the discovery that the tavern was built around a root of Yggdrasil. His other endeavors required far more magic than was needed to simply sunder a tree he was standing in front of."

I signaled the server for the check. "All right, I'll warn Ginny when I see her at Mayor Fred's tonight."

"You would be wise to seek her out sooner, Cassie," Odin said gravely. "My blood-brother earned his reputation as a trickster. He rarely gets what he wants, but he has an unfortunate tendency to leave a considerable amount of carnage in the wake of his attempts."

"Yeah." I sighed.

Just before the check came, Odin leaned forward. "I have observed your progress, Cassie. You have used your gifts as one of the Dísir very well."

I tried not to think about how creepy it was that he'd somehow been observing my progress without my knowing. "Thanks, but it'd be nice to know what those gifts *are*. I've been kinda playing it by ear, and it's *really* annoying."

"It is better this way. You will learn your capabilities in due course."

"Easy for you to say."

"Of course." His eye actually twinkled. "I am the Allfather. Besides, it would not do for you to twist the fate of a god before you were ready for it."

Throwing up my hands, I said, "See, this is what I'm talking about! I can twist a god's fate?"

Odin paid the check, which was a surprise. He paid it entirely with coins, which wasn't. We departed, and I hopped into Rocinante. Odin, for his part, just wandered off the way he always did. Ginny always seemed to walk everywhere, too. Crazy-ass motherfuckers, these Norse gods...

Even as I drove toward Route 1, I realized that I had no idea where to find Ginny. I only saw her at Mayor Fred's, where she'd become the drummer for 1812—the group that Loki's attempt at a band had temporarily replaced as the weekend house band at that Greene Street saloon. I didn't know where she lived, where she worked, *if* she worked, nothing.

Of course, I didn't spend nearly as much time with her as the other members of the band did. So I whipped out my smartphone and called Bobbi—the guitarist for 1812, and one of my best friends since I moved down here. This, by the way, was completely legal in the state of Florida, though it remained spectacularly stupid, especially after also having had three beers. Luckily, at 5'11", it takes a lot more than three beers to impair my driving.

Besides, this was a matter of life and death, possibly. If nothing else, I so very much wanted to bring about Loki's death for what he'd done to my life.

"Hey, Cass," Bobbi said. I could hear the voices of the customers at the store her parents owned, and where she and her six brothers all worked part-time.

"This is gonna sound like a stupid question, but—I need to talk to Ginny before the gig tonight, and I haven't the first clue where to find her."

"Well, she said last night that she was gonna be working a phone bank up in Marathon."

"Phone bank?"

"Yeah, for Greenpeace. It's a storefront on the corner of Route 1 and 29th."

Why was I not surprised that the goddess of earth nymphs was volunteering for Greenpeace? "All right, thanks, Bobbi. See you tonight?"

"Yeah, 'course. Uh, is everything okay?"

Bobbi knew I was a Dís, and knew how much weird shit there really was floating around, so she wasn't asking that lightly. "It should be, yeah."

"Okay." Bobbi didn't sound reassured, but that was mostly because I did a pretty shitty job of sounding reassuring.

When I got to Route 1, I turned right instead of left, heading north through the Keys until I crossed the Seven-Mile Bridge. Right after that was Marathon. I'd only driven through here before, so I was grateful that the phone bank was on the Overseas

Highway itself, the route that went through all the Keys.

I found 29th Street easily enough. At the corner was a store-front with a big-ass FOR RENT sign over the door, but inside I saw a bunch of people sitting at card tables with phones on them. I saw the pale face and red hair of Ginny Blake, née Sigyn, talking on one of them.

The building had its own parking lot, so I put Rocinante in one of the available spots, and headed inside. I was approached by a perky little thing whose head barely cleared my forearms. "Hi! Ohmigod, I *totally* hope you're here to volunteer, because we've still got a few phones left, and the bill goes before the state legislature *tomorrow*. So if—"

I held up both hands, and resisted the urge to smother her with them. "I'm sorry, I'm just here to see my friend—she's right over there?" I pointed at Ginny.

Perky Thing's face fell. "Oh. Well, okay, but she's on until five."

Frowning, I pulled my phone out of the strap of my bathing suit and checked the display, which read, 4:56. "It's five now."

"Is it?" Her eyes widened, y'know, a lot, and she turned and ran off. "Ohmigod, people, it's *five o'clock*, and we've still got to hit the panhandle! Let's *go*, people!"

Since Perky Thing didn't seem interested in me anymore, I wandered over to the small desk where Ginny was sitting.

"Thank you very much for your support, Mr. Mazeroski. Take care." She hung up, and looked up at me. "Cassie, what a pleas-ant surprise! I didn't know you volunteered for Greenpeace."

"I don't. I'm here looking for you. Can we go somewhere to talk? Little Ms. Ohmi*god* over there said you're done now, any-how."

Ginny smiled indulgently. "Do not be so hard on young Elea-nora. She means well. May I trouble you for a lift back to Key West?"

"Sure. To Mayor Fred's?"

She smiled. "A bit early for that. No, we can go to my home."

I finally got to find out where she lived! Yay!

We hopped into Rocinante, and I decided not to bother sugar-coating it. "Loki's back."

Ginny closed her eyes, let out a very long breath, and said, "Of *course* he is! First that one-eyed jackanapes nearly got us all killed because of some idiotic promise he made centuries ago, and now he can't even hold *on* to my dear ex-husband." She shook her head. "Does the Allfather have a plan to stop him from whatever imbecility he has planned next?"

I hesitated. "Loki cast a spell that keeps Odin off Key West itself. He thinks he's gonna go after you tonight at Mayor Fred's."

"After *me?* Does he really think that's going to work *again?*"

Another hesitation as I turned left onto Route 1 to take us home. "Well, from what I understand it's worked once or twice before…"

Ginny looked away, her pale skin flushing. "I've made mistakes in the past…"

"You took him back after he left you in a cave."

Closing her eyes, Ginny moaned and waved her hands up and down. "I know, I know! Look, I can't help it, I fell in love with him the minute I saw him in the forest. He just has this lovely mischievousness about him, and an amazing strength and charisma…" She looked away, staring at the spectacular view of the water from the Seven-Mile Bridge.

About halfway over the bridge, she turned back to me. "You have to understand, he *does* love me, too—but he's an immortal and a born troublemaker. He tries to destroy the world, he fails, he decides he wants to settle down with me, we're happy for a while, he gets bored, he tries to destroy the world again, usually by asking me to help, at which point I leave him, he goes off and forms a cult or a band or whatever his latest scheme is, it fails, and he comes back to me. And I swore that after Woodstock, I wouldn't do it again."

"That was the last time he tried this?" I asked, politely refraining from pointing out that I hadn't been born yet during Woodstock, though my parents were there as little kids with their hippie parents. This was the upbringing that led to them naming their twin children "Castor" and "Pollux."

Ginny nodded and stared back out at the water again.

Joe Cocker had just brought the house down with his cover of the Beatles' "With a Little Help from My Friends," which was his closer.

101

Country Joe and the Fish were setting up for their set. Loki moved effortlessly through the crowd, long blond hair trailing behind him as he sought out his wife.

He soon found Sigyn with a group of musicians, though calling them such was giving them far too much credit. Their lutes were poorly tuned, their singing horribly off-key. Sigyn was playing some manner of hand-drum to accompany them, and she kept perfect time, so there was that, at least. He just stood and watched them play, trying not to wince, and thoughtfully stroking his long, red beard.

After they finished a song, one of the singers looked up and said, "Hey, man, wanna cop a squat and rap with us? Got some good grass."

"No, thank you, I wish to speak to my wife."

Only then did Sigyn look up, her lovely face framed by waist-length, straight red hair.

"Hello, Sigyn."

The singer laughed. "What's a sig-in, man?"

The other one joined the laughter. "This is Gaea."

Loki shook his head and laughed mirthlessly. "What a fitting pseudonym."

"Soo-doe-what?"

"This cat is seriously making a bad scene, man."

Sigyn finally got to her feet. "Don't worry, boys, I'll take care of him, then we can catch Country Joe."

"Groovy."

She grabbed Loki by the arm and they wandered off to stand near a large tree. Several folks wandered by in various stages of undress, and Loki realized there was a swimming hole nearby. "What do you want?" she asked.

"You. I've been a fool, and I want to go back to the way things were in London and in San Francisco, before—"

"Before you decided to destroy the world again? And again?"

Loki closed his eyes. "I let myself be carried away. There's been this children's literature that portrays a version of the Aesir—"

"It's called a comic book," Sigyn said. "You're in it quite a bit, though they made you dark-haired and Thor a blonde." For the first time since Loki arrived at the song circle, Sigyn smiled. Loki's heart melted at the sight, just as it had centuries ago in the forest outside Aegir's hall.

"That gave me an uptick of power that I thought would be enough to bring about Ragnarok."

"And you failed?"

Loki sighed, and then lied through his teeth. "I didn't even try. I re-alized that if I did bring about the end of all that is, I would never see you again." He cupped her cheek with his hand and stared intently at her.

She stared right back. "Dammit."

"It was good for a while," Ginny said as we drove slowly through Stock Island in traffic that kept us at under forty miles an hour, and often under twenty. "But—"

Whatever else she was going to say was interrupted by my suddenly hitting the brakes and bringing Rocinante to a screeching halt just as we were about to cross the bridge to Key West. Luckily, we *were* in traffic, so the SUV behind me didn't rear-end me. The thing was, the car in front of me was actually accelerating.

"Why did you hit the brake?"

I blinked. "I have no fucking clue. But I can't make my foot go to the accelerator." Thinking fast, I hit the hazard lights. Thankfully, there was a shoulder on the bridge, so once I turned the wheel to the right, I was able to move the car to the side. As soon as I turned the wheel back left, I slammed on the brake again.

"What the *fuck*?"

Ginny, for her part, threw her head back and laughed. "Oh, this is *perfect*! You said Loki cast a spell to keep Odin off the island?"

I nodded.

"That was probably too specific a spell for him to manage, given how weak he must be after you and the Allfather spanked him in April. Instead, he just cast a spell that kept *all* Aesir off the island."

I stared at her for a second, and then joined in the laugh. I stopped laughing when I realized the problem. "So I can't go home, either?"

Holding up a finger, Ginny said, "Perhaps not. You are not actually of the Aesir, so it may not affect you—but I am in your vehicle. If I leave, you may be able to proceed."

"I can't just leave you here."

But Ginny was already opening the door. "I will be fine. Go and tell my husband what a colossal blunder he has made."

As soon as she hopped out of the car, I gingerly moved my right foot. Sure enough, I was able to move forward, so I killed the hazards, merged into the traffic, and headed straight for where I figured Loki was going to wind up eventually: Mayor Fred's.

I was also incredibly cranky that I still wasn't gonna find out where Ginny lived.

After parking Rocinante at the Bottroff House, I walked straight from there to the saloon on Greene Street. I might've stopped at the room first, but I didn't want the captain to know what I was doing. He gets into these overprotective moods, and if he knew I was going to talk to Loki without Odin's protection, he'd have tried to talk me out of it. And I might've listened, so why even risk it?

As Ginny had said, it was too early for 1812 to have started. Ihor, the bartender, was playing a classic rock mix over the PA. There were some folks playing pool, the usual combination of tourists and regulars both at the bar and at the tables. We were getting into early evening, so there were lots of people getting their last drink in before heading to the boardwalk for sunset.

Sure enough, there was Loki, sipping a beer at the bar, sitting next to Larry, one of the regulars, who was bitching about the Yankees while sporting his Rays ballcap. It was actually good to see him bitching, as he'd been subdued ever since being reunited with the son he had with a water elemental. That mating made him immortal, so I wasn't surprised that he and Loki had hit it off. They had shit in common, y'know?

"Hey, Cass," Larry said. "This is Sigurd. He's here to see 1812—says he knows Ginny from way back."

I shook my head. "Yeah, I know. Hey, 'Sig,' can I talk to you in private for a second?"

Loki, though, just stared at me, trying the same intense-gaze thing he used on me in April when he was fronting Jötunheim and trying to charm everyone into worshipping him enough to let him break Yggdrasil. For that matter, it was probably the same one he used on Ginny at Woodstock. "I'm sorry, but my new friend Larry and I are having a delightful conversation about baseball."

"It's about Ginny," I added.

"Ah." Loki's face fell. "Will you excuse me, please, Larry?"

"Course. Didn't realize you two knew each other. I need a smoke, anyhow." Larry hopped off his bar stool and went outside to suck nicotine.

Once Larry departed, Loki asked, "What about Sigyn?"

"What're you using another glamour again, so folks don't recognize you as 'Gunnar Rikardsen,' mediocre lead singer of Jötunheim?" One of the side effects of being a Dís was that glamours didn't affect me.

"It seemed prudent, under the circumstances." He leaned forward. "Tell me, little Dís, what has happened to Sigyn?"

"She's not going to be here tonight."

"When will she be here?"

I grinned. "Well, that's sorta kinda up to you. See, she spent this afternoon up at Marathon, volunteering for Greenpeace."

Loki shook his head. "How very like her." Then his face fell. "Wait—Marathon?"

"Yeah, about an hour north of here. Which means the same spell that's keeping Odin from stepping on your head is—"

Slamming a hand on the bar, Loki cried, "Dammit!"

"So it's your choice," I said. "Drop the spell and Odin grabs you; don't drop the spell, and you don't get to make yet another pointless attempt to win your wife back."

Loki grinned. "She caught poison in a bowl for me for eight centuries, little Dís, what makes you think I can't convince her once more?"

"Maybe you can. I'm sure she went to Woodstock swearing she'd never get together with you again, and then you showed up. She told me she was done with you when I saw her earlier, but five minutes with you may change that."

"Then I shall leave the spell intact," Loki said. "What was it that your poet Shakespeare said? It is better to have loved and lost than to never have loved at all?"

"That was Tennyson, actually."

Loki frowned. "Are you sure?"

105

"I have a Master's in English literature, and you were stuck in a cave when Tennyson was alive, so yeah, I'm pretty sure. Look, you can't keep the spell up forever. Odin's probably gonna get impatient and try to stop it. Or I will. Or Ginny'll move on, which would piss me off, as she's become a good friend the last six months, plus 1812 will need to find *another* drummer. And I also just had lunch with Odin, and he's *tired*. I doubt he'd be able to hold you for longer than another six months before you found your way out of wherever he put you."

That got a smug grin out of Loki. "True."

"So drop the spell. I'll convince Odin to let you stay free as long as you don't do anything stupid. And if you hurt Ginny in any way, shape, or form, or if you decide to try the Ragnarok thing again, so help me, I will twist your fate something fierce."

Loki flinched. "You don't even know how to do that—do you?" Those last two words were said with more uncertainty than I'd yet heard from him.

I gave him a smug grin of my own. "I'll learn. Do we have a deal?"

After taking a thoughtful sip of his beer, Loki turned to stare at me. He did have amazing eyes, and if I didn't want so much to rip his face off, I might have found him incredibly attractive. I certainly got the mischievousness and charisma and strength Ginny was talking about.

But mostly I wanted to rip his face off. Which he must've figured out, because he stopped staring at me and looked at his beer some more.

"Very well," he finally said. "I will release the spell, and we shall see what happens."

That night, 1812 played a killer show. Odin, Loki, and I were all in the audience, sitting around the table closest to the ficus around which Mayor Fred's was built—also the section of Yggdrasil that Loki had tried to shatter in April. Odin had agreed to at least let Loki watch the show and speak once to Sigyn before deciding whether or not to go along with my plan. Which, I gotta say, was reasonable, considering it was a plan I came up with while sitting in traffic on Route 1.

They finished their first set with a John Robertson song off his last CD, then Bobbi announced that they were taking a break.

Ginny came to the table and sat with the three of us. "Before you say anything, Loki, I want you to know that I have no interest in taking you back. I've made that mistake once too often, and besides—I have a life here. I *like* it on Key West, and I care about these people. Do you know how long it has been since I had *friends*? It was always the earth nymphs, who are sycophants, or the Aesir, who only saw me as your wife. And then I was alone with you for eight centuries. It took me until now to realize what was missing in my life. I started to find it at Woodstock before you went and derailed me—I have *people*. Mortals are actually very good company, and I prefer theirs to yours."

I applauded. Odin smiled. Loki just stared.

Finally, he said, "In fact, Sigyn, I was not going to tell you I wanted you back."

"Really?" Ginny sounded dubious, to say the least.

"No, not really," he said with a bland smile, "but I knew that saying it would be pointless. And now I know it even more. If the Allfather is willing, I would like to stay and see this new life you have created. Perhaps, in your own time, you may allow me to become part of it." He grinned. "Besides, I rather like this tavern."

I rolled my eyes. "He and Larry were talking baseball for *hours* before you guys set up."

"Well," Ginny said dryly, "if Larry likes you, there'll be no getting rid of you."

Loki, however, was looking at his blood-brother. "Is this acceptable to you, Allfather?"

"No." At Loki's crestfallen expression, he added, "But I will accept it in any case. Cassie is correct in that I have neither the capacity nor the desire to become your keeper once again."

Snorting, Loki said, "Of course not. Eight hundred years ago, you fobbed it off on Skaldi. Today, you do the same to the little Dís."

"Hey!" I barked. "I've had enough of that. I'm half a foot taller than your sorry ass, bucko, and the name's Cassie. I've still got the scale from the Midgard serpent from when I cast the counterspell on you, and if you call me 'little Dís' *one more time*, I'll shove that scale right up your ass"

Loki held up both hands. "I stand chastised."

"Damn right."

A little bit later, 1812 got back up on stage to start their second set. Bobbi went up to the mic and said, "This first song is one our drummer, Ginny Blake, wants to dedicate to someone in the audience she's known for a long time."

They broke out into "With a Little Help from My Friends"— Joe Cocker's arrangement from Woodstock. I shook my head, Loki grinned, and Odin let out a long breath.

After the song ended, Loki leaned over to me. "It seems you've already learned, Cassie."

"What do you mean?"

"That's twice you've succeeded in twisting my fate."

I leaned back in the chair and gave Loki a thoughtful expression. Then I held up my pint. "Then here's to twisting the night away."

Cayo Hueso – Part 1:
A Farewell to Cats

I knew something was wrong when I checked my morning e-mail, and the usual first-thing-in-the-a.m. note from my mother wasn't there.

To make matters worse, Cara Wasserstein, one of my bosses at the Seaclipse dive shop, informed me that nobody had signed up for the 1pm dive. That wasn't a total surprise—Tuesdays were often the slowest day of the week—but I was paid on the basis of how many dives I ran, so that meant no actual income for the day.

The mother thing was way worse, though. I came to Key West more than a year ago as the final part of my post-Master's-degree drive across the bottom of the country, from my home in San Diego all the way across the I-10 to Florida and down to the Keys. I intended to stay for a couple of weeks, and never left.

Starting the day after I drove away from southern California in

Rocinante, my battered old pickup truck, my mother sent me an e-mail every morning, letting me know that everything was okay on the homestead. I'd hear the latest about my parents' work at the law firm, or my kid sister Sunni's latest adventures at the mall or at school, or what my crazy aunt Zelda was doing, or what my parents' best friends Bert and Joe were up to, or how much Grandma hated the nursing home. Every e-mail always ended with, "Can't wait to see you when you come back home."

Sixteen months later, and she was *still* ending every e-mail that way. Until today, one had come every morning, even when she was spending all that time in the hospital after Aunt Zelda's car accident.

"You seem upset."

Shaking my head, I turned to see the ghost of Captain Jeremiah Bottroff, a nineteenth-century wrecker captain who built the house that was now the main part of the Bottroff House Bed and Breakfast. Since dying, he'd continued to haunt the place. Because I'm a Norse fate goddess (yes, really, and trust me, nobody was more surprised than me to find out), I can see and hear him. Well, "hear" is pretty straightforward; "see" can get a bit weird. You know how you see something out of the corner of your eye, but then when you look right at it, it's gone? The captain was like that when I looked right at him.

Anyhow, I'd been his Mrs. Muir since I came to the Bottroff House to stay. Now, in exchange for bits and pieces of work all around the B&B, I lived here for free. With one exception, I'd been his only conversation in a century and a half. It was only occasionally annoying.

"My mother didn't e-mail me this morning."

After more than a year of cohabitation, the captain had finally got the hang of what e-mail was, so at least I didn't have to explain it *again*. "Perhaps you should use that infernal device you're holding to communicate with her verbally."

"Oh, I plan to. But not before coffee. *Never* before coffee."

"That would be wise, assuming you wish to continue your cordial relations with your mother."

I chuckled. "Well, that depends on why she didn't e-mail me."

Sliding open the door, I went down the wooden staircase of

the cottage that had become my home in Key West. Debbie Dellamonica, the B&B's owner, supplied her guests and employees with Hawai'ian Kona coffee, which was the only thing that got my motor running in the morning.

"Cassie!"

It was a very familiar voice, and it came from a woman who practically leapt up from one of the white wicker chairs. She was wearing one of her big floppy hats, massive sunglasses, a plain white T-shirt, and a long flowerprint skirt. Next to her was a balding, pudgy man in a light blue Polo shirt and khaki shorts that exposed hairy knees.

I blinked twice. I rubbed my eyes, and then blinked again. They were still there. At least now I knew why there was no e-mail this morning.

"Mom, Dad—what're you doing here?"

Debbie came over, carrying a mug of coffee. "Your parents are *wonderful*, Cassie! They've been telling me all sorts of stories."

I winced and snatched the coffee mug. "Well, don't believe any of it. I was actually a good kid. It was Paul and Sunni who did all the crazy stuff."

She grinned. "That's not how they tell it."

Mom gave me a huge hug that almost knocked the hat off. "It's *so* good to see you."

"I—" Somehow I managed not to spill the coffee.

After Mom broke the embrace, I noticed that Dad had gotten up from the chair. "It really is good to see you, hon."

"I—" I gulped down some coffee, the hot liquid clearing some of the cobwebs. "I'm glad to see you guys, too, I guess, I just—" I shook my head. "I'm sorry, I'm just—I only just got up."

Mom waved a hand up and down. "Debbie told us about your daily routine. To bed at five, up at eleven, off to the dive shop at noon, running your afternoon dive at one, then off to hang out at a bar." She sat down and put on a smile. "It sounds very—very pleasant."

I knew where this was going. "Mom—"

"It's okay!" She held up a hand. "We're not going to fight. We're here to see you. Out of nowhere, Consolidated decided to settle, so our calendars suddenly cleared."

111

I nodded. Mom had said that lawsuit was likely to take months, and that there was no chance of settling, so this was obviously an unexpected break.

Dad got a word in. "So we figured we'd surprise you and come visit."

"I mean," Mom added, "we figured you weren't coming for Thanksgiving *again*..."

I closed my eyes and sighed. My parents have never been big on most holidays. Christmas particularly was no big deal. As Grandma put it, "It's a pagan festival that was co-opted by Christians, so that's two reasons for us to stay the hell away." We weren't the most observant Jews ever, either, so the high holy days tended to come and go without much going on. And we didn't really care about New Year's or Memorial Day or Independence Day or Labor Day.

Thanksgiving, though, was a different story. That was a big family thing, and Mom's e-mails had gotten ever more frantic last November. After the holiday, the e-mails suddenly got terse, at least until New Year's.

"Look, Mom, I appreciate you coming, but I just wish—" I sighed.

Mom got her pouty face on. "You don't want us here."

"No! It's great to see you, *really*," I said quickly, "but some *warning* would've been nice." That was certainly the truth. I've always hated surprises.

"But if we told you, it wouldn't have been a *surprise!*"

Ah, Mom logic. "All right, look, this is tough to process." I closed my eyes. "Let's sit down and have some breakfast. I don't have a dive today—"

"I know," Mom said, "I called your work and told them you needed today off, but not to tell you why. That nice young lady— Kira?"

"Cara."

"She said that Noel—"

"That's Noah." You'd think someone who named her twin kids "Castor" and "Pollux" would make more of an effort to get other people's names right...

"—could handle your workload."

"Seriously?" I'd like to say I couldn't believe it, but this was a hundred percent in character. "Mom, you cost me a day's work!"

"Oh, please, you can always ask us for money, that's hardly an issue."

I opened my mouth, then closed it. Nothing would be gained by getting into this argument, especially in front of Debbie.

"I was hoping," Mom continued, "that you could show us around the island. Do all that touristy stuff."

"Actually, Mom, I kinda figured I'd help Debbie with the desk, since—"

"No need," Debbie said. "Jorge and Sebastian checked out this morning, and the Kowalskis had some kind of family emergency, so they left, too. It's just your parents—I put them under you in seven—and that snorkeling club, and they're off on their expedition until tomorrow."

I frowned. "What about the Steinmans?" Saying the name out loud, instead of seeing it written down or on my computer screen, made me remember that Steinman was Grandma's maiden name. "You guys are the Steinmans."

"We didn't want to spoil the surprise." Dad gave a small smile.

"All right, fine, you win. I'll play tour guide for you guys. Let me just finish my coffee first?"

We sat through two mugs' worth while I got the rundown that I would've gotten in the morning e-mail. My personal favorite: Grandma's bridge partner set the nursing home on fire, and my grandmother's main complaint was that she'd have to break in a new bridge partner.

Once I gulped the last of mug number two, I asked Mom, "So where do you guys want to go?"

"I am *dying* to see the Hemingway House."

I should've seen it coming. The one place on Key West I had managed to avoid like the plague that its former owner's writing was. "Do we *have* to go there?" To my horror, I heard myself whining that question like a ten-year-old.

Mom glared at me. "Hemingway is the greatest American writer."

"Only if you don't count every other American writer." I

113

sighed. This was another argument I didn't want to have, because I'd had it way too many times before to no good end. The difference was, those previous arguments were on the campus of Revelle College at the University of California-San Diego with my fellow English majors, and several professors.

They were just as wrong about that overrated hack as Mom was now. And that was one of major reasons why I very much did *not* want to go to the Hemingway House.

Dad stepped in before the argument could start. "I could give a damn about Hemingway, but I'd like to see the cats."

"Excuse me?" Mom asked.

"C'mon, Rachael," Dad said with a grin, "didn't you read the web site?"

"What's to read? It's the house Hemingway owned when he lived here!"

"Hemingway owned cats—polydactyl cats, in fact."

We had four cats in the house when I was growing up. They were all Dad's, he just let us feed them. (He even changed the litter box himself, when he had three kids whom he could've forced to do it. That's love, right there.)

I decided to help Dad's cause, even though I didn't really want to go to the Hemingway House in the first place. "They're not just polydactyl, they're specifically six-toed cats."

Dad frowned. "There's a difference?"

"Polydactyl just means more than the usual number of toes. It could mean seven or eight toes. The cats at the museum are *supposedly* descended from Hemingway's cats. He had a thing for six-toed cats."

"Well, then, I want to see it for the literary value, and your father wants to see the cats. It's settled."

A half-hour later (and after I deflected Mom from going to see my room, since I didn't want to subject the captain to her), we headed across Eaton, past Duval to Whitehead, then went several blocks down that street. At one point, we passed a restaurant called the Six-Toed Cat that Mom and I had to physically restrain Dad from walking into. It was obviously going to be *that* long a day...

Eventually, we reached the corner of Olivia. Across the street was the lighthouse—sorry, the Key West Lighthouse and Keeper's Quarters Museum, cha cha cha—which I hoped to talk them into going to afterward. I always liked the lighthouse. The view is simply spectacular up there, and totally worth climbing all those stairs.

The house itself was surrounded by a big-ass brick wall, with an ivy-covered gate right in front of the main entrance. There was a ticket booth in front of the gate, inside of which sat a bored-looking young man farting around on a tablet. He looked kind of put out by Mom interrupting his reading or game-playing or whatever in order to, y'know, do his job.

As we went through the gate and up the stairs to the house, I found myself hoping that Sandy wouldn't be working today. I was, naturally, not so lucky.

"Cassie! What brings you here?" A freakishly tall guy—and as a 5'11" woman, I know from freakishly tall—came bounding down the stairs. He had a shock of curly red hair, horrible acne scars, and big plastic glasses that were a desperate and failed attempt to look hip. He skidded to a stop in front of me and my parents.

"Playing tour guide." I managed not to sigh. "These are my parents, Rachael and Jake Zukav."

He smiled at them with teeth that had way too much yellow in them. "A pleasure to meet you, I'm Sandy, and welcome to the Hemingway Home and Museum! Is this your first time?"

Okay, when I first came to Key West, I checked out the bars on Duval Street. One night, a guy was playing an acoustic guitar at the Bull, playing a decent-if-not-great rendition of "Me and Julio Down by the Schoolyard." He did his damnedest to make it unlistenable with his *awful* whistling. He did one more song I didn't recognize, then took a break. I only stayed because I hadn't finished my beer.

I was staring at the selection of bourbons and thinking that Grandma might like it here when he sat next to me. He was holding a clipboard in his hand. I carefully did not acknowledge his presence.

"Hey there. Did you enjoy the set?"

"I only just got here for the last two songs." I still wasn't making eye contact.

The bartender came over and took his order for a mojito.

"I haven't seen you in here before."

Somehow, I didn't gag on my beer, but it was close.

"I mean, I would've remembered someone as hot as you."

"Look, I just want to finish my beer and move on to the next bar."

"Oh, no, you can't do that! I mean, yeah, of course, you *can* do that, but I wish you wouldn't. I'm gonna be starting the next set with 'Pinball Wizard,' and it's gonna kick some major-league ass-wipes."

I couldn't help but give him a sidelong WTF look at that. "May wanna work on your metaphors, there, Sparky."

"That's close—my name's actually Sandy."

On autopilot, I said, "Cassie."

"May I say, Cassie, that it's an absolute pleasure to make your acquaintance."

"If you insist."

"If I insist what?"

"You asked if you may say it's an absolute pleasure. I answered your question."

He looked confused for a second, then put the clipboard on the table. "Look, if you won't stick around, at least join my mailing list? It'll keep you updated on my gigs and my recordings and stuff. And there's lots of really boss music trivia, too. You should totally check it out."

"Look, I'm only in Key West for a week or two, I—"

"All the more reason to get on my list! We can keep in touch!"

I gulped down the last of my beer, shook my head, and held out my hand. "Fine, but I gotta go."

After I'd been on the island a few weeks, I learned the devious but simple lesson of giving a fake e-mail address if it's someone you don't actually want to hear from, but whom you want to go away. My usual default for those was my UCSD e-mail address, which I haven't checked in ages, and which may even be defunct now.

I've continued to get Sandy's e-mail newsletter for the past sixteen months, and for about a month after that night, he e-mailed me directly a few times. My lack of response seemed to finally give him the hint.

But every time I saw him, he hit on me again. I always deflected it, but it was getting pretty damned tiresome.

"I'll be running the tour," Sandy was now telling Mom and Dad, "which starts at a quarter after. Until then, I'll be happy to answer any questions you might have."

I'd been so busy dreading seeing Sandy and being pissed at my mother that I only just then realized that the place was empty, which was odd. In fact, the only ones here were me, my parents, Sandy, and the study in bored-teenager-with-a-tablet going on in the ticket booth. The emptiness was even greater than that, but I couldn't put my finger on what it was.

Sandy was still talking. "The house was originally built back in 1851 by a marine architect and wrecker named Asa Tift. Hemingway made it his home here in Key West in 1931."

Mom asked, "Why the brick wall? Security?"

"Very good question!" Sandy provided another yellow-toothed smile. "When Hemingway first moved in, there was just a regular chain-link, but he wanted some privacy."

Dad asked, "Where are the cats?"

I blinked, Dad having placed my finger for me. There were usually a whole bunch of felines wandering around the steps in front of the house and meandering around the fountain.

Sandy stammered. "Er—well—you see, uh—"

"Is something wrong?" That was Mom's Jewish Mother Voice. Any second now, she was gonna try to conjure up chicken soup to shove down Sandy's throat.

He raised a hand to his high forehead to wipe away the sweat that had formed there. "No, no, no, no, no, I'm fine. Is there, ah, anything else about Hemingway you wanna know? Like the fountain! Did you know this fountain was built from a urinal that used to be in Sloppy Joe's, the bar where Hemingway used to go drinking?"

My mother made the exact same "ew, ick!" expression I made when I learned that particular fact.

Dad asked, "Are the cats really descendents of the polydactyl—" He grinned and glanced at me. "Sorry, the six-toed cat he had?"

Mom rolled her eyes, as if embarrassed to be with such non-

Hemingway-adoring plebians. "My husband and my daughter are more cat people than aficionados of fine literature, I'm afraid."

I glared at her. "Right, Mom, me and my Master's Degree in English Lit don't have *any* kind of appreciation of good literature, you bet."

Sandy, though, looked like he was gonna throw up right there. He was muttering something to himself.

Suddenly, a voice cried, "*Get out!* I won't have such vermin in my house!"

Turning around, I saw—er, something. Dark hair, muscular figure, thick mustache, but all indistinct, the same way Captain Bottroff's ghost was.

Dad stumbled backward. "*What is that?*"

That was a surprise. I thought us Norse gods were the only ones who could see and hear ghosts. "You can see him?"

"Sort of, yeah."

I hadn't yet told my parents that I was one of the Dísir, as I was still trying and failing to find a way to bring it up naturally in conversation. I still hadn't even figured out how to explain that I had no plans to leave Key West anytime soon.

But that was for later. Sandy stared right at the ghost. "Please, Mr. Hemingway, they're the first paying customers we've had all day!" Based on the pleading tone, I suspected that Sandy had had this conversation before.

The ghost of Hemingway bellowed, "If they are only here for the damned *cats*, they are *not* welcome in my house!" Hemingway then started floating toward my father. I moved to stand between them, but he got to Dad before I could, and grabbed his shoulders.

For a second, I gawked. Ghosts were insubstantial. Captain Bottroff had never been able to affect anything physical in his entire afterlife. He just kind of wafted around the grounds of the B&B.

Yet here was the ghost of an overrated writer physically tossing my father toward the entrance.

"Jake!" Mom cried, running after him.

I glared at Hemingway. "How'd you do that? And how can these people see you?"

"Ah, yes," Hemingway said, "you're Bottroff's young lady. Miss Zukav, yes?"

"You know the captain?"

The sweat was now pouring off Sandy and his voice was cracking. "Cassie, what the hell're you guys *talkin'* 'bout?"

I waved him off. "Shut up, Sandy. As for *you*," I told Hemingway, "you didn't answer my question."

"I'm not at all sure of the reasons for my newfound ability to affect the physical world once again, young lady, but I intend to make use of it. My home is *not* a petting zoo! Now remove yourself, Miss Zukav. Out of consideration to Captain Bottroff, I will not attempt to forcibly remove you as I did your father, but you and your cat-loving family are not welcome here!"

Glancing over at Dad, I saw that Mom was helping him clamber to his feet. Giving Hemingway my nastiest stare, I said, "This ain't over, chuckles." Then I went down the stairs and out the gate. The kid in the booth didn't even look up from his tablet.

"I'm okay." Dad was brushing sidewalk dust and bits of *shmutz* off his clothes.

"He's not okay, *look* at his arm!" Mom pointed at his left arm.

Looking down, I saw that that arm was skinned and bleeding. "C'mon, we've got a first-aid kit at the B&B."

"He should go to a hospi—" Mom started, but I cut her off.

"How do we tell the ER nurse he hurt himself?"

Mom opened her mouth, then shut it. "We can say he tripped on the sidewalk."

"It'll be fine with the first-aid kit," Dad said quickly. "I don't want to deal with a hospital if we don't have to."

We walked quickly back, Dad cradling his arm. Debbie saw us as we came in the door and grabbed the kit without having to be asked. "What happened?"

"Long story," I said quickly.

Mom didn't say anything while Debbie and I treated the arm, and then bandaged it. "It should be fine," Debbie said, brushing a lock of gray hair out of her face.

"Can we go to our room, please, Cassie?" Mom asked. It was the first thing she'd said since we walked away from the Hemingway House, which was an uncharacteristically long silence for her.

I decided to risk the captain meeting my parents. "Sure."

We went into the back, through the garden, past the breeting of Harry S, our parrot, and going under the wooden steps that led to my room upstairs, and slid open the glass door that led to their ground-floor room. It was set up the same as mine, but with blue carpet instead of white, and a roll-top desk instead of a flat letter-writing desk. Otherwise, though, it was the same: double bed, white wicker chairs, bathroom in the back.

As soon as Mom slid the door shut, she stared right at me. "Cassie, what the *fuck* was that?"

Unable to help myself, I burst out laughing.

"This isn't funny!" Mom was getting red in the face.

"I'm sorry, Mom." I managed to get my laughter under control. "Do you remember when Paul and I were kids and Sunni was an infant? You guys decided that kids only cursed because they were told not to, so you didn't censor yourselves at all in front of us, and you figured we wouldn't curse much because it wouldn't be anything forbidden."

"That was a disaster," Dad said dryly.

I nodded. "Right, Paul and I were the most foul-mouthed eight-year-olds in the history of the world, and *then* you started censoring yourselves around us. So I laughed 'cause that's the first time I've heard you use the word 'fuck' in my presence in fifteen years."

She gave me the death glare that so frightened me and Paul both as kids. "You're avoiding the question."

"Yeah, I am." I realized I needed to sit down and plunked myself on the wicker chair. Dad had already sat on the edge of the bed, and Mom was still standing. "Okay, you know how Key West is full of ghost stories? Turns out, they're not stories. There are ghosts on the island—but until today, I thought I was the only one who could see them. Y'see—"

Mom interrupted me with a scream, as she was gaping at something over my left shoulder. Turning, I saw the captain.

"I was afraid of this," Bottroff said.

"You can *see* him?" I asked Mom.

"We both can," Dad said after a moment, when it was clear that Mom no longer had the power of speech.

A very uncharitable part of me wanted the captain to stick around, if he could render my mother silent, but I needed her coherent. "Cap'n, can you give me and my parents a few minutes?"

"Of course, Miss Zukav, however, you should be aware that the young mulatto woman who cleans the linens caught sight of me thirty minutes past."

"Really?" This was just getting weirder and weirder.

"Believe you me, she was as taken aback as I. I made a hasty retreat, and I believe she has rationalized the incident. In any event, I shall take my leave."

A moment later, the captain was gone.

I smiled gamely. "So, now you've met my roommate..."

"You can talk to ghosts?" Mom was talking in a frightened whisper now.

"So can we, apparently."

I shook my head. "That's just it, Dad. Until today, I was the only one who could see the captain. And I guess Hemingway's ghost has been there all along. But Sandy saw him, too, and Lisa-Karen saw the captain." At my parents' blank expression, I added, "That's the 'mulatto' he was talking about. She's the housekeeper. And yeah, he really talks like that."

"I don't understand this." Mom finally sat down at the desk chair. "How can you talk to ghosts?"

I hesitated. "You know how weird shit always happened to me? Well, it turns out that it wasn't just bad luck. I'm a Dís—a Norse fate goddess."

"Come again?" Dad said.

"How much do you guys know about Norse mythology?"

They exchanged a glance, and Mom finally said, "We got *The Avengers* on Blu-Ray..."

"Right. Okay. Well, see, it turns out that there *were* Norse gods—or, at the very least, powerful beings who were worshipped by Scandinavians a thousand years ago. At this point, there aren't that many of them left. I've met Odin, Loki, one of the frost giants, and Loki's wife Sigyn. In fact, Ginny—that's what she calls herself—she's the drummer in the band I always see at Mayor Fred's. If you guys're here until Thursday, you'll get to see them."

Mom shook her head. "Wait, the band you follow has a *Norse god* as a drummer? Cassie this is crazy!"

"Rachael," Dad said, "we just got thrown out of a museum by the ghost of Ernest Hemingway. Can we hear her out, maybe?"

I nodded a thank-you to Dad, and then went on, pacing back and forth across the blue carpet. "Okay, every once in a while? A set of triplets is born on Earth who are fate gods. The Norns are the best known Dísir, they control the fate of all the Norse gods. But turns out I'm one, too."

In a very quiet voice, Mom asked, "And Paul?"

I should've expected that. "I don't know. I haven't heard from him since he called the day of my party."

"And that number isn't in service anymore," Mom said bitterly. My twin brother had dropped out of college and gone off to find himself. His call to congratulate me on achieving my Master's degree was the first I'd heard from him in two years.

Dad sighed, and absently rubbed his bandaged arm. "If he is one of these—what is it?"

"A Dís."

"Right. If he's one of those, maybe that explains why he's had so many problems."

Mom threw up her hands. "How handy for him, he has *another* excuse for why his life's been such a failure."

"Mom—"

She pointed a finger at me. "Don't! Don't you *dare* defend him! We gave him everything—we gave you both, and Sunni, *everything*—and he got rid of his cell phone, his e-mail account's dead, and he never talks to us. What the hell did we do to deserve *that*? I mean, to just *walk out* on your *parents* without a word, and never come back? Who *does* that?"

My heart started beating like a triphammer. "I—" The question wasn't rhetorical, exactly, because the answer was standing right there with the two of them in the room. "I'm sorry, Mom, but—"

She stood up, tears streaking down her cheeks. "You had everything all laid out! You were gonna get your PhD and teach and write papers, and instead you're sitting on this *stupid* island and you're hanging around with bands and ghosts and..." Then she broke, and started crying.

122

I got up and pulled her into a hug, wrapping my arms around her and holding her as close as I could. She wept into my shoulders. "Mom, I'm sorry, I'm—"

"No, no, it's okay." Her voice was muffled, and her tears stained my T-shirt. She broke the embrace. "That wasn't fair, it's your life, you can do what you want."

"It was totally fair." I looked to the ceiling and shook my head. "Fuck, Mom, I wish I could explain to you what this island did to me. From the moment I got here, I felt like I was *home*. Debbie, the regulars at Mayor Fred's, the guys in 1812, Rance, Captain Bottroff—they've become the best friends I've ever had. And besides that—" I cut myself off. No need to get into that just now. "But I didn't think about what it was doing to you guys. Especially after Paul. I should've at least come home at *some* point and explained myself, but—I was scared."

"What could *you* possibly be afraid of, hon?" Dad asked. "You're a *meshugginah* fate goddess."

We all laughed at that. You knew it was bad when Dad started rocking the Yiddish. But it broke the tension enough for me to relax again.

I took a second to compose myself and sat back down. "I was afraid that if I left, the magic here would wear off. That I'd go back to La Jolla and it'd be like it never happened and I'd go back to being the old Cassie. And the old Cassie was fine, but—I like who I've become here. I mean, I saved the fucking world!"

"Excuse me?" Dad said.

I sighed. Turned out I *was* going to have to get into it.

I told them the whole story about Ragnarok and Loki and his band that garnered him enough worship that he could cast a spell that would sunder Yggdrasil, a branch of which was the ficus around which Mayor Fred's was built.

"Wait, that freak snowstorm you guys had in April," Mom said. "That was this—this thimble vedder?"

"Fimbulvetr, and yeah. That was when I found out I'm a Dís."

"That's why you talk to ghosts," Dad said.

I nodded. "But now everyone can talk to ghosts, apparently, and it's got me a little worried."

Eventually, Dad decided he wanted to go be a tourist some more, so we decided to check out the Mel Fisher Maritime Museum. Mom had never held a gold bar in her hand before, so that was nice, and I got to tell them all about Fisher, the crazy-ass treasure hunter who always said, "Today's the day!" He spent *years* searching for buried treasure amidst the reefs, and one day today really was the day.

"So he's this big-shot famous treasure hunter," Mom said as we left the museum after spending more than an hour there. "He's got a museum, people sang songs about him, he got rich. What if he died without finding anything? Then he was just an asshole who sucked his entire family into his stupid obsession."

Dad looked at Mom like she was crazy. Okay, he gave her that look a lot. "Seriously? This is how you discuss a man who followed his dreams?"

"He got lucky."

"And if he didn't follow his dreams, he just would've been some guy. Yeah, he might've failed. But if he didn't try? He *definitely* would've failed."

After that, I took them to the boardwalk so they could experience sunset. Every night on Key West, we celebrate sunset with a big party on the boardwalk, which is filled with vendors, partiers, and the magnificent sight of the sun going down over the Gulf of Mexico.

Then we headed down to the southernmost point—a large red-and-black buoy at the corner of South Street and Whitehead that was the point of the continental U.S. that was farthest south—and then walked to dinner at a Japanese place on Simonton. My parents had never had sushi that was *this* fresh in their lives, which was why I brought them there.

We walked slowly up Duval to head back to the Bottroff House. Having flown a red-eye to get here, and having been tossed around by ghosts and stuff, they called it an early night, and I couldn't really blame them.

Of course, it was only eight-thirty, and it was *hours* before my bedtime. I looked up at the stairs to my room and debated the efficacy of spending some time updating the B&B's web site, which was one of the duties I performed to earn my having a place to live.

Before I could decide what to do, I heard a slight mewing sound. Turning, I saw a gray-and-white cat with six toes sauntering up to me and sitting down on the stone pathway that went through the garden, connecting the two cottages to the main house.

I knelt down by it, petting it gently on the back. "Well hello there."

The cat mewed one more time, then scampered off into the garden before I could get a good look at the tag on its collar.

It had to be one of Hemingway's. They'd been kicked out of the museum, and now they were just wandering about the island. That was a good way to get them killed. I was starting to seriously think I needed to go back and give Hemingway a piece of my mind, calling me "Bottroff's young lady" and—

Oh, fuck me sideways.

I took the stairs two at a time, and practically threw the sliding door open. Sure enough, Bottroff was there. "Are you well?"

Couldn't blame him for asking, as my dudgeon level was pretty damned high. "Cap, remember all the times you told me I was your first conversation in a hundred and fifty years?"

"Of course. What does that—"

"Hemingway said he knew who I was. Called me 'Bottroff's young lady,' and knew my name."

"Yes."

"I thought you said—"

Until I met the captain, I never would've believed that ghosts could sigh. "I was referring, Miss Zukav, to conversation with the *living*. Talking with my fellow shades is—difficult. We are insubstantial, after all, and congress with each other is almost as difficult, indeed nigh unto impossible, as it is with the still-living. I have had fragments of dialogue with Mr. Hemingway, but that is all."

I frowned, my annoyance burned to ashes by him throwing all these facts in my face. But those facts also gave me an idea. "That may be something new."

"What do you mean?"

"Since you started becoming visible to people who aren't me and Odin, have you tried, y'know, having congress with other ghosts?"

"I have not. Indeed, I have been attempting to remain here in

125

your domicile, as I do not wish to risk causing wholesale panic."

Nodding, I said, "Yeah, I get that, but you think maybe you can reach out to Hemingway? Find out who put the burr up his ass?"

"I will endeavor to see what I may be able to accomplish in that regard." Then, with a breeze, he disappeared.

I sat down at the laptop and stared at the source code for the B&B's web site for about ten minutes before I realized that my head wasn't in it. I didn't want to wait for the captain, I needed to know more about what was going on at the Hemingway House.

Luckily, one person who could probably answer my questions was a block and a half away.

I went back outside. One of the reasons why I had gone to the Bull that first night was its proximity. I had been sorry the minute I had heard Sandy massacring "Me and Julio..." but hey, live and learn.

Within a few minutes, I was approaching the corner of Caroline Street and Duval. I could hear Sandy's voice desperately trying to keep up with his acoustic guitar on the rendition of "Pinball Wizard" he'd threatened me with sixteen months ago. It might not've sucked if someone else sang it. Nodding to Lio, the bouncer, I came in.

Only after it was obvious that I was entering did Lio try to stop me. "You sure, Cass? The *good* act starts at eleven."

I chuckled. "I actually do need to talk to Sandy about something."

He snorted. "Your funeral. God willing, his ass'll be takin' a break soon."

I went in to sit at the bar. Sandy noticed me, and stumbled over a couple of notes on "Pinball Wizard." I ordered a pint of beer as he finished that song, then went into "City of New Orleans," which wasn't offensive, and "Me and Bobby McGee," which kinda was. Never mind living up to Janis Joplin, he couldn't even live up to Kris Kristofferson. After a painfully bad rendition of "Blackbird"—again, his voice couldn't keep up with his guitar work—he announced, "We'll take a short break. Please don't let that jar be lonely."

Glancing over at the stage, I noticed that the tip jar had a few bills in it, but not much. I wasn't sure how the Bull paid, but if he had to live off of tips, well, it was no wonder he also worked at the Hemingway House.

Naturally, he made a beeline for me, sitting down in the next stool over unasked, just like the first time. However, since that was actually what I wanted, I said nothing.

"Hey, Cass! It's really great to see you! And hey, thanks for bringin' your parents by, that was totally awesome."

"I actually wanted to talk to you about that. When did the ghost—"

"Hey," he said quickly, running right over my question, "I know you get the newsletter, but you may not have seen? I'm gonna be playing at—"

"Sandy?"

He blinked. "Yeah?"

"I'm here to talk to you about why the ghost of Ernest Hemingway is committing assault on customers at the museum. I am *not* here to talk about what laughingly passes for your musical career, and if you insist on talking about that instead of why the most overrated writer in the language attacked my father, I'm going to leave."

Sandy swallowed. "Okay, uh, whaddaya—uh, whaddaya wanna know?"

"When did the ghost show up?"

"L-l-last week. He just started barreling through and yelling at people and asking what all the cats were doing there, and—" He shuddered. "They're *gone*, Cassie. All the polydactyl cats are *gone*. He threw 'em out, and as soon as someone walks in and asks about the cats the way your Dad did? He throws *them* out, too! It's crazy!" He shook his head. "And it's killing the business. Seriously, the owners're getting *pissed*. We're bleeding attendance, and it's only gonna get worse. Especially since nobody wants to *talk* about it." He put a hand on mine. I gave him a death glare and he quickly pulled it back. "I'm so glad you believe it really happened. Most people think it's some kind of trick, but because he's so *violent*, nobody likes it, and they leave and don't come back and tell their friends how awful it is…"

127

"Bad word of mouth?"

"The worst. The place'll have to close if this keeps up. As it is, we keep closing early, and they're talking about not opening again until Friday, hope we get a decent weekend crowd." He sighed. "Are your parents enjoying it here?"

The very last thing in the universe I wanted to do was discuss my personal life with Sandy. Luckily, I had an easy out, as I was down to my last gulp of beer. "They love it. Thanks for the help, Sandy." I threw back the last of the beer, let out a very unfeminine belch, and then hopped off the stool.

"That was awesome!" he said after the burp, which was kinda gross. "Hey, why not stick around for the second set?"

"Maybe another time," I said lamely. He'd actually provided some useful info, so I didn't want to totally let him down by saying what I was thinking, which was, *Never in a billion fucking years.*

Nodding a goodnight to Lio, I headed back to the B&B, only to find the ghosts of two old white guys in my room.

"Well, look who's here." I shook my head as I slid the door shut behind me. All I needed was a little green Muppet, and I had the final scene from *Return of the Jedi* in my room.

"Captain Bottroff tells me that I owe you an apology."

"Actually, you owe my father an apology. What I want is an explanation."

"Of what?"

"Why you're being such an asshole."

Hemingway turned to Bottroff. "You told me she was a lady."

To my shock, the captain actually smiled. "I told you she was a *young* lady."

Folding his arms, Hemingway said, "What is it that requires explanation? I believe I have the right to dictate who is allowed in my own home!"

"In fact, Mr. Hemingway," the captain said, "it is no longer your home. Believe me, I have had quite the lesson in *that*. Miss Dellamonica owns this residence now, and she—"

"Hogwash!" Hemingway bellowed. "This is as much your home as it was then—it even has your name on it, as does my home on Whitehead. It perpetuates my reputation, and a man has a right to protect that."

"All right, so how's causing bodily harm to patrons protecting your rep? Or are you *trying* to cultivate a reputation as a spectacular jackass?"

"Hardly, but nor am I cultivating a reputation as a cat lover."

I raised an eyebrow. "You *don't* like cats?"

"Of course I do, and I had quite a number of them in Cuba. But the house is overrun with them! And when given the opportunity to do something about it, I took it!" Hemingway clenched his fists in a display of machismo that was depressingly predictable.

"So now the world can appreciate you for your genius and not for your predilection for cats?"

"It was only the one damned cat anyhow! My home was never festooned with the blessed things! And I refuse to allow it to become a haven for *cat-lovers*."

I couldn't help but chuckle. "You do realize that the people who *run* the place are cat-lovers? They've already started closing early, and they'll be closed tomorrow and Thursday. It's supposed to be open seven days a week. At this rate, you're going to put the people who've kept your legacy going out of work. Even if they do manage to reopen, most of the people who show up will be coming to see what happened to the cats. Not to mention the fact that the island's gonna be full of homeless six-toed cats now."

"What do you mean?"

"I mean, you just kicked the poor cats out. What happens to them now? It's supposed to rain tomorrow, and you've just dumped dozens of felines out onto the street with no home."

Hemingway just stared at me for several seconds, then turned to look at my roommate. "Captain Bottroff, I must ask you. Is this woman—this *young lady*—always so damned infuriating?"

"No, she's usually worse."

I snorted. "Fuck you too, Captain."

"You see?" Bottroff indicated me with an outstretched hand.

That got Hemingway to chuckle. "I'm impressed. I can see why Captain Bottroff seeks out your company. In less than a day, you have given more thought to the consequences of my actions than I have for the last several decades."

My eyes went wide. "You've been planning this that long?"

"Yes, but my comparative corporeality is a recent development."

"You have any idea why?"

"None."

I sighed. He didn't have any more insight into the supercharging of ghosts than Bottroff did. But he was damn sure taking more advantage of it.

"I do see your point, Miss Zukav I'll allow the cats to return and refrain from causing harm to the patrons—up to a point."

"I'll take what I can get. There's too much of you on this island already without you messing things up."

Hemingway folded his muscular arms. "Is that an insult?"

I pretended to think about it. "Pretty much, yeah. I always thought your work sucked, by the way."

"Captain Bottroff," the ghost of Ernest Hemingway said, "you never told me your friend was a critic." And then he laughed, even as a breeze kicked up. A moment later, he was gone.

If I was lucky, he wouldn't come back.

Somehow, I managed to haul my ass out of bed at eight and have breakfast with Mom and Dad. I told them about my second encounters with both Sandy and Hemingway's ghost, and the latter's promise to stop being a douchenozzle and let the cats back.

Dad dunked a croissant in his cappuccino. "You sure he'll keep his promise?"

"I have no fucking clue. Seriously, this whole Dís thing did *not* come with an instruction manual. Odin tried to tell me that it was better this way, but I think he was just trying to abdicate responsibility."

"But you're not," Mom said softly.

For a second, I just stared at her. "Mom, it's way too damn early for cryptic. I'm not what?"

"Abdicating responsibility." She took a sip of her tea. "The way you've been acting, it's almost like you're responsible for the—" Then she shook her head and smiled. "—the weird shit."

"Maybe I am." I refilled my coffee mug. "I dunno. But I have the ability to see things that other people don't—like Captain Bottroff, like Loki's true face—so I guess I do feel responsible, yeah. And I try to do something about it, when I can."

I stared at Mom for a second. She seemed all weirded out, and frankly, so was I.

And then we both said, "Look, I'm sorry for—" at the same time.

All three of us burst out laughing at that. "Go ahead," I told her.

"No, you go ahead," Mom said.

Dad threw up his hands. "Oh for fuck's sake, both of you, will you stop it? Cassie, your mother is sorry for being such a *nudzh* about you coming home because she didn't know you were so happy here. Rachael, your daughter is sorry for not letting you know she was so happy here, which is why you kept being a *nudzh*. Now will you two shut up and eat your breakfast?"

Both Mom and I gave Dad sidelong glances. I pointed at my father. "What he said."

"Yeah." Mom stared at Dad. "How do you always manage to cut through the crap?"

"Thirty years of my wife and three children producing plenty of crap for me to cut through."

She leaned over and kissed Dad on the cheek. Then she looked at me. "There's a part of me that's in denial about all of this. I mean, it's more than a little crazy. But then I look at your father's arm, and I remember what happened, and—" She let out a long breath and took a sip of tea. "And I worry. I carried three of you around for nine months. I lost one of you right away, and I lost Paul—hell, I lost Paul *years* ago. I don't want to lose you, either."

I put a hand on hers. "You won't, Mom. I promise."

"That's not the promise I want. I want you to promise you'll tell me *everything*. Even the Dís stuff."

"Okay." I smiled at her.

Dad held up both hands. "Me, you don't have to tell. I'll just get *agita*."

As I grinned at my old man, my smartphone beeped with new e-mail, and I checked it out. There were five e-mails, but only one that I cared about. "Finally. Okay, that was Andy at the dive shop pinging me. I gotta run a dive at one, so you guys are on your own for the afternoon."

"Well, from the sounds of it," Dad said, "we can give Hemingway another shot. And maybe do the lighthouse, too."

"You'll be okay without me?"

"We have been for over a year," Mom said.

I shot her a look, and she immediately got all crestfallen.

"I'm sorry, Cassie, but—we'll be fine. Go do your work."

I gulped down yet more coffee. This was my fourth mug. Or maybe my fifth. The fact that I couldn't keep track bespoke the need for it.

Dad finished off his cappuccino. "Did you really tell the ghost of Ernest Hemingway that he owed *me* an apology?"

I nodded.

"Quite the life you're leading, hon," he said with a grin.

But I was still wondering about how it got to the point where Hemingway needed—or indeed was *able to*—apologize to anyone. And I needed to find out before there was a lot more at stake than a single museum and a bunch of cats.

To Be Continued...

Cayo Hueso – Part 2:
The Buck Stops Here

"This is *not* a Ram Jam song," Jana Naha told the crowd. "This is a Leadbelly song."

Chet Smith, playing the bass, rumbled in his deep baritone: "Oh, Black Betty, bam-a-lam, oh Black Betty, bam-a-lam, Black Betty, Black Betty, bam-a-lam, Black Betty, Black Betty, bam-a-lam, jump steady Black Betty, bam-a-lam, look yonder Black Betty, bam-a-lam."

Jana and Bobbi Milewski were just slamming on the power chords. Notably, they were *not* the ones Ram Jam used on their cover version, which could be heard in sports arenas all across the country, but a killer three-chord progression that sounded more like it came from Leadbelly's twelve-string in the 1930s.

My mother, sitting next to me in Mayor Fred's Saloon near the ficus tree around which the open-air bar was built, leaned over. "Okay, I get why you spend so much time watching these guys."

133

I laughed. 1812 was the house band at Mayor Fred's on Greene Street on Key West, playing every Thursday through Sunday night. Whenever real life allowed, I was present for their performances.

My parents had dropped in for a surprise visit two days ago. Since I had come to Key West over a year ago for a two-week visit, and hadn't yet come home, they decided to drop in on me.

They got more than they bargained for, but this is what happens when your daughter is a Dís. Yes, I'm a Norse fate goddess, something I found out at the same time I found out that the ficus we were sitting next to was a root of Yggdrasil, the world tree of Norse myth.

After "Black Betty," Jana replaced her electric guitar with an acoustic, and she started a nifty version of "Who Are You," which was just her guitar and some light cymbal fills by Ginny Blake, the drummer, for two verses. Then she yanked off the acoustic and went to rock out the remainder of the song on the keyboards while the rest of the band joined in. Jana's junkyard growl on the lead vocals contrasted beautifully with Bobbi's sharp soprano on the "who are you" echoes.

After that, Bobbi rested her left wrist on the strings of her left-handed guitar while strumming the chords to "Edge of Seventeen," and I grinned, remembering the day Bobbi finally figured out how to duplicate Waddy Wachtel's distinctive guitar playing. She'd been practically jumping for joy. She also sang lead on it, and it was awesome to watch this 5'2" blonde completely dominating the stage as she belted the lyrics and pounded through the sixteenth-note guitar riff.

When the song was done, Bobbi, sweat plastering her hair down, stepped up to her mic. "We're gonna take a short break. Back in a bit!"

Jana ran outside to smoke a cigarette, and Chet went to the bathroom, but Bobbi and Ginny came over to our table. We'd arrived after the first set started, so I hadn't had the chance to introduce them.

Bobbi grinned. "So these must be the parents."

"Yes, we must," Dad said. "That was some amazing stuff."

"Thanks!"

As Ginny and Bobbi pulled two chairs over to join us, I said, "Jake and Rachael Zukav, this is Bobbi Milewski and Ginny Blake."

Mom looked at Bobbi. "That song you were playing when we came in, right before 'Black Betty'—I didn't recognize it, but it sure sounded like a John Robertson song."

"It was." Bobbi gave a broad smile.

I added, "1812 was Robertson's backup band for his last CD. It should be out, when?"

"Early December," Ginny said. "Just in time for holiday shopping."

Mom's eyes went wide. "Wow! You know, we took Cassie to see him and the Dead way back when."

I nodded. "They know, Mom. Had to share that detail once they got the gig."

"Such a shame about his dying," Mom said.

Ginny and I exchanged a glance. "Not as much as one might think," Ginny said softly.

Dad frowned. "That's an awful thing to say."

"Not as awful as what he did." Then I added to Ginny and Bobbi: "They know."

Bobbi's eyes went wide as saucers. "Oh!"

Mom looked at Ginny. "We also know that you're some kind of goddess yourself."

Ginny smiled demurely. "Some kind of, yes."

I grabbed my beer and took a big gulp. "These days, she sticks with being a drumming goddess."

"Well, that's for sure," Dad said. "The drum work you did on 'Who Are You' did Keith Moon proud."

"I'm grateful." Ginny inclined her head. "Keith was one of my mentors."

I blinked. "I didn't know that."

"I've lived for well over a thousand years, Cassie, you could hardly be expected to know *every* detail."

"She's got a point, hon," Dad said.

Bobbi looked at Mom. "How long you guys on the island for?"

"Not sure. We were planning to have a quiet Thanksgiving at home—Sunni, Cassie's sister, is off with her boyfriend's family this year—plus we had this legal case, but then it was settled…"

"Wait a sec." I leaned forward in my chair. "Sunni's going to Malcolm's place for Thanksgiving?"

Mom nodded.

"I thought she was gonna break up with him."

"Your sister," Mom said in a long-suffering tone, "didn't think it would be kind to break up with him so close to the holidays."

I rolled my eyes. "Translation: Sunni wants to get presents from him before she dumps him."

"Yeah, probably." Dad shook his head.

Bobbi said, "Well, if you want to stay through Thanksgiving, you can always join our feast."

"Uhm…"

Holding up both hands, Bobbi laughed. "It's not remotely an imposition. Every year, my parents have a *massive* Thanksgiving in the back yard. First of all, just the base family that's there includes my parents, my grandfather and his boyfriend, and all seven of their kids, including me. Of the seven, we all are bringing at least one person—spouse, significant other, or, in my case, Jana."

"Jana," I added, "hasn't been on speaking terms with her family since high school."

"And my parents consider her their second daughter."

Dad winced. "Oh lord, your parents have six boys and one girl?"

Bobbi nodded. "And I'm smack in the middle. Barry, Bernie, and Bart are older, Bo, Ban, and Barney are younger."

"I'm detecting a pattern…" Dad grinned.

"Yeah, well, blame my parents, B.J. and Bonnie."

"And," I said grumpily, "people who name their twin kids 'Castor' and 'Pollux' shouldn't throw stones."

"You're never gonna let us live that down, are you?" Dad shook his head.

I leaned forward. "You named me *Castor*."

"Well, yes, dear," Mom started, "but—"

"Castor was male!"

Bobbi laughed. "Let it go, wouldja, Cass?"

"Feh." I wasn't really angry, but I also hadn't snarked them

136

about it in more than a year. I had some lost time to make up for.

Mom sounded desperate to get back on topic. "We appreciate the invite, but we don't want to impose."

"It's *really* not imposing." Bobbi sat up straighter in her chair. "Okay, like I said, we *start* with eighteen people, plus some of my siblings have kids, which brings the total to twenty-four. The current guest list of friends, hangers-on, extra family, and Grandpa's boyfriend's great-grandson makes it thirty-five."

I stared at her. "Do I count as a friend or a hanger-on?"

Bobbi grinned. "We're still working on that. Anyhow, thirty-seven isn't qualitatively different from thirty-five. Honestly, Mommy and Daddy have enough food to feed fifty."

Mom and Dad exchanged glances yet again, but this time I could see that they were doing their usual telepathy. "I'll call the airline tomorrow morning," Dad finally said.

Only then did I realize that, of course, they had to have plane tickets home, but I never asked how long they were staying. "When *were* you gonna go home?"

"Monday," Mom said. "We figured if we hadn't convinced you to come back with us by then…"

"Which," Dad added quickly, "we're not even gonna try to do now. Hell, if listening to these guys four times a week is how you spend your off-hours, *I* may want to retire down here."

Mom shot him a look. I recognized it as the *we'll talk about this later* look—which really meant Mom would lecture him about it later—and then Jana came in and Chet came over, I did the introduction thing again, and conversation shifted a bit. After about fifteen minutes, they got back onstage.

By the middle of that next set, my parents' eyelids were obviously drooping. After two days, they'd adjusted to east coast time, but a normal day for them was to be in bed by eleven, since they had to be at their law office by eight. I told them to get their asses back to the Bottroff House Bed & Breakfast, where they were staying (and where I'd been living since I got here), while I hung out for the rest of the evening.

"So those were your parents," said a voice from behind me. I turned to see the blond hair, red goatée, and short body of Loki. He was trying to make amends for trying to destroy the world.

He was also trying to win Ginny back. Back in the day, they used to be married, and over the past seventy years, they had an on-again-off-again thing.

Loki was walking around free again mainly because I promised to keep an eye on him and make sure he didn't try to bring about Ragnarok again. That didn't mean I wanted to be in his direct company, but he kept seeking out mine.

"Yes, those were my parents. You get within ten feet of them, I'll rip your throat out."

"Calm down, Cassie, I have no malicious intent."

"And I'm supposed to just believe that?"

Loki smiled. He had a really nice smile, but that just increased my great urge to punch him in the neck seventeen times.

He headed over to the bar to chat another of the regulars. Larry also was an immortal thanks to a dalliance with a water elemental decades ago. They probably were taking about the good old days of the Korean War or the Dupont Network or Elvis Presley or whatever other nostalgic nonsense they got into. One time I overheard them talking about how much better football was before they improved the safety equipment.

After the set ended, 1812 did their usual: Chet to the bathroom, Jana to suck nicotine, and Bobbi to my table—solo this time, because Ginny went to talk to Loki and Larry instead. Loki was trying to win Ginny back, and she was provisionally letting him, against my very loud advice.

Norse fate goddess or yenta? You be the judge!

Bobbi sat down just as Adina, one of the servers, came by, having noticed that my pint was almost empty.

"Two beers?" Adina knew us both way too well.

I grinned. "And whatever Bobbi wants."

Adina rolled her eyes. "Tcha, Cass, that joke wasn't funny the *first* six hundred times, either."

We both, however, laughed—Bobbi, though, didn't. She seemed distracted. "What's wrong, Bobbi?"

"I wanted to talk to you alone. I'm worried about Barney."

That was Bobbi's youngest brother. He was only eighteen, but he was already married with a kid. "What about him?"

She shook her head. "There's something about Deirdre that I

don't like—and I don't like what Barney's becoming. I just think there might be something—y'know, *bad* about her."

Deirdre, the wife in question, was twenty-two. Theirs was a proverbial shotgun wedding. "Bad in what way?"

"I just want to know if she's gonna hurt him. I'm already seeing all kindsa personality changes—"

I really didn't like where this was going. "He's eighteen and just had a kid, Bobbi. I'd be more worried if there *weren't* personality changes. Look, I'm not the significant-other-scanner for Key West."

"Oh, come *on*." Bobbi threw up her hands. "You're the one who figured out that Seymour's girlfriend was a nixie—"

I winced. I didn't find that out in time to save Seymour's life from her, unfortunately.

Bobbi went on: "—you're the one who figured out that Jana's fiancé was a water fae. Not to mention that you make a face every time Ginny talks to Sigurd."

I sighed. Ginny had asked me not to tell anyone that "Sigurd Jarlsson," who was hanging around with Larry and hitting on her, was really the same guy who tried to destroy the world in April. She said it would unfairly prejudice everyone against Loki. I'd pointed out that that would be a completely fair prejudice, all things considered, but I went along with it.

"Look, they'll be at Thanksgiving, right? I'll—"

"Actually, Barney's been wanting to show Deirdre the band, so they're coming here tomorrow night. Just—just check her out, okay? Do that Dís thing you do."

I threw up my hands. "I don't *have* a 'Dís thing.' And even if I did, it doesn't always work. I didn't see Robertson coming, did I?"

Bobbi nodded. I'd had no clue that John Robertson was sucking away the souls of his backup bands until *after* he pulled it on 1812 and I had to stop him.

"Why are you making a big deal out of this?" Bobbi sounded genuinely confused by my discomfort.

"I'm not," I lied. "I just—"

"Look, I'm sorry if I just want the person I thought was my friend to help me keep my kid brother safe, but hey, if that's too much, fine." She got up. "Tell Adina I'll get my beer later."

With that, she stormed off and went to talk to Chet and Ginny, who were now congregating by the stage.

Maybe I really was a yenta.

More than anything, I wanted to sit alone and stew for a bit, so of course, Loki chose that moment to sit down next to me.

I glared at him. "I don't recall saying you could join me."

"Now you're starting to understand, little Dís."

"Which is more than I can say for you. I told you not to call me that."

He smiled. "Apologies, but it seemed appropriate in this case. You weren't prepared for this, were you? The tedious, tiresome, *constant* begging from your worshippers."

"Bobbi isn't a worshipper, she's my *friend*."

"Gods' only friends are other gods. Mortals are here to worship us—or ignore us, as I've learned to my annoyance. But you can no longer think of any of these mortals as your equals. And this constant whining for boons will *not* cease for as long as you remain accessible to them and have these gifts." He chuckled. "All-father didn't warn you about this, did he?"

Adina came over with just one beer. "I saw Bobbi over there. Sig, you need anything else?"

"I'm fine," Loki said. "Larry is keeping watch over my bourbon."

After Adina walked off, I stared at Loki, wondering what the fuck I was thinking taking on responsibility for him. Especially when I had no clue what my responsibilities even *were*. The bastard tried to destroy the world, and I really just wanted to rip his goddamn face off. His and Odin's both. I just came down here to scuba dive and listen to good music, why the fuck does this have to be *my* problem?

"I asked Odin about why there wasn't an instruction manual. He said I'd learn on my own 'in due course.'"

Loki shook his head. Great, now he was *pitying* me. "Ah, how like my blood-brother. The next time he accepts responsibility for his actions will also be the first. If you wish any guidance, Cassie, I am more than happy to provide it."

"I'm sure you are. Just as sure as I am that I'd rather sip hot lead through a straw than ask you for help."

"Of course." He rested his hands on the small table and rose to his feet, returning to the bar without another word.

Damn, but that "Of course" was smug.

Cara Zimmerman and Andy Wasserstein, my bosses at the Seaclipse dive shop on Stock Island, gave me Friday off. This was so I could spend the day with my parents and also to make up for how hard they were going to work me over the next five days. Thanksgiving week was always a busy time at the dive shop, and it'd be all hands on deck (so to speak) from Saturday to Wednesday. The shop was closed on Thanksgiving itself.

Crawling out of bed at nine in the morning—two hours before my usual—to have breakfast with my parents proved easier than I thought it would be, as I'd slept for shit the whole night. I'd had bad dreams before I met Odin and Loki back in April, but I'd had a shit-ton more of them since.

My parents had actually been up for hours when I came stumbling downstairs, so they'd eaten, and I didn't usually do breakfast anyhow. We all gathered 'round one of the tables in the garden, sipping our respective caffeinated beverages.

"What's the plan for today?" I asked.

Dad said, "I was thinking the Little White House." Mom and I exchanged nervous glances, which got Dad all defensive. "What?"

"Okay, Dad? You have to promise me and Mom something."

"I will *not* correct the tour guide."

Mom looked at me. "Do *you* believe he won't correct the tour guide, Cassie?"

"Believing it would fly in the face of twenty years of evidence."

Dad folded his arms. "This is not at all fair. Did I correct that red-haired guy at the Hemingway House?"

"No, but there wasn't a president involved."

I need to explain about my father and presidents. When my twin brother Paul and I were six years old, we started learning about the presidents of the United States in school. I didn't care much one way or the other—it was just something else that led to homework—but Paul? He became the world's second-biggest president geek. Dad had to keep up with his millions of questions.

So Dad did all that research, and then Paul moved on to other things because, y'know, he was six and had the attention span of a gnat with ADD. But in helping Paul out, Dad turned himself into *the* biggest president geek in the world.

This meant every time we went somewhere that had to do with a president—Mount Rushmore, say, or anywhere in D.C.—we got endless descriptions, explanations, trivia. And heaven help the poor tour guide, whom Dad would proceed to nitpick to death.

I never did ask if my parents flew into Miami and drove down Route 1 or if they flew to Atlanta and took a puddle jumper to Key West Airport. If they'd driven, there was a very real possibility that, as soon as their rental car hit I-95, Dad started his lecture about President Eisenhower and the interstate highway system. Again.

Anyhow, with Dad swearing up, down, backwards, and sideways that he would absolutely not pester the tour guide, we headed to the entrance to the Little White House on Front Street. We paid our admission and joined a tour group that included a mother with her kid; two men in white T-shirts and shorts, holding hands; and four senior citizens wearing matching yellow T-shirts that said TAMPA TRAVELERS.

Our guide was a perky young blonde with a little nametag that read BECKY, and she spoke in a squeaky drawl.

"*Originally* the Little White House was built for the U.S. *Navy*. The naval base here was a *very* important part of the United States' defense against sea attack from our *enemies*. What is *now* the Little White House was *then* the quarters for *important* people who served the base. By the turn of the *century*, it was converted into a single-family dwelling for the base *commandant*."

One of the seniors raised her hand. "Didn't Thomas Edison live here?"

"Yes, he did!" Becky squealed so loudly I winced, and wondered if dogs all over the island were barking madly now. "During the *First* World War, Thomas Edison—the father of modern electricity—lived here while helping the U.S. Navy in their effort against the *evil* Axis powers."

Dad tensed, but said nothing. I smiled at him.

The taller half of the gay couple was less reticent than my father, however. "Lady, Edison wasn't the father of nothin' 'cept stealin' from smarter people. And we fought the Axis powers in World War *Two*."

I turned to look at Dad. He shrugged and whispered, "What? It wasn't me!"

"Wouldn't put it past you to hire the guy," I whispered back.

"Be fair," Mom whispered, "he wasn't arguing about presidential stuff."

"True," I agreed grudgingly.

Becky had moved on. "President Harry S Truman *first* visited here in 1946, looking for a place for rest and relaxation. For President Truman, the buck *didn't* stop at Camp David." Becky smiled at her half-witticism, which was more than any of the rest of us could dredge up.

Dad, though, tensed, his fists clenched. "Don't do it," I whispered.

However, the short half of the couple decided to be Dad's understudy. "Actually, Becky, it wasn't called Camp David back then, it was Shangri-La. That's what FDR named it."

"He's right," one of the old men said. "It was Eisenhower, who came *after* Truman, who renamed it Camp David after his son. I remember it well."

The woman next to him smacked him gently on the bicep. "You were five years old when that happened!"

"I was very precocious," the man said defensively.

"Moving *on*." Becky spoke almost sternly, though the squeaky voice diluted the effect. She took us through a bunch of rooms, giving the history of the place. Dad stayed stone quiet, but he could afford to. The seniors and the couple were doing their best to correct everything Becky said—or, at the very least, comment on it. Truman signed some bills and worked on State of the Union addresses here, among other things.

At one point, I heard the tall member of the couple mutter to his boyfriend, "This is bogus. This chick's like Wikipedia—just dull facts."

"Yeah, and she's about as accurate as Wikipedia, too," the other one said, shaking his head.

Becky was drawling on. "In addition, after President Truman left office, *other* presidents used this site, from President *Eisen-*

hower, who came here to recover from a heart attack, to President *Kennedy*, who came here after the Cuban *Missile* Crisis, to President *Carter*, who held a family reunion here. It's still available for any president to use, and in fact Secretary of State Colin *Powell* held peace talks here between the presidents of Armenia and Uzbekistan."

"That was Azerbaijan," the tall one said in a tight voice.

Becky had taken to just ignoring the comments, and so she went on, leading us into a massive space with plenty of chairs and a big window that looked out onto the Gulf of Mexico. There was also this large round table in the center. Becky walked in backward, droning on and on. "President Truman *loved* to play poker, and he had a table in this room that he used for games. But he had to be *careful*, because of course the president couldn't be seen to be *gambling*, so there was a cover for the table for when *reporters* came by."

And then I felt a breeze in the room. So did Mom and Dad—they both shivered, as did a couple of the other tourists.

An older white guy with short gray hair, large round glasses, and a bright smile walked into the room, behind Becky, so she couldn't see him. He was wearing a straw hat, a white button-down shirt, and white pants, and he was holding a deck of cards. He walked over to the big round table.

Becky's pert little face scrunched into a very mean-looking frown. "What are you all staring at?"

I looked around, and yeah, everyone was staring, because this guy had the kind of odd not-really-there look of a ghost. I knew because I lived with one, and up until last week, I was the only one who could see him. Then two days ago, the ghost of Ernest Hemingway literally tossed my father out of the Hemingway House and Museum in a misguided attempt to get rid of all the cats and cat lovers from the place.

I still had no idea who'd been supercharging the ghosts on the island, but now there was another one. Great.

"Fuck me sideways," Dad said, "that's Harry Truman!"

"It—it *can't* be!" Becky turned around to see the dead president approaching the poker table. Her eyes glazed over and her lips were twisting oddly. It was as if her brain, such as it was, had short-circuited. "Isn't he, like, *dead?*"

Meanwhile, the ghost of Truman put the cards in his pocket, and took the top off the round table, revealing the decorated green felt of a poker table that was hidden underneath. I'd taken this tour before a year ago, with a much less vapid guide, and part of the gig was that the guide would dramatically remove the covering that they left on the table whenever cameras were around.

Truman sat down and started shuffling the deck. "Well? Want me to deal any of you folks in? It's five-card draw, jacks or better to open, trips or better to win."

Dad was practically bouncing. "Can you believe this? That's Harry Truman playing poker! God, it was like a whole different world in the forties. There's no way a president could hide something like this the way Truman kept the poker under wraps. Of course, I don't think anyone today would give a damn if the president gambled, either."

"Yes, young man," Truman said to my father, "it's a brave new world. Now you in or not?"

"Me?" Dad put his hand to his chest.

"This is insane!" Becky cried, her voice echoing off the windows. "You're Harry Truman!"

The ghost of a dead president smiled. "'Course I am, little lady. It's *my* vacation home, isn't it? Now, who's being dealt in?"

Becky ran off, blubbering incoherently.

"Hell, I'm in," one of the old-timers said, taking a seat to Truman's right, followed quickly by the couple.

One of the old women looked at the other one. "Boys will be boys."

Dad took a step toward the table, but I grabbed his arm. "I think we need to leave."

"Cassie, I've just been invited to play poker with the ghost of Harry Truman—which, I don't mind saying, is a sentence that *nobody* ever expected to say in the history of whatever."

"Yeah, but this place? It's still somewhere that presidents go and other members of government. Which means that security is handled by the Secret Service."

Mom said quickly, "We should leave."

"Yeah," I added, "our friend Becky the Godawful Tour Guide

will probably be back with guys in Ray-Bans and ear-pieces any second, and I don't wanna try to explain *that*," I jerked my thumb at Truman as he dealt five cards to each player, "to them."

We beat a nervous retreat out onto Front, and decided to calm our nerves with a spot of shopping, eventually winding up at Em's. I hadn't taken my parents here yet, even though it's my favorite place to eat on the island.

They know me there, so even though there was a big lunch crowd, we got seated quickly. Our order came fast too. At my suggestion, we all got conch fritters and fries, as that's Em's speciality. Mom and I got beer, while Dad, against my sage advice, got the house white wine.

Mom asked, "So do you have any idea what's going on with all the ghosts? I mean, Hemingway, Truman, your Captain Bottroff."

I sighed and munched on one of Em's great fries. "I have no idea. The problem is, don't know what to do. I mean, I've had people I could ask in the past, or I was able to stumble through on my own—but on this? I got nothin'."

Mom frowned. "You said it was Odin who told you that you were a fate goddess, right?"

I nodded. "You think maybe he'll have something to say about the ghosts?"

"Or Sigyn," Dad added, having just sipped his wine. "What *is* this garbage?"

"Did I, or did I not, warn you that this was a beer place and not a wine place?"

Dad shrugged. "I always drink wine with lunch."

After lunch, we did some more shopping. I was able to take them to the really good crafts shops and steer them away from the tacky tchotchke places, which were sometimes difficult to differentiate on the outside. I mean, if they had a shitload of T-shirts with funny sayings in the window, it was a safe bet to avoid, but some tourist traps had better camouflage.

After a really nice dinner (with a stupendous view) at the high-end restaurant in the Hyatt at the end of Duval Street, we went to Mayor Fred's to catch 1812's Friday set. This time, we arrived before they started, but that gave me the chance to meet Barney's wife.

Deirdre Milewski was a petite little waif of the type I tended to hate on general principles. Not that it was their fault, it's just that clothing stores actually have things in *their* sizes. Every other female diver I knew was like her, an itty-bitty thing, while I had to struggle to find a neoprene suit that was built for somebody 5'11" who actually has boobs.

Anyhow, she didn't need to suffer for my being an amazon—or, since I was a Norse fate goddess, valkyrie? I guess?—so I put on my best smile when Barney introduced us.

"Jesus, you're tall," was the first thing she said. "Must suck to buy clothes."

"It can, yeah." Great minds think alike. Or something.

"You should get breast-reduction surgery so you can just buy men's clothes and be done with it."

Okay, I was starting to understand why Bobbi didn't like this one.

My usual table by the ficus wasn't really geared to seat five comfortably—sure, for Bobbi and Ginny to sit for a minute between sets, but not long-term, the round tables weren't big enough— and the tables around it weren't suited to put together, as it would block server traffic.

I went back toward the merch table. "C'mon, let's put a couple tables together, so Barney and Deirdre can join us."

"Aw, thanks, Cass!" Barney said. He had the same blond hair and blue eyes as his older sister, but he was built like a truck. While he was actually shorter than me, he was really stocky. Basically, Deirdre could fit in his forearm.

Bobbi helped me move the tables together and shot me a grateful smile. "I gotta go tune up. I'll see you guys between sets, okay?"

Deirdre sat next to Barney. "I don't like these seats. We can't see anything."

"We can see half the stage, honeybunny," Barney pointed out, "and it's the half Bobbi usually stands on."

"I *know* what Bobbi looks like! I wanna see the rest of the band."

The whole rest of the evening went like that. Her beer was too cold, then when Adina brought her a new one, it was too warm. The music was too loud, she couldn't hear the drums. Then dur-

147

ing a drum solo she complained about how lousy the drumming was. She hated Led Zeppelin songs, why do they have to do those? (They did "Kashmir," "Whole Lotta Love," and "The Immigrant Song," which were specifically requested by a couple in the audience celebrating their wedding anniversary.) And on and on and on.

By the time the first set finished, I was ready to commit several acts of homicide. Didn't even have to be Deirdre, I was more than happy to kill anyone handy.

And then Loki walked in. It was like he knew I wanted to commit murder and there he went and provided himself. Sadly, there were witnesses, and I couldn't count on *everyone* in the bar staying quiet to protect me.

"Not at your usual table, I see." Then Loki noticed Barney and Deirdre. "Ah, company!"

Explaining why I wanted to punch this guy in the neck would take too long, so I just went with polite. "Sigurd Jarlsson, these are my parents, Rachael and Jake Zukav, and this is Bobbi's brother Barney, and his wife, Deirdre."

Deirdre shot me a look. "You had to introduce me to the cute guy last?"

"Why thank you." Loki gave her his suave smile.

Barney put an arm around her, more than a little protectively. "Cassie was just saving the best for last, honeybunny."

She made a "tch" noise. "Well, of course you *have* to say that."

I winced. So, amazingly, did Loki. When you've offended the sensibilities of the trickster god who tried to destroy the world last spring, how far have you fallen?

Bobbi and Ginny came over, then. "Well, hello there." The smile modulated into a feral grin at the sight of Ginny.

"How'd you like it?" Bobbi asked Barney.

Of course, Deirdre answered. "I've heard better. Why do you have to do so many *covers*? The only one I liked was that original."

How long had she lived on Key West? The only place that had original music was Jimmy Buffett's place—everywhere else thrived on cover bands.

Bobbi frowned. "We didn't do any originals."

"Right after *all those* damn Led Zeppelin songs."

"Oh!" Bobbi chuckled. "That was a John Robertson song, 'Old Man's Blues in a Young Man's Body.' It's the title track on his last CD—we were his backup band on it."

Deirdre scoffed. "Shyeah, right, like you guys would ever get anywhere *near* someone like *him*."

"Actually, it's true, honeybunny. Remember, when Bobbi was gone for a few weeks in August?"

"No, I don't remember. Whatever."

Bobbi looked right at me with a seriously intent look on her face. "I gotta pee."

Getting the hint, I climbed up from my chair. "I'll go with."

Next to me, Mom rose as well. "Me, too."

Dad looked at both of us with a look of murderous rage, since he was now stuck with the Demonspawn of Satan and her dumb-but-loyal sidekick, Barney.

Of course, then I was worried *she'd* come along, but all she did was mutter, "God, I *hate* when women do that."

Once we got into the rest room, Bobbi asked, "So?"

I let out a long sigh, which gave Mom an opportunity to answer first. "She's a total bitch on wheels. Why the hell did your brother marry her?"

Bobbi shook her head. "Barney has a thing for girls so small he could swallow them whole. This is just the one he happened to knock up, so he married her."

"There are other options," Mom said.

"Not for Deirdre. She insisted on having the kid, and Barney didn't think he had a choice."

I gave Bobbi a sympathetic look. "Well, that may make her old-fashioned, but that's all it makes her."

"It's gotta be *something*, Cass!" Bobbi was pleading now. "Barney's always careful, and always uses protection."

"Protection isn't a hundred percent," Mom said.

I snorted. Sunni was a total accident, something I knew and my twin brother Paul knew, and which Sunni would go to her grave not knowing.

"Please, Cassie." Bobbi was pleading now, and I felt like a total heel.

"I'm really sorry, Bobbi. Look, I still don't know much about this whole Dís thing, but I know for sure that I can see people for what they really are—or at the very least, tell when they're trying to be something they aren't. That's why I knew something was hinky with the nixie, and why I knew something was up with Jötunheim and with Jana's guy. But I couldn't see through Robertson, because he wasn't hiding what he was, exactly." I put what I hoped were two friendly hands on Bobbi's shoulders. "Deirdre is a bitch queen from the lowest reaches of hell, but she's not a monster."

"You're wrong. You've *got* to be wrong."

"I *don't know*, Bobbi! Like I said, I'm not an evil-SO Geiger counter. All I know is that *I* can't sense any weird mojo off her, except for the dark cloud that everyone's picking up on."

"Fuck." Bobbi stormed out of the bathroom.

For the rest of the night, Bobbi didn't speak to me. That was the bad news. The good news was that Deirdre was tired and wanted to go home, and so she and Barney left, thus making my parents' and my evening two billion percent better.

After Bobbi deliberately avoided speaking to me for the third time, I gave up. At one point, Loki walked up to me, leaned over, and said, "I *did* warn you…" Only the fact that we were in public kept me from strangling him. Well, that, and I've never actually strangled anyone, and I wasn't even sure I knew how to do it.

Saturday was a blur. There were, as expected, a metric fuckton of dives to run at Seaclipse, as all the folks visiting the Keys for the Thanksgiving holiday had started to show up. Mom and Dad, meanwhile, went on a glass-bottom boat tour in the morning, had lunch at Em's, and then went to a couple more museums. They'd planned to go to the Audubon House, but it was closed, which was ridiculous on a Saturday. I had a bad feeling that the ghost of John James Audubon or Captain Geiger (who built the place) was making it hard to stay open, though I had no basis for that without actually going there.

I had to run some night dives on Saturday, so I didn't make it back to Mayor Fred's until they were breaking down at the end of the last set. Bobbi *still* wasn't talking to me, but she wasn't who I wanted to speak to anyhow.

"What can I do for you, Cassie?" Ginny asked as I went up to her while she packed up her snare drum and cymbals. (The drumkit belonged to the bar, with each drummer supplying his or her own snare and cymbals. Ginny had a glorious brass snare that she treated with the utmost care.)

"I don't know if you've noticed, but the ghosts on the island are getting more—more active."

"I hadn't noticed, actually. I try not to pay the dead much mind. That's the realm of Hela and the valkyries, not me."

I frowned. "Are they even still around?"

Ginny shrugged. "I've no idea. But I have always been able to speak to spirits, just as Allfather and my former husband can."

Smiling at her use of "former," which meant there was hope that she *wouldn't* get back together with Loki, I told her about what happened at the Hemingway House and the Little White House, not to mention what I suspected was happening at the Audubon House.

Ginny then got a faraway look in her eyes. "What is it?" I prompted.

She shook her head. "One of the volunteers at Greenpeace is married to a police officer. He told me that his wife was first reporting officer at a murder where the victim was strangled with a net—except the net disappeared right in the middle of the investigation. Everyone saw it, but none of the photographs taken had the net in it."

"Great, now the ghosts are getting homicidal." I had a close friend who was a federal agent, I'd ask him to look into it. In fact, come to think on it, he had signed up for tomorrow afternoon's dive with me.

"Ma'am, we're closed—*ma'am!*" That was Ihor, the bartender.

I turned to see a woman in a gray nightgown walking through the bar. Ginny and I exchanged worried glances.

"Damn homeless people," Ihor muttered, and walked out from behind the bar. "Ma'am, *please*, you need to—"

He reached for her, and his hand went right through.

She kept walking right toward the stage, just as Jana and Bobbi came back inside from loading up Bobbi's cargo van. Jana's cigarette-scratched voice actually squeaked. "Fuck me, it's the fucking lady in gray!"

"The lady in gray?" I asked. Ginny just shrugged.

Before anyone could explain what the lady in gray was, said lady walked up to the stage and looked right at Ginny and me. "This is your fault."

Then she was on the stage. At no point did she step up, just one moment she was on the dance floor, the next right in front of us.

She repeated: "This is your fault!"

I held up my hands. "What the hell did I do?"

One of my hands brushed her, and suddenly the lady in gray threw her head back and screamed. A big-ass lightshow, and then she disappeared, the scream fading more slowly, leaving me to blink spots from my eyes.

I turned to Ginny. "What the fuck was that? Was she a demon, too?" The last time I touched something that disappeared like that, it was a demon.

"You can disrupt ethereal creatures who can alter fate, but I do not know what this—this 'lady in gray' is."

Jana was standing with her mouth hanging open. "What the fuck just happened?"

Wincing, I looked helplessly at Bobbi. We'd both agreed that telling Jana about my being a Dís wasn't the best idea.

But Bobbi ignored me and looked at Ginny. "The lady in gray is one of the ghosts that's supposed to be haunting the island. Supposedly, she was hanged on the ficus for killing her husband."

I nodded. Besides being a root of Yggdrasil, the ficus around which Mayor Fred's was built was Key West's hanging tree in the nineteenth century.

"Perhaps that is why. Murderers by definition alter fate." Ginny didn't sound particularly convinced, and neither was I. The demon's *purpose* was to alter fate. This was just a woman who committed murder, and had already paid for the crime. It didn't make sense.

Jana threw up her hands. "Will someone please explain to me what the *fuck* just happened?"

I sighed. There wasn't really any hiding it. "Okay, you know how I've always noticed weird-ass shit? And been able to fix the weird-ass shit?"

"Like finding Russ's mother?"

I nodded.

"I just figured you were into all the spooky crap, Zukav."

"It's more than that." I let out a long breath. "I'm a Dís—a Norse fate goddess."

"And Ginny's also a Norse goddess," Bobbi added. "Cassie didn't want to tell you."

"What?" I stared at Bobbi. "Actually, Bobbi and I *both* agreed to keep it under wraps."

"Whatever." Bobbi waved a hand dismissively.

"What the fucking *fuck*, Zukav? You couldn't tell me? You neither, Blake?"

Ginny drew herself up. "Until I joined this band, I did not reveal my true nature to anyone. Bobbi and Cassie's parents are the only mortals currently alive who are aware."

"And me," I added. "And whaddaya mean by 'currently alive'?"

She smiled. "I believe I mentioned that Keith Moon was my mentor?"

Jana stared at her. "Fuck."

Bobbi turned to leave. "Obviously, you goddesses need to work shit out. We'll leave you alone." Then she stopped and turned around. "By the way, you two need to make other plans for Thanksgiving."

She left. Jana stood for a moment, staring at us with a hurt look on her face. Then she took out a cigarette and headed for the exit as well.

Almost as if on cue, Loki came out of the men's room. I hadn't even realized he was in the damn bar.

"Well done, Cassie," he said with a supercilious smile. "I was actually looking forward to this harvest festival at the Milewski home. But then, mortals do not know the true meaning of a feast in any event. We shall have to make our own. Perhaps even invite Allfather!"

"Fuck you, 'Sigurd.' Those are my friends you're talking about."

Ginny was shaking her head sadly. "Sadly, my former husband is correct. Gods and mortals may not be friends. If we lie about our true nature, then we are not truly friends, for friends do not maintain falsehoods. And if we tell the truth, they are no longer our friends, but our worshippers."

"Exactly," Loki said triumphantly. "Bobbi is angry because you did not answer her prayer."

I clenched my fists hard enough for my fingernails to dig into my palms. "It wasn't a fucking prayer, it was a favor! And she'll get over it."

"Of course," Loki said patronizingly.

Snarling at him again, I turned to leave. This was eighteen kinds of fucked up. Why were the ghosts on the island all supercharged? Why did this lady in gray say it was *my* fault? And how was I suddenly able to disperse a ghost like that?

Then I saw Bobbi and Jana at the van—

—but Bobbi wasn't just standing at the van, she was also somehow at the same time hobbling around her parents' back yard on crutches, with a cast halfway up her leg.

—and Jana was loading the van at the same time she was sitting in the middle of what looked like Key West Cemetery, sitting next to Bobbi and me, all of us dressed in black while two caskets were lowered into the ground.

What. The. Unholy. *Fuck?*

It was just a moment, and then Bobbi and Jana were only loading the van and studiously ignoring me without anything else going on.

I walked away from there as fast as I could. For some reason, my B&B cottage with the ghost of a wrecker captain in it felt like it would be a bastion of normalcy.

As I turned away from the bar, I saw a single figure walking slowly up Greene Street toward me. For a second, I thought it was another weird-ass vision—and when the *fuck* did getting visions become part of the package?—because I hadn't seen this particular person in a couple years. Like me, he had curly hair, though his was more brown than my blond, and he had the same mix of Dad's long nose and Mom's hazel-green eyes that I had.

He came right up to me hit me with that grin that looked just like Dad's. "Hey, Cassie."

It was my twin brother Pollux Abraham "Paul" Zukav.

Son of a bitch.

To Be Continued...

Cayo Hueso – Part 3:
Twisting Fate

The last time I saw my twin brother Paul, he was driving away on Comet, the Harley Davidson motorcycle my parents got him. He didn't even say goodbye to me or our baby sister Sunni as he drove away from the house in La Jolla, California where we grew up. He had a backpack and a couple thousand dollars in his pocket.

Within a month, his cell phone number was out of service and messages to his e-mail address bounced. He even disabled Comet's GPS.

That was three years ago. I hadn't heard hide nor hair of him in all that time except for one call two years ago to congratulate me on getting my Master's Degree. I didn't even know how he knew that I'd gotten the degree, especially since it happened a semester later than expected. That call was from a different number than the old one, and it was out of service a day later.

Until one Saturday night when he showed up at Mayor Fred's Saloon on Greene Street in Key West, Florida just as the place was closing. Because my life apparently wasn't fucked up enough.

I wanted to take him home, but he said he was starving, so we went to Em's, my favorite place on the island to eat. It gets a little crowded after the bars close, but I'm a regular. As soon as Frieda saw me, she led us to a table.

I stared at him. We were fraternal twins, obviously, what with us being different sexes and all, but we were very noticeably siblings. I was actually the taller of us—at 5'11", I had an inch on him—and his hair was a dirtier blond and less curly than mine. But we both had Dad's long nose—more's the pity—and we both had Mom's hazel-green eyes.

After we sat down, I ordered conch fritters, two orders of fries, and two coffees. "Just one coffee," Paul added. "Herb tea for me, please."

"Okay, *you* were the one who got *me* into coffee."

He shrugged. "I lost the taste for it."

"No problem, babe." Frieda jotted down the order on her pad. "You want raspberry, chamomile, or mint?"

"Raspberry, please. You serve chamomile?"

Frieda smiled sweetly. "We get a *lotta* people in here with upset tummies. I'll be right back with the coffee and tea, 'kay?"

After she went off, I shook my head. "I don't even know where to start. Where the fuck have you been for three years?"

"Where haven't I been?" Paul sighed. "All right, there's something you need to know. I've got—well, for lack of a better word, I guess you could say I've got super-powers."

I chuckled. "Really?"

"You don't believe me."

"Oh, you have *no* idea how much I *do* believe you. In fact, I can do you one better—I can tell you where those powers come from."

"What?" Paul leaned forward and put his right arm on the table. Back when I was a teenager, whenever I got excited about something, I'd do the same thing, only with my left arm. Then Paul started doing it with his right to make fun of me. I'd broken myself of the habit by grad school, but Paul never did, which both amused and depressed me. "You mean, you can see the future, too?"

I choked back what I was going to say, because that was *not* what I was expecting. I had to clear my throat before taking a second shot at words. "Uh, no, I—"

Then Frieda came with my coffee and his tea. Even as I saw her place the coffee cup in front of me, I also saw her walking into what I assume was her house, exhausted after her shift, and then confused upon seeing one of the closets emptied out, and then angry upon seeing the note from her girlfriend taped to the bathroom mirror saying she'd moved out to be with someone named Annie.

After Frieda walked off, Paul gave me a significant look. "You saw it too, didn't you? Her girlfriend is moving out while she's working."

I nodded quickly and snatched my coffee, suddenly wishing there was Scotch in it. "That's the second time that's happened tonight. What the fuck *was* that?"

"You couldn't do that before?"

"No!"

"But I thought—"

"I can—" I hesitated. "I can see things for what they really are, I guess. I can see ghosts, I can see through glamours, I can dispel demons that affect people's fate, and I can cast spells."

Paul just stared at me with his mouth hanging open.

I raised an eyebrow at him. "You had that exact same look on your face when we were twelve and I asked you if you'd kissed Sarah Rae Rosenthal."

He stuck out his tongue at me. "Well, that's quite a list. I can't do any of those things."

"Yeah, well, until you got here, I couldn't tell the future, either."

"How'd this happen? And what's a glamour?"

I hesitated. "How much do you know about Norse mythology?"

"Just what I got from those old *Thor* comics you used to steal."

I drew myself up in outrage. "I did *not* steal them. I borrowed them."

Glowering at me, Paul said, "You took them without permission. That's stealing."

"I gave them back when I was done. That's borrowing. Anyhow, the comics only got some of it right."

And then I told him about all the weird-ass shit that had happened to me since I drove Rocinante into Key West: the dragon, the UFO, the nixie, John Robertson, the water elemental, and most importantly Loki, Odin, Sigyn, and the attempt to destroy the world. I told him about 1812, the band I hung out with and saw, the drummer for whom was the aforementioned Sigyn. And then the kicker: Odin's revelation that I'm one of the Dísir, a Norse fate god, which happens sometimes to triplets born on Earth.

By the time I was done, our fritters and fries had arrived. "All right, two things," he finally said, "one, these fries are fucking amazing, and two, if our brother hadn't been stillborn—"

"He'd have had funky powers, too."

"Sonofabitch." He popped a fry into his mouth. "It's amazing, these don't even need ketchup." He swallowed another, then: "So that explains that, then. Fuck, it's been making me crazy for *years*. Honestly, that's why I had all the problems with drinking and the drugs and all the rest of it—and why I finally just left. I thought maybe it was something at home, and if I got away, maybe it would stop. And even if it didn't—I couldn't stand knowing what was gonna happen without being able to *do* anything about it." He sipped his tea. "The straw that broke my back was Grandpa."

"Yeah, that was so out of left field." Dad's father died of a heart attack, and he was a health nut, never smoked or drank and was a fifth-degree black belt in some martial art or other. "We never saw it coming."

"I did." Paul packed a lot of feeling into those two words.

"Fuck." Frieda walked by, and I flagged her down and ordered a beer.

"You sure, babe?"

"Yeah." Caffeine was not gonna be enough for this conversation.

Frieda looked at Paul, but he shook his head. "Just got my two-year chip from AA."

I blinked. "Seriously? It actually took this time?" Paul had tried AA several times in college, but he and the wagon never really got along.

"Yeah. Turns out the whole seeing-the-future thing isn't as intense when I'm sober."

"So after Grandpa died you left." I hadn't seen the connection between the two events before. We weren't all that close to the old man—he lived on the east coast, so we only saw him once every other year or so—but if Paul saw his death coming...

"I couldn't tell anybody about it, either. Everyone *already* thought I was nuts, claiming to tell the future just would've made it worse."

Frieda brought my pint of beer. I quickly gulped about a quarter of it, then wiped the foam from my mouth with the back of my hand. "Well, you're not crazy. You're just a Dís."

"Apparently." Paul ate the last of his fries, then reached for mine.

"Hey!" I smacked his hand. Some things don't change.

"All right," he said, "so how the hell'd you wind up living down here? What're you doing with yourself, anyhow, teaching?"

"Not exactly." I shifted uncomfortably in the wireframe chair and then sipped some more beer. "After I got my Master's, I took a break, doing an I-10 tour along the bottom of the country. I hit the Grand Canyon, Albuquerque, Austin, New Orleans—then I came down Florida and arrived here. My *plan* was to spend a week or two diving during the day and checking out live music at night. That was sixteen months ago."

"Mom and Dad must've shit themselves." Paul grinned.

That got a glower from me. "Well, when I left home and didn't come back, I kept my cell phone and e-mail address and I talk to them every day, so they're not quite as beside themselves as they were."

Paul didn't even let that bother him, the fucker. "Still, I never would've guessed that you'd wind up here. I figured you'd be most of the way to your PhD by now, TA'ing for what's-his-name—"

"Liverakos." He was the English professor I'd been teaching assistant for when I was working on my Master's.

159

"Yeah, and scaring the undergrads. How're you making a living? Or are Mom and Dad—?"

I shook my head. "They've offered, but I've been managing. I do some work for the B&B where I'm living, and that's enough for Debbie to give me a place to stay. I make money working part-time at a dive shop."

"Well, thank goodness Mom and Dad paid for all that education, then." Paul grinned as he said it, which was the only reason why I didn't punch him in the nose.

"Fuck you too, baby brother. And how've *you* been making *your* living, since you didn't even finish your Bachelor's?" I held up a hand. "No, wait, lemme guess—you worked as a psychic!"

"Actually, I tried that." He grinned ruefully. "It didn't really work out."

That surprised me. "Why not?"

"People don't go to psychics to hear the future, they go to psychics to hear what they want to hear. Turns out that actually knowing the future is the kiss of death for a professional psychic. But it's great if you want to make shit-tons of money at casinos. Just gotta be careful not to go to the same casino twice." He absently rubbed his left shoulder. "Besides, living on the road is kinda cheap. Worst part is paying for gas for the Harley."

"That why you came here? You saw it in the future?"

"Pretty much. I knew that Mom and Dad were going to be in Key West and would be seeing both of us here. So I came on down."

"Well, you're the last one to the party—Mom and Dad have been here since Tuesday."

"Really?" Paul's face fell.

"Yup. They're staying at the B&B with me. Well, not *with* me, they're one flight down, but, well…"

Paul sighed. "I guess I should've expected that. I was hoping I'd get here first and talk to you."

"Well, you did that, sort of. Where you staying?"

"Uhm, nowhere. I was in Charlotte when I got the vision yesterday, and I just hopped on the bike and drove till I got here—which just happened to be at three a.m. I parked Comet on Greene Street."

I regarded him with annoyance—a look I hadn't had to give in three years, and I had to admit to kind of missing it. "And how the fuck were you gonna find a place arriving at three in the morning?"

He shrugged. "I have an in at a local B&B."

"Like hell. It's the weekend before Thanksgiving, all our rooms are booked." If it hadn't been for a last-minute cancellation, I'd have had to stay in the main house's living room for the weekend. Debbie was more than happy to give me a free room in general, but if a paying customer needed it, it was the fold-out couch for me.

Staring at me with his big blue eyes, he said, "But my twin sister will help me, right? Like a rollaway in her room?"

"Rollaways are on wheels. I'm on the second floor of one of the cottages, and I sure as shit ain't carrying that thing up the stairs at four a.m." I went over the B&B's inventory in my head. "How-some-ever, we do have an airbed that isn't being used. You can sleep on that on my floor." I grinned. "And you get to meet my roommate!"

Paul looked very confused. "Where's the roommate gonna sleep?"

"Not really a factor—he hasn't needed sleep since the nineteenth century."

From there, we finished off our conch fritters and caught each other up on what we'd been doing. He told me about how working as a barista at a coffee shop showed him that the service industry was a bad choice for someone who can see people's futures. I told him that John Robertson—the very same guy our parents took us to see play with the Grateful Dead when we were little—was really Robert Johnson whose deal with the devil turned out to be *way* more complicated than legend would have you believe.

Frieda brought us the check. Paul asked her, "How do you guys make those fries so amazing?"

I rolled my eyes. But Frieda just gave the sweet smile. "Trade secret, babe."

She took my debit card. Paul reached for his wallet, but I said,

"Nah, this one's on me. Besides, you're the one who gets to explain to Mom why you haven't called for years, I figure that'll cost you plenty."

"I had my reasons."

"Yeah, but they're sucky reasons, Paul."

"All right, I know that *now*, but—"

Frieda dropped off the card and receipt. As I signed the bill, I asked Paul, "Should we tell Frieda what—"

"No!" Paul nearly bit my head off. "No fucking way, Cass. Seriously, that *never* ends well. She'll find out soon enough. Us telling her will *not* help her. *Trust* me."

I nodded quickly. I honestly wasn't entirely sure it was a good idea, and Paul had had this particular ability for years, where I'd only had it for an hour, so I trusted his judgment.

On that, anyhow.

We headed out to Greene to recover Comet.

The Harley needed a good cleaning, but the bike seemed to be in decent shape otherwise. "Glad you still have her," I said. "And still call her by name."

Thrusting his index finger upward, he said, "Tradition!" in a perfect impersonation of Dad.

On cue, I did likewise. "Tradition!" All the cars in our family were named after horses from pop culture. My parents' silver Rav4 was named Silver, after the Lone Ranger's faithful steed. (Dad always cried, "Hiyo, Silver, away!" when he drove somewhere no matter how many times Mom threatened him with bodily harm if he ever did it again.) Sunni's Jaguar was Starsong, after one of the *My Little Pony* characters, and my pickup truck was Rocinante, after Don Quixote's mount.

We were all fans of the short-lived Western from the 1990s, *The Adventures of Brisco County Jr.*, so Paul went with Brisco's horse when Mom and Dad bought him the Harley.

Grabbing the spare helmet, I got on the back of the bike behind him, and we went the three blocks to the Bottroff House. I hoped we didn't wake too many of the paying customers; motorcycles ain't quiet. We parked right alongside Rocinante in the driveway.

We went into the main house first. I had a key, and we quietly

162

got an airbed out of a closet. Then we walked through the garden toward one of the cottages in the rear. We passed the parrot cage, which was thankfully covered. Harry S would've gone batshit if he'd seen us, and woken everyone up.

Sitting on the staircase was a man with one eye, but no eyepatch, a bald pate and wild white hair along the temples. He was, like most people on the island, wearing a T-shirt and shorts and no socks.

I stopped short, and Paul nearly crashed into me. "Well, this isn't good," I said.

"You know this guy?"

"Yeah, and you kinda need to also." As we approached, I said, "Y'know, the last time you were sitting on my stairs in the wee hours of the morning, it was to tell me that the world was gonna end if I didn't save it."

Odin almost smiled at that. "Nothing *quite* so dire this time."

"But it is something dire?"

"Yes. And the presence of your twin is part of the proof that it *is* so dire."

Paul looked baffled. "Uhm…"

"Sorry." I shook my head. "Odin, this is my twin brother—"

"Pollux Abraham Zukav. I'm aware. You no doubt have questions—both related to yourselves, and to the manifestation of ghosts."

That got Paul to shoot me a look. "Ghosts?"

Lamely, I said, "I was getting to that."

"Let us go inside." Odin rose to his feet.

The three of us trundled up the stairs and I unlocked the sliding door into the room. Waiting for us, as usual, was the ghost of Captain Jeremiah Bottroff, the wrecker captain who built the main house.

"So this is the roommate?" Paul said, a hitch in his voice.

"Yes. Captain Bottroff, this is my twin brother Paul."

"My goodness," he said, "you really do have a twin."

I regarded him with annoyance. "You didn't believe me?"

The captain didn't reply to that, instead looking at my brother. "It is a pleasure to make your acquaintance, sir."

"Uhm, thanks, I, uh, I guess." He swallowed. "Sorry, never

talked to a ghost before."

Now Bottroff looked at me funny. "I was under the impression that he had the same capabilities as you yourself."

"Not exactly."

"Not at all, in fact." Odin took a seat in the big wicker chair, and Paul went to sit at the desk chair, leaving the edge of the bed for me. I tossed the airbed and pump onto the white-carpeted floor. Odin went on: "Separate, the twins have different aspects of the Dísir. Together, they share all aspects."

A huge feeling of relief washed over me like a wave. I mean, I'd figured that was the case, but having Odin say it made it real. "That's why I can see people's future now?"

"Indeed."

Paul added, "And why I can see Captain Bottroff here?"

"Yes and no," I said. "Right now, everyone can see him. Somebody's been supercharging the ghosts on the island. On Tuesday, Ernest Hemingway physically threw Dad out of the Hemingway House, and then on Friday we saw Harry Truman deal a poker game at the Little White House. Plus I've been hearing weird things from people at Mayor Fred's and at Seaclipse."

Odin nodded. "Sigyn also mentioned a strange death where a net disappeared."

"Yeah. You got any idea what's going on?"

"I know only that strong magic is involved." Odin shook his head. "But I do plan to investigate further. However, your assistance may be required to deal with it."

"Yeah, 'cause that went so well last time." I rolled my eyes.

"It did. Do not underestimate your own contribution, Cassie. Loki was using strong magic. It was as much your own power as mine that allowed the counterspell to work."

I was not even a little convinced. If Odin had just done the counterspell in the first place, everything would've been fine, the world would've gone on, and I'd live in blissful ignorance about being a Dís which would, if nothing else, mean my two best friends would still be speaking to me.

"There is another issue," Bottroff chimed in. "A consequence of these recent events is that we of the dead have been able to speak to each other with an efficiency we were heretofore denied. One such was the ghost of a Mr. Fisher, who apparently made a career of treasure hunting."

Both Paul and Odin looked blank. I filled them in briefly on Mel Fisher, one of the great characters of Key West, who spent years searching for sunken treasure. Lots of ships had crashed and sunk on the reefs hereabouts over the centuries. In fact, back when he was alive, Bottroff made his living as a wrecker captain, whose ship went out and rescued vessels that had been damaged out there in the 1800s.

"This morning, he disappeared. The owners of his museum appeared relieved, but there is no sign that ever he was there. And Mr. Hemingway informed me this afternoon that he had lost touch with Captain Geiger, whose shade has haunted the so-called Audubon House."

I smiled. Geiger had built the house, but the museum on the site was named after the famous ornithologist, who probably never even lived there. Bottroff had always been a little cranky about that.

Aloud, I said, "Our parents tried going to the Audubon House today, but it was closed."

"Apparently, Captain Geiger's shade has caused issues similar to those of Mr. Hemingway, disturbing the clientele."

"But now he's gone?" Paul asked.

"Yes."

"Maybe whoever cast the spell is taking it back?" Paul asked.

Odin shook his head. "The spell cannot be 'taken back.' It may be reversed, but that would simply return the previous state of affairs. No, what concerns me is that someone might be providing the dead with additional power only to then take that power away."

I stared at Odin. "Gee. Who do we know like that?"

Odin stared at me with his one good eye. "You believe my blood-brother is behind this?"

"I believe that Loki's tried to destroy the world about half a dozen times, and his first step toward doing it is to build up the power needed to cast the spell. I wouldn't put this past him at all."

"Great," Paul said glumly, "so where do we find this Loki guy?"

Odin stared at me. I straightened and got a little defensive. "Why you looking at me?"

"I believe you accepted responsibility for making sure Loki did not do something very much like this."

"Yeah, okay, but he hasn't *done* anything that I've seen! And it's not like I'm an expert on this shit." I shook my head. "Look, he'll be at Mayor Fred's tomorrow night. We'll nail him, then."

"Are you sure of this?" Odin regarded me more than a little skeptically.

I nodded. "He hasn't missed an 1812 gig that I'm aware of since he came back. Not always there the whole time, but he spends the between-sets breaks putting the moves on Ginny." I slapped my hands into my lap and then got up. "On that note, I'm exhausted. I need to sleep, and so does my brother."

"Hm?" Paul looked up like he'd just come out of a trance. "Uh, yeah. Yeah, I'm wiped. And, uh—I got a lot more than I bargained for tonight. It was, uh, nice meeting both of you."

Odin also got up. "I will meet you at the tavern tomorrow evening."

"*This* evening, you mean," Paul muttered.

"Feh," I said. "It's not tomorrow until after you've slept. As far as I'm concerned, it's still Saturday."

"Goodnight," Odin told us. "And be prepared, Castor Lisbeth and Pollux Abraham. The challenge before you will be great."

"Call me 'Castor' again, and you'll lose the other eye."

That got another almost-smile out of Odin. "Of course. Goodnight, Cassie, Paul."

Odin left through the sliding door. The captain stared at me. "Will you be well, Miss Zukav?"

He rarely called me by name. That meant he was worried. "We can take care of ourselves."

"Very well." A sudden breeze, and he was gone.

Paul had brought in the same backpack he'd been wearing when he left home three years ago. He grabbed it now off the floor and went into the bathroom. I unfolded the airbed and started the pump. I also started up the ceiling fan.

By the time the airbed was inflated and settled at the foot of my bed, he came out wearing sweat shorts and a plain white T-shirt.

He stared at me for a second. "So we're Norse fate gods, and I just met the Allfather of Norse myth and the ghost of a wrecker captain."

"Yes."

"And tonight—sorry, *tomorrow* night, I get to meet Loki and Sigyn and stop them from destroying the world?"

"Just Loki, Ginny's good people. But again, yes."

"And this is a normal day for you?"

I smiled. "More or less, yeah." I climbed into bed, still fully clothed except for my bra, which I'd removed with the old trick of pulling it out through the sleeves of my shirt. I usually slept in the buff, but that was my brother on that airbed. Y'know—ew.

"Tomorrow night's gonna be interesting." Paul covered himself with the bedspread that I'd tossed down.

"Not as interesting as tomorrow morning. That's when we get to tell Mom and Dad that you're here."

My usual morning routine was a bit messed up by my twin brother taking up most of my floorspace. The airbed prevented me from even pulling out the chair of my desk to sit and use my laptop.

Instead, I checked my email on my smartphone before showering and getting dressed in the bathroom. After so long, I didn't bother with modesty around Captain Bottroff, but for some reason, I was self-conscious of being undressed or doing my morning toilette in front of the guy I shared a womb with.

The human brain is seriously fucked up. Well, at least mine is.

Of the various emails I got, the only one I actually read was the one from Seaclipse, telling me who'd signed up for the one p.m. dive. That was when I realized how much awkwardness was afoot. Seaclipse was slammed due to the upcoming Thanksgiving holiday. They were running three dives at one, and they only had four dive-masters, one of whom had to stay behind to keep the shop open while the three boats were out. If it was an emergency, Cara, Andy, and Noah could run the dives and they'd just close the shop, but then I'd a) let my employers down, b) cost them business they might've gotten if the shop was open for those two hours, and c) cost myself a day's income.

Question was, did Paul's reunion with Mom and Dad constitute an emergency?

By the time Paul got ready, I had decided on a course of action.

Leaving him in the room and telling him to wait for my signal, I went downstairs. I'd composed a text message to him (which had the added benefit of me finally getting his new cell number). The signal would be me hitting send on that message.

Mom and Dad were waiting for me at one of the tables outside in the garden. The main breakfast rush was long gone, but Debbie, the B&B's owner, kept some pastries and coffee, tea, and juice on the table for the late risers like me. My parents were both wearing damp bathing suits, my mother with an unbuttoned blouse over it, my father also wearing a T-shirt. Mom was in her usual big floppy hat. I noticed bits of sand here and there.

"Went to the beach, did you?" I asked as I passed the table and went for the coffee.

Dad leaned over to Mom. "Toldja she should've become a detective."

"I hate guns, remember?" I took the first sip of the blessed hot beverage, and the cobwebs cleared a bit. I know it's totally psychosomatic, but that first sip just makes all the difference. It blasts away the bleariness.

Sitting down alongside them, I placed my phone in front of me on the table. "Listen, Mom, Dad—something happened last night. Actually, a couple somethings," I added, remembering that Bobbi's grumpiness at me extended to disinviting us from Thanksgiving at her parents' place. I quickly mentioned that, which got a look of concern from Mom, but I waved her off. "That's not the big news, though." I activated my phone and hit send. "I also had a surprise visitor last night."

The light thunk of sneakers hitting wooden stairs could be heard behind us. Mom and Dad saw me look over toward the cottage where we were all staying and turned around.

Paul came down and walked to the table. "Hi Mom. Hi Dad."

"Oh, *baby!*" Mom leapt up from her chair and wrapped Paul in the most enthusiastic bear hug I've ever seen. It knocked her floppy hat to the ground. "Oh, thank God, you're *alive.*"

"Alive, and apparently a Norse god." He smiled. "Who knew?"

"Well, I did." I leaned over to pick up Mom's hat off the ground.

Dad looked up at Paul, who was still wrapped in maternal arms. "You look like shit, son."

"Thanks, Dad," Paul said wryly. "I was driving all night."

"Still got Comet?" Dad asked.

"Of course. She's a great ride."

"Good."

Mom *finally* broke the embrace and cupped Paul's jaw in her hands. "Let me look at you." She chuckled. "Your father's right, you do look like shit."

"Some tea will help."

"We've got just the thing."

The next fifteen minutes were just like old times, sitting around the breakfast table on a late Sunday morning. Paul told a condensed version of what he'd been doing, and mentioned how relieved he was that he got the vision to come here because now everything made sense.

"You knew about Pop?" Our father's voice was slightly strangled when Paul revealed that particular thing.

"I saw a vision of him dying," Paul said, "but I didn't realize it was an actual premonition. I was always seeing weird stuff and—"

"Why didn't you *say* anything?" Now Dad was sounding pissed.

"Dad—" I started.

Paul held up both hands palms-up in frustration. "What was I supposed to say? How would you've reacted if I said, 'By the way, Grandpa's gonna die of a heart attack next week'?"

Dad opened his mouth as if to yell, closed it, shook his head. "I'd'a said you were crazy," he finally said in a softer voice.

"Exactly." Paul let out a long breath. "I just wish I'd *known* about this whole Dís thing."

"You and me both," I muttered. Louder, I said, "Look, I need to go run a dive. You three gonna be okay?"

"Are you kidding?" Mom asked. "I've been dreaming of this day for three years! We've got *so much* to catch up on."

"Lucky you." I stood up. "You're gonna get the *Reader's Digest* condensed version of the emails I've gotten every morning for the past couple years."

Dad gave me an *are you serious?* look as he got to his feet. "You honestly think she's gonna condense it? I'm gonna need more cappuccino."

I went back to the room to get my dive gear, tossed it in the back of Rocinante, and headed to Seaclipse.

Each of the three dives had six people, which was generally the max, though sometimes they squeezed another one or two on. In fact, mine was supposed to have seven—the extra being a good friend, Rance Demitrijian, but he never made it. Usually he texts me when he's gonna miss a dive, but he's also a federal agent. Sometimes the job gets in the way and he isn't in a position to text.

Since there were an even number of customers, I stayed with the boat while everyone dove. Mostly I spent the time they were down thinking that I really needed to introduce Mom and Dad to Rance. He and I weren't dating, though we'd been flirting for the better part of two years, I'd seen him naked (when I saved him from a nixie who almost fucked him to death), and we'd seen a lot of weird shit together.

I was also grateful that I did this dive without Paul. For the first time since he got here, I wasn't seeing flashes of people's futures. At the Bottroff House I kept seeing Mom and Dad walking down Duval Street with Paul. But once I got away from Paul, it stopped.

Mom, Dad, and Paul hadn't moved from the same spot in the garden when I got back, and I convinced them that we should go out for a celebratory dinner. Mom and Dad took a long overdue shower, as did I, we all changed into nice clothes (for Key West, that meant a T-shirt that didn't have words or a picture on it and shorts that didn't have a waistband), and went to the sushi place I'd taken my parents to when they first got here.

After dinner, my parents decided they wanted to see some of the other musical acts on Duval Street—there were plenty, and some of them were even good—and Paul and I left them to it. They invited us to come along, and I made noises about joining them eventually, but I wanted to see if I could patch things up with Bobbi and Jana.

Leaving Mom and Dad at the Bull, Paul and I wove our way

through the tourists en route to Mayor Fred's. "I notice," Paul said, "that you didn't mention the part about confronting Loki with his evil plot to make ghosts more real?"

I just glared at him as I narrowly avoided being slammed into by a drunken coed. I'm 5'11", you'd think they'd notice me...

The night went downhill from there. First, we arrived at Mayor Fred's to find no sign of Loki. I asked Larry, one of the regulars, if he'd seen Sig around—Loki was going by the name "Sigurd Jarlsson"—and he said no, not since closing time last night, which was also when I saw him last. That didn't bode well.

Second, 1812 sounded like hammered shit. Seriously, I'd seen about eighty-five percent of their performances since I arrived in Key West sixteen months ago, and even though they were off some nights, they were never horrible.

Until tonight: Bobbi's guitar playing was lackluster, and she broke a string three times. Ginny and Chet Smith, the bass player, couldn't get into any kind of rhythm together, and Ginny kept going to the high-hat every five seconds, which just was *weird*. Jana was the only one who seemed to be on, but she was a musical prodigy—she could be bleeding out from a gunshot wound and still play great.

The first set ended with a Blacklight song called "One Hour Too Far," during which Bobbi just butchered what had always been a favorite guitar solo of mine. Just as the tune wound down, the third crap thing happened: Rance came in.

Normally, Rance's arrival at Mayor Fred's was cause for celebration. We may not have been dating or anything, but I was pretty fond of the jackass, and he was fun to talk to and listen to music with. And I wanted him to meet Paul.

But Rance was dressed up. And I don't mean Key West dressed up, but actual pants, button-down shirt, jacket, and socks and shoes dressed up.

Which meant he was on the job. He'd only been on the job in Mayor Fred's once before, and that was part of the same incident that led to me saving his life from the nixie.

There were two other guys with him, whom I didn't recognize. They stayed at the entrance to the bar in the back, Rance studiously avoiding eye contact with me. That pissed me off for about half a second before I realized that, if he was on official business, flirting with me was probably not something he could be seen doing in front of his buddies.

1812 finished "One Hour Too Far," and Bobbi muttered, "We're takin' a break," and they all wandered off the stage. Chet, as usual, went straight to the bathroom. Jana was pulling out a cigarette and heading to the exit, where Rance and Frick and Frack were waiting for her.

"Hey, Demitrijian, how—"

"Ms. Naharodney, I'm sorry, but I'm afraid that we need to speak to you for a few minutes. This is Detective Malloy and his partner, Detective Reed, from the Key West Police. May we speak with you in private, please, Ms. Naharodney?"

"The *fuck*, Demitrijian? Ain't nobody calls me Naharodney no more, all right? And we don't need to speak in private, I ain't got shit to hide from these people."

Any other night, I'd have thought Jana was nuts, but Sunday night was a quieter crowd, with a ratio of regular to tourist that was much more in favor of the former than on any other night 1812 played.

At this point, Bobbi had noticed what was going on and had moved closer. "Rance? What's going on?"

Rance let out a long breath, and then said, "All right. I'm afraid I have some bad news. It is the sad duty of the FBI and the Key West Police to inform you that your parents, Melissa Kolikoski and Augustus Naharodney, were found dead in their house this morning."

Jana shook her head and snorted. "Thought you said you had *bad* news."

Paul and I exchanged glances. I felt my stomach clench, and the beer I'd just sipped went sour in my mouth. Last night, just as Paul arrived, I'd seen Jana attending the funeral of two people some time in the future.

One of the detectives asked, "When was the last time you spoke to your parents, Ms. Naharodney?"

"Day before my eighteenth birthday, 'cause that was the last time I had to. Moved out after that, never looked back. Look, it sucks that they're dead, but it ain't got shit to do with me. I ain't

172

seen 'em, spoke to 'em, thought about 'em, or given two shits about 'em in eight years."

"Nevertheless, Ms. Na—" Rance cut himself off. "Jana, you are going to have to go with the detectives here to identify the bodies. You're listed as their next of kin."

Jana's eyes widened. "Seriously? Why the fuck they have *me* as that?"

"I couldn't begin to explain that, Jana, but the fact remains that you're their heir, and it's up to you to identify them, and then also deal with the remains once the KWPD have completed the case."

"Fucking joy. I gotta do this now?"

"No," the other detective said. "You can come to the medical examiner's office in Marathon in the morning."

"Yeah, okay, we'll do it then. I need a fucking cigarette."

"That's fine," the first detective said, "we'll follow you out. We've got a few more questions."

Rance held up a hand when Bobbi tried to come out with her. "I'm sorry, Bobbi, but the detectives and I need to speak with her alone for the moment, all right?"

With that, he turned and left. Ginny had come over to our table without my noticing at first, and then Bobbi came over as well. I got nervous, as I wasn't sure how she was gonna react to us.

But mostly, she was just stunned. "I can't believe it. I always got along with Mel and Gus. Honestly, I think they kept wishing I was their daughter instead of Jana. I just liked going to their house 'cause there weren't six brothers in it, y'know?" She shook her head. "Fuck." Then she noticed Paul for the first time. "Who're you?"

"Uh, Bobbi, Ginny, this is my brother Paul. Paul, this is Bobbi Milewski and Ginny Blake. Paul came into town—"

"Wait, he was the guy you met up with last night after you left, right?" Bobbi stared at Paul. "Yeah, I can see the resemblance. Hey, mind if I sit?"

"Like you have to ask," I said.

"Oh, thank *God*." She sat down. "I was worried you were pissed at me."

173

After you go diving, you have to remove your neoprene suit and the bathing suit underneath it. Once the dive is done, they're both so soaked that it's like carrying the weight of another person, and taking it off is the biggest load off ever.

I kinda felt like that now. "Oh, for fuck's sake, Bobbi, I've been sitting here worried all night that *you* were pissed at *me*."

She winced. "I know, I know, I'm sorry, I was a total fucking bitch last night. I shouldn't have put all that on you—on both of you," she added to Ginny. "And besides, dammit, it's cool having two goddesses as friends. So forgive me? Please?"

Ginny closed her eyes and let out a long breath. "Of course, Bobbi. And thank you. I was worried that—" She wiped away a tear that was welling up in her eye. "I cannot believe this. I've been wandering Midgard for seven decades, and I've only been with you all for seven months. I've started and ended more friendships than I can count. Yet I've never been so emotionally distressed over losing mortal friends as I was about the possibility of not being in this band anymore."

Bobbi snorted. "You kidding? You're in as long as you wanna stay in. Not to speak ill of the dead or anything, but Zeke was okay—you're fucking amazing."

Zeke Bremlinger had been 1812's drummer when I first got to Key West, and Bobbi summed it up nicely: he was good enough. I didn't really notice how mediocre he was until Ginny joined up, though.

Now that *that* was settled, I found my brain wandering to what brought law-enforcement here. "Okay, I'm a little confused about something. Jana's parents lived on the island, right?"

Bobbi nodded. "I still get a card from them every Christmas. They're in the same house down on Seminary Street that Jana grew up in. Why?"

"I'm just wondering why Rance is in on this."

Paul spoke for the first time since Bobbi and Ginny came over. "Weren't we wondering something else, too?"

I pointed at him. "Yes!" I turned to Ginny. "Have you seen your boyfriend today?"

"What," Bobbi said, "are you and Sig dating?"

"No!" Ginny was emphatic in that negative, and I was grateful.

"And I have not seen him since last night. We went our separate ways after we closed down this place."

Jana came back in, and looked down at the tableau. "Please fucking tell me we're back to bein' friends again? 'Cause I can't take sittin' through another shit set like that."

Bobbi nodded quickly. "We're fine."

I introduced Paul, and the five of us crammed around the table. Mira came by and took a drinks order, and then Bobbi asked, "So what happened?"

"Somebody strangled 'em." Jana shrugged. "Fucked if I know what happened. They said it was a fishin' net that did it, but they didn't find the net at the scene. Those two don't own any fishin' stuff anyhow, least they didn't before, so fucked if I know."

Paul frowned. "How do they know it was a net if they didn't find it?"

Jana shrugged again. "One'a the cops mentioned the net, and then the other one talked over him."

I asked, "Did Rance say why he was involved?"

Ginny spoke quietly. "Because it's a serial killer. This is the third instance of a person being murdered by a fishing net that I've heard of in the last two days."

"Shit." I remembered our conversation from the other day. "That Greenpeace friend who's a cop, right?"

"A cop's husband, but yes." Ginny nodded. "I also overheard two people at the bar discussing something similar when I arrived this afternoon."

"Damn." Bobbi shuddered. "We don't get a lot of murders around here, so the local cops probably called in Rance to help out."

Paul and I exchanged glances. This did not sound particularly good. I then asked Jana, "Want some company on the trip to the M.E.'s?"

"You sure?" Jana asked. "Means gettin' up before eleven."

"I'll manage it. You're my friend."

Bobbi pounded a fist on the table. "All right, that's so not fair! You're not supposed to be so wonderful the day after I was a bitch and a half."

"Oh, shut the fuck up, Barbara Ann." Jana only called her best friend that when she wanted to snark her off. "C'mon, I wanna get back up and wash the taste'a the first set outta my mouth."

Within a few minutes, 1812 was back on stage. Bobbi walked up to the mic and said, "Okay, we kinda didn't do Blacklight justice at the end of the last set, so let's do it right. This one's called 'Liplock.'"

It was like night and day. On the first set, they were all over the place, totally out of sync. Now? They were like a well-oiled machine. Bobbi buzzed through the guitar parts, Chet's deep voice just coated the song like chocolate on a candy bar—which kinda fit as a metaphor, since the song was about a guy getting a blowjob—and Jana's organ filled things out beautifully. And Bobbi's solo between the bridge and the final verse was by far the best one of the night.

Once "Liplock" was done, Jana stepped out from the keyboards and put on her electric guitar. She, Bobbi, and Chet all yelled into their mics: "Wipeo-o-o-o-o-o-o-o-o-out!"

Then they slammed into the famous chord progression of the instrumental classic "Wipe Out," with each of the four taking a solo at different parts of the song. The song hadn't been part of 1812's *oeuvre* until after Ginny joined, as she loved riffing during the drum solos, and tonight, she rolled and tumbled through a killer solo. Best of all, she lost the high-hat fetish.

The rest of the night went much better, as the awkwardness was all gone. My parents even showed up around twelve, just in time for the traditional midnight playing of "The Weight" by the Band. That was followed by the inevitable audience request for Van Morrison's "Brown-Eyed Girl."

Dad laughed when they started playing it. "We *just* heard that at Irish Kevin's."

"Not surprising," I said. "Seriously, you can't go forty-eight hours on this island without hearing 'Brown-Eyed Girl' at least once, and sometimes as many as four or five times in a single night. Guy from New York was in here about five months ago, he said he heard it in every single bar he hit up and down Duval and he put a twenty in 1812's tip jar and specifically requested that they *not* play 'Brown-Eyed Girl' the whole night."

Our parents tuckered out around one-thirty and went back to

the Bottroff House. Paul seemed to be enjoying himself, but I honestly couldn't tell. Finally, as 1812 did a string of quiet, acoustic songs, starting with the Who's "Blue, Red, and Grey," I went with the direct approach. "You doing okay?"

"Actually, yeah. Honestly, Cass, this is the most fun I've had in ages. Probably not since I was in New Orleans last. Thanks for this. For everything."

"No problem. I'm glad you came. Mostly."

Paul frowned. "What do you mean?"

"Well, you've been seeing people's futures since you were a teenager. I've only had a day, and it *sucks*. I saw Bobbi in crutches at Thanksgiving dinner, and I'm just waiting for something bad to happen."

After 1812 finished Extreme's "More than Words," the electric guitars came out and they did "I Heard it Through the Grapevine." As Jana snarled through the song in her junkyard growl, Odin came into the bar and sat down with me and Paul. Mira came over and he ordered bourbon—for some reason, this Kentucky beverage was the drink of choice for all three of the Scandanavian immortals in my life, which amused the crap out of me—and then leaned forward. "Something dire is afoot."

There was that word again. "What does 'dire' mean in this particular context, exactly?"

"There are *two* powerful spells at work here. One that tethered the spirits of this island more closely to the world of the living, and a different one that comes from a source I do not recognize."

"Wait," Paul asked, "so you *do* recognize the first one?"

He nodded gravely. "My blood-brother."

"Motherfucker." I leaned back in my chair and shook my head. "I'm gonna kill him."

"We must find him, first. I had hoped that he was gathering power to himself to make another attempt to bring about Ragnarok. That is how I was able to find him in the past. But I can find no sign of him, which means he *isn't* gathering power to himself."

"What if he found a way to hide himself from you?" Paul asked.

Odin smiled. "A wise question, but my blood-brother could

not possibly have accumulated sufficient power to cast such a spell."

I didn't like the sound of this. "Okay, you keep mentioning that he's your blood-brother. Like you wanna remind us that you swore an oath not to harm him."

Paul shot me a look. "He did?"

I nodded. "And he broke that oath in April."

"To save the world. It is unlikely that such a great calamity will ensue on this occasion."

"I dunno, people are *dying*. We've got a bunch of people murdered with fishing nets that disappear. That sounds like a ghost to me."

Odin nodded gravely. "We must find Loki quickly. I believe we should conscript Sigyn to this purpose."

"Okay, but we'll have to wait until the set's done at three."

The rest of the set maintained the high level of kickassery. This being Sunday, the last song of the evening was going to be "Quinn the Eskimo," which was also how the Thursday shows ended. If it was Friday or Saturday, they ended with "Zip-a-Dee-Doo-Dah" (yes, really).

As they broke down, and the few people that were left on a Sunday night filed out of Mayor Fred's, Odin, Paul, and I approached the stage.

Before we could say anything, though, I heard Ihor, the bartender, say, "Dude, we're closed. You can— Holy shit, *Sigurd?*"

I whirled around to see Loki stumbling into the bar. The clothes he was wearing were—odd, to say the least. Flowing white robes and a large cape, and his hair was much wilder than before. He was also horribly beaten up, cuts and scrapes all over him.

And then a second later, he looked like he normally did: blond hair, red goatée, and wearing the usual Key West outfit of T-shirt and shorts. But they were ripped, too, and the cuts and scrapes hadn't changed.

"Loki!" Ginny cried, jumping off the stage.

Bobbi and Jana exchanged a glance. "What did she say?" Bobbi asked.

I decided to pretend I didn't hear that, especially since I was more worried about what did that to him. Ginny was on top of him before I could move, but the three of us went over to "Sigurd" right away.

"I'm—I'm sorry, I didn't mean—"

Then he collapsed. As soon as he did, he was back to the white robes.

"I don't believe it," I said, "the fucker cast a glamour even I couldn't see through."

Odin shook his head. "It is not a glamour. Loki is a shape-shifter. We must bring him somewhere safe. Perhaps your abode—"

"No!" I snapped. "My parents are there, not to mention a full house of guests. No fucking way we're taking this guy there."

"We will remove him to my dwelling," Ginny said.

I stared at her. I'd managed to never learn where it was she lived in the seven months since I met her, so this came as something of a surprise.

We propped him up in one of the chairs while the band got everything into Bobbi's parents' cargo van. Chet wandered off with some white chick like he usually did. Seriously, every night he brought a different woman back to his boat, and it was almost always a white woman. If I sound stereotypical and/or cynical, it came from watching this play out four nights a week for over a year. Chet was a fucking man-whore, and a lot of the women who came to the island—well, it was harder to get into community college than their pants, y'know?

Anyhow, we weren't getting any help from Chet, but whaddaya expect from a bass player?

Once we loaded the gear, and Paul and I got Loki's unconscious form into the back of the van. We all clambered in. It being a cargo van, only Bobbi and Jana got to sit in the driver's seat and shotgun, respectively. Odin, Ginny, Paul, and I crammed ourselves in amidst the instruments in the cargo section.

Ginny directed Bobbi down Greene to Elizabeth, down Elizabeth to Fleming, and left on Fleming. I asked, "What, you live by the cemetery?"

Worryingly, Ginny didn't answer that question, just telling Bobbi, "Turn right on Margaret."

That brought us to the spot where Margaret turned into Passover Lane, right by the entrance to the Key West Cemetery.

"Park anywhere here," Ginny said.

Bobbi turned around. "What the hell, Ginny?"

Ginny sighed. "I'm not simply the ex-wife of Loki, I'm also the goddess of the earth nymphs. My home is—not here. Exactly. I need the earth to access it, and the cemetery is simply the nearest pure ground to Mayor Fred's."

Reluctantly, Bobbi parked the van—luckily, there was a spot on the street in a residential parking area. Since the van had Monroe County plates, it would likely be safe. We pulled Loki out of the car.

"We all have to stand on natural ground—dirt or grass."

"Seriously?" Jana just stared at her.

"Just trust me, please?"

Jana turned her stare to me. "This the sorta shit you do all the time?"

Lamely, I said, "Kind of?"

Once we all had our feet planted on cemetery ground, Ginny closed her eyes and her body tensed briefly.

A second passed, then two. And then we were somewhere else.

It looked like a cave, but it was well lit—from a light source I couldn't find—and with lots of bean-bag-style furniture. Oh and a big flatscreen TV mounted to one of the rock walls.

Jana looked around at the space, which had no doors or windows. "You fuckin' *live* here, Blake?"

"Yes." Ginny pointed at one of the bean-bag chairs. "Put him down there."

Paul and I gently placed Loki down on it. Well, Paul was gentle, I would've been happy to just drop the sonofabitch on the floor.

He moaned as we did so, which I took to be a good sign. "Yo, Loki! Wake your ass up."

His eyes blinked open and he moaned again. "Where'm I?"

Ginny stepped forward. "You are in my dwelling, along with Bobbi, Jana, Cassie, the Allfather, and Cassie's brother."

Loki smiled raggedly. "S'this's what it takes t'getcha t'take me t'yer home."

Before Ginny could reply to that, I stepped between them.

180

"Loki, I'm about five seconds from kicking you repeatedly in the balls. Start talking. I *know* you're the one who supercharged all the ghosts."

Now he laughed, which was followed by a quick cough. "Ah, the Dís does it again. Yes, I cast th'spell that made th'ghosts more active."

Odin spoke up. "Yet another attempt to bring about Ragnarok?"

"Actually, no." Loki sat up now, and I noticed that his cuts were mostly healed. He was also speaking in close to his normal voice. "I simply wished to give the people of this island a bit more of a proper ghost experience." He grinned. "Why should the Dís have all the fun? The mortals tell such ridiculous stories of ghosts, so why not give them something to *really* talk about?"

Jana stared at him. "Why the *fuck* would you do that?"

"Not that I need answer to you, minstrel, but why shouldn't I?"

Jerking a thumb at Loki, Jana looked at Ginny. "You were *married* to this asshole?"

Staring at her ex, Ginny set her face hard. "It seemed like a good idea at the time."

"Still and all," Loki said quickly, "I had no intention of making another attempt at Ragnarok. And then I met the Last Calusa."

Simultaneously, Paul and I both said, "The *what?*"

Bobbi spoke up. "The Calusa are the Native people who lived in the Keys before the Spanish got here. By the 1800s, though, they all died out. They wouldn't trade with the Spanish, but their enemies did, and so they got wiped out by superior weapons."

"Indeed." Loki looked upon Bobbi with something vaguely resembling surprise. "Apparently, the last of them is one of the many spirits that wander this island. But there was magic in that spirit I didn't recognize. So I approached it, realized how incredibly powerful it was, and endeavored to take its power for my own."

"And failed?" I added.

"Yes, little Dís, I did."

I winced. I'd threatened him with bodily harm if he ever called me that again. But looking at him, injured, weakened, looking like his normal self instead of the "Sigurd Jarlsson" persona, I wasn't sure what I could do to him at this point that the Last Calusa hadn't already done.

"The spirit managed, instead," Loki continued, "to take all *my* power for *itself*, leaving me drained and bloody. It couldn't kill me, of course, but it did trap me in a fishing net and throw me into the water. It took quite some time to swim back."

"Looks like you ripped your skin open on some coral," I said. "Well, it couldn't happen to a nicer—"

"You do not understand, little Dís! From me, the spirit learned that it could consume other spirits as well! Soon it will be incredibly powerful! It told me it was going to spill the blood of its enemies."

Bobbi frowned. "The Calusa's enemies were the Creek and the Yamasee. There aren't that many left around here—it's mostly Seminoles. The Creek moved west, and the Yamasee died out, too."

"Fuck," Jana muttered. "My parents were both part Muscogee."

From sheer habit, I whipped out my smartphone, only to be stunned to find that I had four bars. Shooting Ginny a look of respect, I then went to my contact list. "I'm calling Rance. I need to find out if the other victims are Natives."

"First off," Jana said, "why the fuck would he tell you anything, Zukav? Ain't like you actually slept with the guy."

"He knows I'm a Dís." I spoke without thinking, belatedly remembering that Jana had only known this for twenty-four hours.

"Fuck, did *everyone* know but me?" She shook her head. "Also, Demitrijian ain't gonna answer the phone at three-thirty in the fucking—"

"Hey, Rance!" I said, when he answered.

I might also have stuck my tongue out at Jana, who finished with a lame, "—morning."

"Cassie, I was just finally about to get to sleep. It has been a quite excruciatingly long day, and I really have a tremendous need to—"

"I need to know if the other victims of the disappearing fishing net killer had Native blood."

A pause. "Cassie, I can't even confirm to you that there even *are* other victims of—"

"Rance, I *need* to know, it's *important*."

182

Another pause. "Is this—?"

"Yes, it's a Dís thing."

"Dammit. All right, look, Cassie, I have to be incredibly careful about this, because this is considered a major case, and I'm just consulting. It's truly KWPD's case, so I could get myself in—"

"Rance!"

"All right, all right." He sighed. "There have been eight victims so far. Six have Native blood— mostly Seminole or Muscogee. The other two, though, are Spanish—not Latin American, but from Spain."

"Yeah, that fits," I said.

"I'm sorry, Cassie, but on what planet does that sort of thing make—"

"Gotta go. I'll talk to you tomorrow, I promise."

I ended the call. Rance was definitely going to have words with me next time he saw me. And, since Rance was a firm believer in using five sentences where one would do, he was going to have a *lot* of words...

Jana was fixing me with a nasty stare. "So what the hell'd Demitrijian have to say at three a.m.?"

I told everyone what Rance told me.

Ginny was the first to respond. "We must cast a counterspell."

Odin shook his head. "It is not that simple. The Last Calusa is obviously a collective spirit of great power. By casting the spell he did, Loki made it even more powerful, and now it is wreaking havoc, destroying other spirits and mortal lives. A mere counterspell will be insufficient."

"Then what do we do?" Ginny asked.

Loki slowly got to his feet and stood unsteadily for a moment. "There is only one thing *to* do."

And he looked right at me and Paul. "What?" I asked.

"We cannot ask them—" Odin started, but Loki interrupted him.

"You were perfectly happy to ask that young woman to risk her life to stop *me*. With two of them here, the risk is far less."

This was starting to piss me off. "Risk of *what*?"

Odin turned to me and Paul. "It is possible for the Dísir to twist a being's fate."

183

I blinked. "Wait, we can really *do* that?" I had thought Odin was joking about that…

"It's not possible," Ginny said.

"It is *possible*, but very dangerous," Odin said.

We were now well into the middle of pissing me off. "If somebody doesn't start giving straight answers—"

Odin held up a hand. "Twisting a being's fate is something that requires all three Dísir in a set."

My heart ached, suddenly. "That's—that's gonna be a problem…"

Paul's jaw fell open. "You guys aren't gonna make us fly to San Diego to dig up our brother's body, are you?"

Jana stared at Paul like he'd grown another head. "Dude, *that's* where you went?"

I was, sadly, not surprised, having grown up with him. I also now had the image of digging up the grave in question and was just nauseated. After twenty-six years, would anything even be *left*?

"That," Odin said dryly, "will not be necessary. However, I believe that, among the three of us, we can provide the extra power that will be required."

Loki raised a hand. "Excuse me, but *three* of us?"

I whirled on the toga-wearing bastard. "Excuse *me*, chuckles, but this was *your* fucking idea! What makes you think you get out of helping?"

"It is not a question of desire, little Dís, but rather of capability. It is taking everything I have to maintain my mortal disguise."

Bobbi winced. "Uhm, about that? Not so much."

Jana grinned. "Like the toga, though. *Really* hot."

Looking down at himself, Loki noticed for the first time that he was in his true form. "Hel's teeth. Well, that settles that, then. I have *nothing* to give."

Odin regarded him with his one eye. "You will try."

Loki turned to his former wife. "Sigyn, you explain to him what—" Then he saw the look on Ginny's face. "Very well, I shall try."

Ginny's expression softened as she turned to Odin. "The risk is still great."

Paul's voice was softer than I'd ever heard it when he asked,

"Define 'great,' please?"

"You could both die," Odin said bluntly.

I didn't even hesitate. "And if we don't do it, how many more people die?"

Neither did my brother, bless him. He moved to stand next to me. "Why are we even still talking about it? What do we have to do?"

"The first thing we have to do," Ginny said, "is leave here. If I am to provide magical assistance, I must absorb the power of my current home." She sighed. "I will miss this place."

I frowned. "Where will you live after this?"

Ginny smiled wryly. "Assuming we all survive, I will simply have the earth nymphs construct me a new dwelling. But it will take some time."

A nanosecond later, we were all back in the cemetery.

Jana shuddered and pulled out a cigarette. "That's some fucked-up shit, right there."

Staring at Bobbi and Jana, Odin said, "You mortal women will be required as well."

"No," I said. "Odin, you can't—"

"I *must*," Odin said emphatically. "The spell will place all five of us in a trance-like state. Our physical forms will be vulnerable. Barbara and Jane Anne must guard us against harm."

Puffing on her cigarette, Jana said, "Call me 'Jane Anne' again, I use my ciggy to see how deep that eye socket goes."

"Understood." Odin stepped away. "I will seek out this Last Calusa. Loki, you will assist."

"I *told* you, Allfather, I—*ow!*" That last word came when Odin grabbed Loki by the arm and dragged him away.

Ginny, meanwhile, had her eyes closed and started muttering an incantation that sounded somewhat familiar.

Paul looked at me. "You recognize that language, don't you?"

It is impossible to have a poker face with your twin brother. "Sort of. I mean, I don't know what any of it translates into English as, but I know the language from the counterspell I cast against Loki to keep him from ending the world."

Jana was staring at us. "So lemme see if I got this straight, Zukav—that asshole was both Sig *and* Gunnar? And if you hadn't stopped his band that night when it snowed, the world woulda ended?"

I nodded.

"Fuck me backwards. That's some *serious* shit, there." She took another puff on her cigarette.

"I may need one of those before this is over," Bobbi muttered. "I can't believe this is *happening*. I mean, we're talking about—what the hell *are* we talking about?"

"Ultimately?" I sighed. "We're talking about stopping a murderer. The rest of it is window dressing." Then I chuckled mirthlessly. "Least that's how I get through this shit. Listen, you two don't have to—"

"Yes, we do," Bobbi said. "This thing is killing people."

"Including my parents," Jana added. "Didn't like the fuckers all that much, but they were still my parents." She took a final drag of her cigarette and tossed it aside. "'Sides, I still owe you for saving my ass from marrying Russ. So we're doing this, so you can shut the fuck up about being noble and shit, all right?"

I shook my head and chuckled. "All right."

Paul had his head in his hands, and I noticed tears welling up in his eyes. "Paul?" I asked, putting a hand on his arm. "What's wrong?"

"Besides the obvious?" He managed a smile at that. "No, I just—I really don't wanna die, Cassie. I just figured out who I am—*what* I am. And besides, if we die doing this—then I'll never get to apologize to Mom and Dad."

For a few seconds, I stared at him. Then, rearing back, I hit his arm as hard as I could.

"Ow! What was that for?" He stared at me with annoyance, rubbing his arm.

"You spent *all fucking day* with them! It woulda killed you to say 'I'm sorry'?"

"I was waiting for the right moment." He sounded pathetic saying it, and based on the sheepish look on his face, he knew it.

"Well, waitasec—shouldn't we *know* what happens? I mean, we can tell the future, so why can't we—"

But Paul was shaking his head slowly. "We can see *other people's* future, Cass. Not our own."

186

"That sucks."

"Until today, I wouldn't have agreed with you."

Odin and Loki came back. "We have located the Last Calusa. He is quite powerful, and we must move swiftly before there are more deaths."

"Where is he?" I asked.

Odin hesitated. "The inn where you live."

My stomach was doing flips. The beers I'd had at Mayor Fred's started to well up in the back of my throat.

"Mom and Dad." Paul's voice was a throaty whisper.

I finally found my voice. "And the captain—he may need another ghost to suck up." I clenched a fist. "I'm fucked if he's doing that to my roommate. Let's *go*."

My smartphone insisted it took less than three minutes to drive down Margaret to Eaton and down Eaton to the Bottroff House. Felt more like three hours. Or maybe three years.

Or maybe just the rest of my life.

Bobbi pulled into the driveway behind Rocinante. Technically, it was blocking the sidewalk, but under the circumstances, a parking ticket was the least of our problems.

There was no sign of anything wrong. The B&B was deathly quiet, as it generally was after midnight when the front door was locked and before five when Debbie showed up to make breakfast. The entire gaggle of us—two Dísir, three gods, two musicians—moved as quietly as seven people could through a garden. When we came in sight of my cottage, my heartrate went up.

I always turned everything off when I left the room, but there was light coming from my windows.

I whispered to Odin, "How close do we need to get?"

"Your patio should suffice."

Seven people moved even less quietly up a wooden staircase than they did across a garden. I was stunned that the entire clientele of the B&B didn't come out to find out why a stampede of elephants was coming through.

I was first up the stairs. I peeked through the window. Behind me, Odin, Loki, and Ginny had begun muttering an incantation. I didn't really pay close attention to what they were doing—I wanted to see what we were up against.

The first thing I saw was the captain, but he looked—well, stuck. Normally he kind of floated around the room, but now he was utterly immobile. Honestly, I hadn't even realized how much he moved until that moment when he couldn't.

He also looked really pissed.

The other guy in the room was taller than the captain, and damn well built. I could see almost all of him, as the only parts of his bronzed body that were actually covered were his naughty bits by a small leather loin cloth, which was bound at the waist by a belt decorated with, I kid you not, human bones. Fingers and toes, mostly, with a skull right in the center.

I also couldn't see his face. He wore a wood mask decorated with a really elaborate, and I gotta say, really cool design of red and white and black. His arms were raised, and it sounded like he was chanting something. Probably the spell that was going to cost Captain Bottroff his un-life.

Over my dead body. Possibly literally.

Paul was standing next to me, also looking into the window. "That is a really cool mask."

I was thinking the same thing, but I still snapped at him. "Focus, pinky—that's the *bad guy*."

"Yeah, yeah. So how do we—?"

And then, all of a sudden, the porch was no longer under our feet. Neither was anything else.

The world shifts and changes all around Cassie and Paul. Together they float through the air, with the porch of the cottage at the Bottroff House Bed & Breakfast below them…

…but also beneath them is the garden as it was before Debbie Dellamonica bought it and turned it into a B&B, adding the two cottages in the back…

…but also beneath them is the empty lot it was before Captain Bottroff bought it and constructed the cottage…

…but also beneath them is the grassland occupied by Calusa…

…but also beneath them is a pathway used by Spanish and Bahamian fishers on their way to and from the sea…

Paul and Cassie float together, their movements in perfect concert. A blue thread connects them, with a third blue thread that remains just out of sight. No matter how many times either of them turn to look at the thread they can never see where it leads...

Cassie's room in the cottage (also an empty space) (also a huge building) is below and she and Paul see the Last Calusa. White threads stretch away from him. Paul looks to see where the white threads lead and so does Cassie when he does.

The threads go back to another island in the Keys, but also straight to the eighteenth century. Two hundred and fifty years of nothing and then a tall man wearing a loincloth very much like that of the ghost, though with animal bones around the waist instead of human ones. He wears a mask of blue and white and red with an open mouth.

(The voice of Odin whispers in Paul and Cassie's ear, telling them that this was the chief priest of the Calusa, and the open mouth represents his ability to speak to the Three Gods.)

(The voice of Loki mutters that he met the Calusa's Three Gods once, and found them humorless and annoying—rather like Thor but without the bombast.)

(Sigyn points out that all Thor is is bombast, to which Loki says that's the point.)

There is a boy with the chief priest, wearing a mask of red and black and white. Priest and boy chant and dance in a circle, each moving three times—one for each god, Paul and Cassie realize. The priest holds two daggers while the boy holds a third.

After three circles, the priest and the boy each lunge for each other. Paul jumps in shock, but Cassie understands that this was the creation of the Last Calusa.

The spirit, created by the dying act of the chief priest and the boy, bided its time for two and a half centuries. Waiting for the right moment.

They follow the white threads back to the present, the Last Calusa standing in front of Captain Bottroff (who has white threads behind him, but no threads in front of him, which worries Cassie, and therefore also worries Paul).

Red threads stretch forward from the front of the Last Calusa, showing hundreds and hundreds of dead bodies, and a Key West that has no more ghosts—except for one.

Paul looks at Cassie. Cassie looks at Paul. Cassie reaches for the white threads, but they will not move.

(Odin says that they cannot change the past.)

Paul knows that they must change the future, not the past. Cassie knows that they must act quickly before they lose Captain Bottroff.

Cassie and Paul both reach for the red threads—

—and they scream together, their cries of agony echoing through time. Cassie feels the white-hot pain slicing through Paul's arm, Paul feels the burning sensation on Cassie's hands, and they both let go.

The voice of the Last Calusa is deep and resonant, the sound of hundreds speaking as one. "You will not interfere!"

"We have to interfere." Paul and Cassie speak as one, also. "You're killing people!"

"Of course. We are a spirit of vengeance, and long have we awaited our time to reawaken! The outsiders with their foul diseases and their absurd religion! The Creek and the Yamasee, once respected foes who consorted with the outsiders and took their weapons. Once, the Calusa were mighty, for our weapons were made of the shells from the sea. But the metal shells of the outsiders were stronger, and we were defeated."

Cassie and Paul move between the Last Calusa and Captain Bottroff and also simultaneously flank the spirit. "None of these people had anything to do with that. It was hundreds of years ago. You have to stop!"

"The Three Gods have blessed our endeavor, providing us with the outsider god who showed us how to take the spirits of others."

Paul points at Captain Bottroff even as Cassie's voice comes to the fore. "The spirit you're trying to take now is my friend! We won't let you destroy him!"

"He is already dead and dust."

"So are you! What gives you the right to carry out your vengeance at his expense?"

"His reflection and shadow have moved on, leaving his eye soul trapped in this place. We will free it as we did the others, and use them for our grand purpose!"

"Not if we stop you."

(Loki tells them that now is the time.)

Cassie and Paul hold hands and reach together for the red threads. They have stalled long enough, their godly backing providing extra strength, and it is time to try again.

With all four hands, the two together and the two separate, the twins grab the red string.

They concentrate.

They focus.

The red string turns black.

The Last Calusa screams with the voice of thousands, reaching not only through time, but through all the Nine Worlds.

There is a blinding flash of light—

—and then we were back in the real world, about eight feet over the porch.

Fuck!

My arms flailing, I fell to the porch in bone-jarring agony, my left shoulder wrenching really badly as I landed right on it.

From a few feet away, I heard a blood-curdling scream. Paul had landed on Bobbi, and the two were all tangled up. The scream was Bobbi's; she sounded like she was in as much pain as we felt when we first grabbed the red string.

Clutching my shoulder, I clambered to my feet. Jana was kneeling next to Bobbi, while my brother disentangled himself from her. Every move he made caused her to wince or scream.

"What is it?" Jana asked.

"Leg," Bobbi said through gritted teeth. "Hurts like *fuck!*"

"Allfather!"

Whirling, I saw Ginny and Loki running to Odin, who had collapsed onto the porch.

"What the hell's going on?" That was Dad, who had run out along with Mom. They were both completely naked, which was a sight I never ever ever needed to see.

"We kinda saved the world again, Dad." I ran across the porch to see how Odin was. "Call 911, wouldja please? And, uh, put some clothes on, maybe?"

"Right." He ran back inside, and Mom followed, covering herself once she belatedly realized that she had forgotten to toss a robe on.

I knelt down next to Ginny and Loki over Odin. The Allfather of the Aesir was fading fast—and I meant that literally. He was turning transparent before our very eyes. "Odin, what's—"

"...Last Calusa..." he muttered, "...gone forever...well done...Cassie..."

He stopped breathing and closed his eye. And then he faded away.

I stared at the empty space where he had been, and then turned to Ginny. "Is he—is he dead?"

"It is—difficult to say," Ginny finally said.

"Allfather," Loki added, "has been dead before. But that was when the Aesir were at the height of their powers. Of course, in those times, we would have crushed this upstart ghost—"

"Loki," Ginny said gently putting a hand on his.

"Of course."

Mom and Dad came back out, this time in bathrobes, thank goodness. "Ambulance is on the way."

"Good." Jana was holding her best friend's hand, "'Cause Bobbi's in bad shape."

Paul was on the other side of Bobbi, looking miserable. "Bobbi, I'm so sorry."

"S'okay…" she said, teeth still clenched. She was sweating even more than she did when she performed, which I wouldn't have believed possible. "Wouldn'ta missed that for nothin'. That was fuckin' *awesome*."

"It is well that you arrived when you did."

I jerked my head around and saw that Captain Bottroff had materialized on the porch. As if enough wasn't happening. He looked—well, normal, which was actually a good thing.

"Another few moments, and we would no longer be enjoying each other's company."

"You're welcome, Cap."

Jana stared at me. "Who you talkin' to, Zukav?"

I exchanged a look with Paul, who shrugged. I realized that we'd really done it. The Last Calusa was gone, which meant that things were back to normal on the island.

Well, as normal as we get around here.

The ambulance took Bobbi away, Jana not leaving her side, and by that time, everyone in the damn B&B was up. Of course, by then it was after five, and Debbie had come in, and we spent the rest of the night and the early morning talking to paramedics and Debbie and cops. Even Rance came by, as he hadn't been able to get to sleep after I called. It was a huge mess.

Somewhere in there, Loki and Ginny disappeared. But more subtly, not the way Odin did. And somewhere else in there, I managed to call Seaclipse and tell them I couldn't do any dives on Monday. And then Paul and I went into my room at about nine in the morning and collapsed, not waking up for another fourteen hours or so.

Thanksgiving at the Milewski house was amazing.

Yes, I'm jumping ahead. We slept away all of Monday, and Tuesday and Wednesday were a blur of exhaustion. Changing the fate of the collective spirit of an entire tribe of Native people turned out to be pretty goddamned tiring. And I had to run a bunch of dives over those days, since Seaclipse was overbooked, and I had to make up the time I missed Monday.

Jana wound up missing her appointment to ID her parents' bodies Monday morning. She refused to leave Bobbi's side until she was released from the hospital, even though there was a steady stream of family and friends coming by. They let Bobbi out in time for Thanksgiving, but she was on crutches—just like I'd foreseen.

My parents and I crammed into Rocinante—it was an old truck that only had a single bench seat in front that barely fit three—while Paul followed on Comet as we drove to the house on Cow Key where the Milewski clan lived.

Walking around to the back, we saw the party in full swing when we got there at noon. Which, by the way, was when we were told to be there. But there was this sea of blond-haired people everywhere.

Others arrived right behind us, and it hit me that it was just the immediate family who had been here when we arrived. The blond got a bit more diluted at that point.

Their back yard was filled with dark wooden picnic tables that Bobbi's father joked about having stolen from parks all over the country. At the center table was Bobbi, Jana by her side, left leg covered from knee to foot in plaster, crutches leaning against the bench next to her.

"Hey, Cass!" she said brightly as we approached.

"You're in a good mood," I said with a ragged smile.

"It's Thanksgiving!" She grinned. "And I'm on the *good* drugs."

"Chased with beer," Jana added, grabbing Bobbi's empty plastic cup. "Speaking of which, you need another."

"I really really really don't, Jana." She put a hand on Jana's shoulder to keep her from getting up. "Let me get some of Grandpa's turkey in me before I drink anymore, 'k?"

"Yo," came a voice from behind us. I turned to see Chet with a beautiful, chocolate-skinned woman on his arm.

"Chet brought a date," I said with a certain amount of surprise.

"'Course I brought a date. You think I ain't bringin' my girlfriend to Thanksgivin'?"

"This is your girlfriend?" I shouldn't have sounded as shocked as I did. But then, I remembered how he tended to end every night.

Chet introduced the girlfriend—whose name was Beholi—and we all introduced each other. Beholi looked at Chet. "I'm gonna get something to drink. You want anything?"

Shrugging, Chet said, "Just a beer."

"What kind?"

He tilted his head. "You know what I like, baby. Corona."

She raised an eyebrow. "I thought you said you wanted *beer*." Her eyes twinkled at him as she walked off.

"I like her," I said with a grin.

"Yeah, 'cause your approval was keepin' me up nights," Chet said with a snort.

"I thought you only dated white women," I said, remembering the skin color of every single woman he went home with after a gig.

"No, I only fuck white women. I only date black women. And before you get all self-righteous and shit, Beholi knows all about how I spend my gig nights. That ain't when we see each other."

I held up both hands. "I wasn't gonna get self-righteous. Your problem, not mine."

"Ain't a *problem* at all." He sat next to Bobbi. "How's the leg?"

"Broken," Bobbi said with a chuckle. "But we're back on stage tomorrow night regardless."

"How you gonna do that?" Mom asked, incredulous.

But Paul and I just exchanged smiles. We'd both seen premonitions of Bobbi performing on stage with 1812 while sitting on a stool. I was almost kinda sorta starting to get used to seeing glimpses of the future.

Of course, right after that, I got a flash of how Chet and Beholi were spending their night. An image I will likely spend the rest of my life trying and failing to scrub from my brain.

"I'm sorry we won't get to see it," Dad said. "We're flying back tomorrow morning."

Paul said, "And I'm going with them."

I blinked. "What?"

"Well, not *actually* going with them, 'cause I can't bring Comet onto the plane, plus I need to head back to Charlotte to finish off some stuff, and then drive out there—but I should be back in La Jolla by the time you light the menorah."

Dad stared at Mom. "We even know where the menorah *is*?"

I rolled my eyes. "Well, good. I'm glad."

"Not nearly as glad as I am," Mom said emphatically. "I'm so glad we came."

"Except for the part where I got manhandled by a crappy writer, anyhow," Dad added.

Mom smacked him on the arm for that. "The point is, this is the best Thanksgiving I could've asked for. I'm finally getting my son home again."

To my relief, Mom didn't emphasize "my son" in a way that made me feel guilty about not coming back with them. I think she finally got that I was staying here.

"And Mom? Dad?" Paul said. "I'm sorry. Really. I wish I'd known—"

Dad held up a hand. "It's okay. You know now, that's what matters."

The afternoon continued from there, with me introducing Paul and my parents to all the various Milewskis and Milewski hangers-on, food being brought out in droves to the picnic tables, alcohol of various sorts flowing freely, and a good time being had by all.

At one point, me, Ginny, Loki, and Paul were sitting at one of the tables. The one oddity today had been Loki, who'd been very subdued. At least he looked like Sigurd Jarlsson again.

"What's wrong, Sig?" I asked. "Sorry you can't use the ghosts of Key West to end the world this time?"

Loki just stared at me angrily.

"Oh, don't give me that look. Tell me you *weren't* thinking that."

"I wasn't, as it happens," he said in as soft a voice as I'd heard him use since he was pretending to be Gunnar Rikardsen and leading the band Jötunheim. "I'm saddened by the loss of my blood-brother."

That deflated me something fierce. "Yeah." I raised a bottle of amber beer. I had no idea of the brand, as it had been in a plastic tub filled with ice that had melted, so the label was long gone. "To Odin. He was a crappy teacher and an annoying mentor and he usually only showed up when all hell was breaking loose—but he was all right."

"To Odin!" Paul said, while Ginny and Loki both said, "Skaal!" We clinked our various drinks together and gulped down.

Eventually, Bobbi's parents brought all the turkeys out (there were three), and we all gobbled it up. (Sorry.)

I looked around at all the people, including me and my brother and my parents, all together for the first time in years. We just saved Key West from Loki being an asshole—again—and things were looking good.

I had a lot to be thankful for. Mom was right, this was the best Thanksgiving.

God of Blunder

There was a hush over Mayor Fred's Saloon as Ihor and Jana Naha helped Bobbi Milewski onto the stage. Bobbi wore her trademark plain white T-shirt and blue shorts. Her left leg was covered from the knee downward with a plaster cast.

As she sat on the provided stool, Jana hopped up onto the stage. She handed Bobbi her left-handed Les Paul electric guitar.

Ihor turned to head back to tending bar, but Bobbi called out after him. "Hey, can I get a beer?"

"Like hell, girl. You're on, what, Percocet? Darvocet?"

"Percs. What's the big—"

"No chance. You're cut off. And I already told Adina and Mira that if they get you any booze, I'm gonna fire their asses." Ihor then continued back to the bar while Bobbi gave him a pissed-off look before turning her attention to tuning up.

I was sitting at my usual table by the ficus tree that Mayor Fred's was built around, and as Ihor passed by me, I got his attention. "Aren't you being a little hard on her? I broke my arm once back in San Diego, and I still had a beer or two to wash down the painkillers."

"Yeah, and you've got about eight inches of height and fuck knows how much body weight on her. Shit, her BMI's in negative numbers, for fuck's sake."

Body mass index was one of those bullshit weight measurements that always pissed me off because doctors kept telling me that mine was too high, even though I'm a 5'11" woman with boobs and hips. There's only so low my weight's gonna get, y'know?

But Ihor had a point about Bobbi. She was only 5'2", and had the minimum amount of body fat you could have and still be at all identifiable as female.

I considered and rejected telling Ihor that she'd spent most of the previous day drinking quite a bit of beer amidst the painkillers at her family's Thanksgiving shindig and didn't seem worse for the wear. He was the guy responsible for the bar; I couldn't blame him for being cautious. Yesterday, Bobbi was at her home if something went screwy. Tonight, she was in Ihor's house, and he wasn't gonna take any chances.

While Bobbi was tuning, Jana was arranging the pedals in such a way that Bobbi could still step on them with her good foot. I thought she was out of her mind for playing so soon after breaking her leg. Part of that was guilt. She broke it while helping me, my twin brother, and three Norse gods stop a psychotic, mass-murdering ghost. Mostly, though, it was worry that someone as active onstage as Bobbi would go nuts having to play sitting down.

I was also worried about the show, generally. Jana was mostly behind the keyboards, and when she played guitar she didn't move around that much, and Ginny Blake (a.k.a. Sigyn, one of the aforementioned Norse gods) was behind the drumkit. As for Chet Smith—well, you know the stereotype that bassists are automatons who just stand on stage and never move? They use Chet to illustrate that stereotype. Bobbi was the one who had the most stage presence, despite being the smallest person up there. She was constantly moving about the stage, playing her guitar with passion, always. I kinda figured it was her way of compensating for her size, but it worked. Even though three of 1812's four members took turns singing lead, Bobbi was in many ways the front person.

However, Jana had texted me to make sure that I was there for the beginning of the set because, as she put it, "we're opening with Bobbi's fuck you I don't care about my leg set." My curiosity was, to say the least, piqued.

Once Bobbi's guitar was in tune, she looked around. Ginny was ready at the drumkit, Chet had tuned up his Ibanez bass, and Jana had tuned her own Gibson electric guitar, which meant they were opening with a two-guitar song that had no keyboards. Bobbi gave Ihor a nod, and he said over the PA, "All right, ladies and gentlemen, hope you all had a great Thanksgiving, and now it's back to the routine—put your hands together for 1812!"

Mayor Fred's was pretty full, with lots of tourists who were spending their Thanksgiving weekend in Key West. Some of them were looking funny at the guitarist with the busted leg, wondering exactly what kind of show they'd get.

Then Bobbi and Jana nodded at each other and slammed into the opening chords of AC/DC's "Back in Black." Bobbi also sang that, her sharp soprano fitting nicely into Brian Johnson's lead vocal from the original, and man did she kill it on the guitar solo.

The place burst with an explosion of applause, but the band didn't even wait for it to die down. Jana went to the keyboards and Ginny started the rat-tat-tat of the opening to Led Zeppelin's "Rock and Roll," which Bobbi also sang, and she slammed through guitar on. When she sang the final "lonely, lonely, lonely, lonely, lonely" *a cappella*, then took a great dramatic pause before "time," I got goosebumps.

Bobbi took a break from melody singing as she started up the guitar riff that opened the Rolling Stones's "Gimme Shelter." Chet's deep bass provided the lead for that one, but Bobbi sliced through the harmonies and yet *another* killer guitar solo. She was always good, but she just basically took over three great riffs by Angus Young, Jimmy Page, and Keith Richards and made them her own.

After "Gimme Shelter," Bobbi leaned her left wrist on the strings, and I grinned. It was Waddy Wachtel's turn to be supplanted by a short, skinny blonde chick in a Key West bar. Bobbi sang this one, too: "Edge of Seventeen" by Stevie Nicks.

Half the bar was on their feet, several people were dancing in the area directly in front of the stage, everyone was cheering and screaming and yelling, and I looked down to realize that I hadn't touched my beer since the first chord of "Back in Black."

You gotta understand, 1812 has been the house band at Mayor Fred's for a bunch of years now. Except for two breaks—in April when they were between drummers, and in the summer when they were in Mississippi recording tracks as the backup band for John Robertson's last CD—they'd been there every Thursday through Sunday night, and I'd seen most of their performances since I first arrived in Key West sixteen months ago. I hadn't thought there was a helluva lot they could do to surprise me at this point.

Holy shit, was I wrong. To say they were on fire tonight was to give fire way too much credit.

I gulped down about half my beer as Ginny started another drumroll, one slower than "Rock and Roll," but only a bit. This time it was Sweet's "Ballroom Blitz," which Chet and Jana split the lead vocals on—Chet did the quieter first half of the verses with Jana taking over the louder second half. All three sang the chorus in magnificent harmony.

By now, I was exhausted, and I was just sitting. Luckily, they slowed it down a bit, with Jana starting the piano bit that began Warren Zevon's "Werewolves of London," followed by Jana and Bobbi both donning matching black Takamine acoustic guitars for a stellar rendition of Bob Dylan's "Tangled Up in Blue." For that, Chet, Jana, and Bobbi each sang three verses, with the three of them singing every two lines of the final verse. The two guitars rang out through the saloon.

So much for my worry about Bobbi retaining her front-person status.

They closed the first set with "Till the Walls Come Tumblin' Down," a J. Geils Band number that gave Jana a chance to re-mind everyone how awesome *she* is: she snarled out the lyrics while playing a mean-ass piano. But it ended with another killer guitar solo, while Chet and Bobbi belted the "Ooooh, yeah!" that alternated with each line of the chorus.

The crowd whooped and cheered louder than the guitar solo, and half a dozen people moved to assist Jana in helping Bobbi off the stage. I was sitting alone, so I stayed put. Bobbi had plenty of help and I didn't want to lose the table.

Ginny handed Bobbi down her crutches and the two of them slowly worked her way over to me. Chet had already gone into the men's room, and Jana was outside smoking.

Adina came over with two beers and a bourbon. She put one of the beers in front of Bobbi and smiled. "This one's on the house."

Bobbi, Ginny, and I all looked over at the bar, and Ihor gave Bobbi a thumbs-up, mouthing the words, *You earned it.*

Grabbing the pint glass, Bobbi gulped down about half of it. "*Shit*, I needed that."

I regarded her with amusement. She was just as sweat-soaked as she usually was after a set, staying seated notwithstanding. "That was fucking amazing."

Two tourists passed by the table. "You guys were awesome!"

"Thanks!" Bobbi raised her pint glass. "Yeah, that set didn't suck."

After a twenty-minute break or so, they headed back up. The bar was emptier—a bunch of people left after the set was over, which always happened, but the musicians *really* needed breaks in order to play for five to six hours...

As they were tuning up, a group of five tourists came in. I recognized them from both the Bottroff House Bed and Breakfast where I lived and worked part-time, and also the dive shop where I worked part-time as a dive master. I'd checked them in when they'd arrived on Tuesday afternoon, and recommended both diving at Seaclipse (I took them out on Wednesday) and seeing 1812 at Mayor Fred's.

It was three men and two women, all college students from Baltimore. Two of the guys, De'Andre and Anwan, and one of the girls, Dravon, were siblings. Dravon's boyfriend was named Steve, and De'Andre's girlfriend was Rosita.

"So this is the place, huh, Cass?" De'Andre asked as they came in.

"Yup. Good timing, too, the second set's about to start."

Steve wiped some sweat off his shiny bald head. "Wouldn't'a found this place without you tellin' us."

"Yeah, well." One of the things I liked about Mayor Fred's was that it was around the corner from Duval Street, which meant the average tourist had to think to come here. Most just wandered up and down the main drag without ever venturing down the side roads like Greene Street. Which worked for me, because that limited the tourists to the ones who either had heard of the place and knew what to expect or to ones who actually made an effort.

Rosita was looking up at the wall, to which hundreds of business cards had been stapled over the years—as were assorted other things. "Is that a—a bra?"

I followed her gaze to the bra that had been stapled to the wall right near the merchandise table and grinned. I didn't even notice that stuff anymore. "Yup."

De'Andre gave his girlfriend a toothy grin. "You wanna hang yours, baby doll?"

"*Fuck* you." But she was smiling as she said it.

The table behind mine had been abandoned, and it was slightly bigger, but only had three chairs. I gave the quintet my two spares, since Bobbi and Ginny wouldn't need them for a while and I knew that Special Agent Rance Demitrijian, my occasional companion for 1812's shows, wasn't going to be here tonight, as he was still on a case.

As Anwan took one of the chairs over, he gave me a huge smile and said, "Thanks a *lot*, Cassie." He was leaning over, giving me a very nice view of his muscular arms—he was wearing a sleeveless T-shirt—plus his smile could've powered the whole island.

"My pleasure." And I meant it. I found myself remembering what a good diver he was—I'd gone under with him as his buddy, since the two couples paired off—but I hadn't really noticed *him* before. At the B&B I was exhausted from stopping that psychotic ghost, and at Seaclipse I was focused on working, but now?

Yeah, he was hot. And the only unattached guy in the group.

I decided to go for it before he went away with the chair. "Hey, Anwan, where's *your* girlfriend?"

The smile fell, and I was suddenly sorry I asked. "Bitch broke up with me. Week before Thanksgiving, she goes tellin' me she wants a—" He cut himself off and looked away. "Nemmind."

"Oh, come on, you can tell me." I gave him my best smile. "If you can't tell your dive master, *who can you tell?*"

That got the smile back, which was the idea. Then he shook his head. "Nah, she was just all, 'you're too physical' and shit."

I raised an eyebrow. "Too physical?"

"Yeah, well, she's a short shorty, na'mean?" He indicated the stage with his head. "Like that little girl with the cast up there. Guess she don't like her men strong."

"Too bad for her. I certainly do."

The smile widened. "A'ight." And then he headed to his table.

After about seven or eight songs, they all got up and left. Dravon said, "We're gonna bounce. Wanna check out the Hog's Breath, then maybe hit one'a the dance clubs."

"Oh, you should stay." I admit I was looking at Anwan as I spoke.

"Nah. I mean, they're good an' shit, but we need to be *dancin'*."

"Shoulda been here for the first set." 1812 had been a bit more low-key for the second set, going for songs that were still intense and rockin', but not really toe-tappers that would get people on the dance floor.

"It's a'ight. We'll catch you tomorrow?"

"You bet." They had signed up for my Saturday afternoon dive.

As I watched them leave, Anwan turned and gave me one last bright smile. I figured I had another two hours to spend with him in a skintight neoprene suit, which wouldn't suck.

Maybe I'd get the opportunity to find out what "too physical" meant, exactly.

Another group took over their table, only there were six of them, so they had to steal another chair. Bobbi leaned into her mic. "This one's for Cass."

Uh oh. I braced myself, and Bobbi slammed into the opening chords for "Holy Diver." Then I just laughed. Well, hell, I am a goddess and a diver, so why not? Making it even funnier, Chet sang lead, and he was the only bandmember who didn't know the specifics of my being a fate goddess.

As Bobbi did the final descending chords of the Dio song, this big guy who made Anwan look like a ninety-eight-pound weakling walked up to the table, holding a chair. He was close to seven feet tall—seriously—wearing a plain white T-shirt that was straining against his bulging muscles. His red hair was shaved down to a buzz cut, but he had a thick red beard. Seriously, he looked like every Bear I'd ever met—and given that Key West had a homosexual population equivalent to that of San Francisco, there were quite a few Bears (though a lot more Twinks). He wore cargo shorts and, oddly, there was a small ballpeen hammer hanging off a loop on his belt.

Putting the chair down so the back was facing my table, he straddled it, leaning his redwood-sized arms on the chair's back.

"So, *this* is the mighty Dís who saved us all!"

I just stared at him for a second, both impressed and appalled by the audacity—and not *at all* comfortable with his identifying me as a Dís. About seven months ago, I found out I was one of the Dísir, a Norse fate goddess—which is why weird shit has been happening to me all my life in general, and why I was helping Norse gods stop crazy ghosts in particular. Only a few people knew about it. I told Rance, Bobbi, and Jana. Ginny already knew, being a Norse goddess herself, ditto Loki and Odin, obviously. In fact, Odin was the one who told me right before he conscripted me to help stop Loki from destroying the world. And my parents and twin brother knew, the latter being a Dís himself.

But that didn't explain how this asshole knew.

"Who the fuck are you and why the fuck are you sitting at my table?"

The Bear threw his head back and laughed to the ceiling loud enough that it briefly drowned out 1812's rendition of "Bang a Gong." Everyone around me looked at us funny.

"Seriously, who the fuck—"

"You were there when the Allfather died, were you not?"

I just sat there with my mouth hanging open. I had no idea how to respond to this, although I seriously considered throwing my beer in his face, before rejecting the notion as a waste of a perfectly good drink. Odin, the Allfather of the Aesir, died—sort of—when we stopped the ghost.

"All right, listen, I don't know who—"

"You must come with me this evening. There is *much* to do." He held out one massive hand.

I looked at it like it was diseased. "Sorry, I don't know where that hand's been."

A huge grin spread behind the thick beard. "More places than you could possibly imagine, beautiful Dís. Now, shall we be away from this place to somewhere quieter where our business may be discussed?"

"We don't have any 'business'! Look, I'm not sure what your game is, but in about seven seconds, you're going to find out how good I am with a dive knife." I didn't actually have my dive knife on me, but I was hoping he wouldn't call my bluff.

That just widened the asshole's grin, only now he had a lascivious look in his eyes. Maybe he wasn't a Bear. "Excellent. You have spirit. That will serve you well."

While I was trying to figure out how to manhandle someone who was twice my size, Adina came over. "Can I get you something, big guy?"

Before I could say that he wasn't going to be sitting here long, he barreled forward. "Ah, of course! Before we adjourn there must be a toast! Two pints of the same ale that she is drinking. And a fresh one for her as well."

Adina's eyes grew wide. "Uhm, two pints?"

"The toast is for the recent death of my father."

I squinted at him. Son of a fucking bitch.

"Oh, I'm so sorry!" Adina's face got all scrunchy. "I'll bring those three pints right away."

She went off and I glowered at him. Odin's son, knows what I am, red hair, carrying a hammer. Shoulda figured it out right off. "You're Thor."

"Of course I am!" He regarded me with confusion, apparently surprised that I'd only just put it together. "Odin's beard, woman, who else *would* I be but Thor Odinson, god of the storm?"

"Bang a Gong" ended and the bar filled with more raucous applause. I noticed that Ginny was looking right at my table with a murderous expression on her face.

Bobbi leaned into the mic again. "We got two separate requests for this next one." Tapping on a pedal, she started in on the opening chords for "(I Can't Get No) Satisfaction." Ginny was still staring daggers at our table. I wondered what the history was there.

Adina brought the three pints, putting two in front of Thor and one in front of me. Thor lifted one of the pints, and I decided what the hell, and raised my almost-empty one.

"To Odin, the Allfather, ruler of the Nine Worlds, my father, and the greatest god that ever lived!"

I recalled what Loki and Ginny said when we did a similar toast yesterday at Bobbi's. "Skaal!"

We clanked our pints together, Thor's glass hitting mine hard enough that for a second I thought they both were gonna shatter. As we did so, thunder rumbled in the air and I caught a flash of lightning through the open roof of Mayor Fred's.

I sipped the rest of my beer, which was less than a third of the glass.

Thor guzzled the entire pint in one shot. Yowza.

Slamming down the now-empty pint glass, Thor laughed. "Ah, lovely Dís, you are fortunate, to have fought alongside my father in battle, and been there for another triumphant death!"

That was the second time someone told me that Odin had died before. "How many triumphant deaths has Odin had, exactly?"

Thor grinned. "Far too many to keep track of—that's the task of the Norns. Or you, actually, magnificent Dís, for fate is your purview."

Looking around furtively, I said, "Okay, look, my name's *Cassie*. I'd rather you didn't call me 'Dís' like that. Or any other way." It wasn't quite as annoying as Loki calling me "little Dís," as he liked to do. The funny thing is, I wouldn't have minded it as much coming from Thor, since compared to him, I *was* little. Hell, compared to him, aircraft carriers were little.

And yeah, okay, it was nice to be called lovely, beautiful, and magnificent. But still, we were in public.

He slammed a hand on the table and it jumped. That got us our second set of funny looks, only more of them this time. "Very well! To you, beautiful Cassie, the Dís who averted Ragnarok!"

206

I picked up my full pint. "You know about that, huh?"

"My father informed me when last we spoke at midsummer. You are to be commended, lovely Cassie. Loki Laufeyson is a trickster of the highest order."

"Tell me about it," I muttered. It also looked like I was getting the complimentary adverbs no matter what, and I was honestly okay with that. "I'm supposed to keep an eye on him, make sure he doesn't cause trouble. And I've already failed at that once."

"Wait—the foul trickster is no longer imprisoned?"

I shook my head. "In fact, I'm surprised he's not here to drool over Ginny some more."

Again, Thor pounded on the table, but this time it almost fell over, and I practically fell out of my chair. "Curse his infernal shifty eyes and his damnable hide! When I see him, I'll pull out his entrails and strangle him with them!"

"Give me some advance warning, I'll sell tickets."

Thor just stared at me for a second, then threw his head back and brayed a laugh that made his previous one sound like a titter. Now it wasn't just people around us looking at us like we were nuts. Over at the bar, both Thor behind it and Larry sitting at it gave me a WTF expression. I just shrugged sheepishly.

1812 had, at this point, finished the Stones song. Jana had put on an acoustic guitar and started strumming the rhythm chords for "You Ain't Seen Nothin' Yet."

"But enough!" Thor declared once he was done scaring the tourists with his guffaws. "We must away to our business posthaste!" He reached into one of the pockets of his cargo shorts and tossed a huge pile of money onto the table, most of which were dollar coins.

I shook my head. "What is it you guys have against paper money?"

Thor ignored my question and got to his feet, once again holding out his hand. "Will you accompany me, magnificent Cassie of the Dísir?"

Staring at the hand that looked like a giant slab of meat with fingers, I kept going back and forth in my head about what to do. The last time a Norse god came to me with a great mission, it was to save the world. I still wasn't a hundred percent recovered from twisting the crazy ghost's fate so that it would stop killing people.

But I had to admit to being intrigued.

I got up, pointedly not taking his hand; I *still* didn't know where it had been. "All right, let's go."

Casting one glance back at the stage to wave goodbye to the band, I got a lascivious smile from Jana, a quick smile from Bobbi (she was singing), utter indifference from Chet, and an even more murderous glare from Ginny.

We stepped out onto Greene, and Thor just stopped moving.

"Uh, where *is* this mission, exactly?" Remembering the comics I'd read as a kid, I took a step back and held up both hands, as if to ward him off. "We are *not* flying."

"Of course not! We are simply awaiting my chariot."

After being told I was a Dís, I dive-bombed into everything I could find about Norse mythology, and I knew about Thor's chariot. Flying wasn't looking so bad. "All right, there is no fucking way I'm getting in a chariot pulled by two goats named 'Teeth-Barer' and 'Teeth Grinder.' We can go get my tru—"

A car came blazing down Greene, nearly running down a couple of tourists. (And yes, after living here sixteen months, I can tell a tourist on sight.) It came to a screeching halt in front of Mayor Fred's, right under the NO STANDING ANYTIME sign. There was *nobody* inside it.

Once it was idling in front of me instead of blazing down the street frightening pedestrians, I recognized it as a Pontiac Tempest GTO. Which went by a very particular nickname.

I just stared at Thor. "A goat? Seriously?"

He grinned again. "One must change with the times, mighty Cassie."

"Apparently." I liked "lovely," "beautiful," and "magnificent" better, but "mighty" wasn't bad.

Thor moved around to the driver side. "Come, we will ride in Tanngnjostr."

"What, not Tanngrisnir?"

"The car is Tanngnjostr only on my own day, as well as Odin's and Freya's days." Thor squeezed himself into the front seat. "It is Tanngrisnir the other four days."

I nodded as I did likewise and fastened my seatbelt. He was talking about Wednesday, Thursday, and Friday, and calling the goats that pulled his old chariot by their Old Norse names. "This is a '64, right?"

From his position behind the wheel, he regarded me with a look of respect. "Well spotted, lovely Cassie." I noticed that his seat was as far back as possible, and also that he *hadn't* fastened his seatbelt.

"Yeah, well, I used to be a car nut."

"Whyfor 'used to be'?" He threw the car into gear and gunned the accelerator for the thirty feet to the intersection with Duval, then he stomped on the brake and screeched around the corner. I found myself reaching for the "Jesus bar," but the '64 goat was a convertible and didn't have one.

"Uh, yeah." I closed my eyes, not wanting to actually see it when he ran someone down on the crowded thoroughfare of Duval on a Friday night. "Since I was a little kid, was always seriously into cars. Had models, Matchbox cars, the works. That was how I met my ex-boyfriend Greg, back in college, we were both geebling over this '66 Dodge Dart one of the other students had. It was the two-door postless model they only did that year."

"A fine vehicle."

I winced as he just missed clipping a pair of co-eds. "Uh, yeah. Our first date was to go to the San Diego International Auto Show. Anyhow, he cheated on me, and I caught him. What's worse, when I walked in on him liplocked with the little bitch, he just blithely introduced me as his 'friend.'"

"And did you smite the varlet for his impertinence?"

"No, but I'm totally stealing that way of describing it next time I tell this story. Anyhow, I may've thrown something at him, and I never spoke to the shitheel again. Kinda lost interest in cars after that."

Thor made a sharp left onto Eaton. We passed the Bottroff House on the left—at this point, my stomach had been left behind and was probably going back up to my room—and went careening down the less-well-travelled street, taking it to the end, then zoomed right onto Palm Avenue, which intersected with Route 1.

As we drove over the bridge onto Stock Island, I asked, "So—where are we going again?"

"Our mission will take us to the isle that you refer to as Summerland Key."

"And what, exactly, will we be doing there?"

Thor just grinned.

Suddenly, I was very conscious of the fact that—contrary to every instinct I'd built up over twenty-six years of being female—I had just gotten into a car with a strange, aggressive man whom I'd just met.

"Look, I got enough of the cryptic-ass shit from your old man. Will you just *tell* me what we're doing?"

"Fulfilling your wildest dreams, lovely Cassie. Consider it your reward for the role you have played in protecting the world and serving the Aesir in these dark times."

I threw up my hands. "Why is it that when I ask you fucknuts for clarity you just get *more* cryptic? And what dark times are you talking about?"

As he barreled down the Overseas Highway as fast as traffic would allow, Thor spoke in a graver tone than he'd used since he sat down next to me. "There are very few of us left, Cassie. Myself, Loki, Sigyn, Geirrod, Tyr, the Sons of Ivaldi, Vali..." He shook his head. "Asgard is lost to us, the Nine Worlds reduced to a story told to children." Then he shook his head a second time, grinning through that ridiculous beard again. "But enough of this maudlin mewling like old women."

I winced at "maudlin mewling," but said nothing as Thor zoomed over the bridge from Cudjoe Key to Summerland, and a few minutes later, swerved right onto West Shore Drive. After that road turned into Ocean Drive, he slammed right onto a dirt road for about a quarter mile, which led to a small cabin.

This was starting up what my uncle Harry used to call a queasy feeling in my gizzard.

Thor screeched the goat to a halt just outside the cabin. Unfolding himself, he got out of the car. "Come, lovely Cassie! The greatest adventure you will ever encounter awaits you within those walls."

I stood next to the goat, facing the rather bland-looking cabin.

Couldn't make out many details, as it was dark. The only light came from the goat's headlights, which were now out.

"Okay, you *do* realize that I've corralled dragons, stopped nixies, twisted the fates of ghosts and immortals, banished demons, and stopped the end of the world, right?"

Thor was now standing in the doorway, fumbling with a set of keys he'd removed from one of the many pockets in his cargo shorts. "I'm aware of that—well, perhaps not all the specifics, but you *are* a Dís."

"Right, and what I'm saying is, my 'great adventure' bar is pretty fucking high."

"Rest assured, this will be greater than all of them." Thor got the door open, and it swung inward. "Come, enter, and be amazed!"

The gizzard was on overdrive, but this was Thor, for crying out loud. Odin's son and one of the great figures of Norse myth. Hell, he has his own comic book and movie series. Sorta.

So I went in.

The cabin had a big living room with a galley kitchen against the back wall. On the left and right were doorways to bedrooms. There was a couch in the middle of the living room, making it look just like a sitcom apartment—seriously, on television, they *always* put the couch in the middle of the floor, and I've seen maybe one dwelling in real life that did that before now—and an easy chair next to it.

As soon as I closed the door behind me, Thor took his shirt off.

I just kind of stared for a second, not entirely believing what I was seeing—until he undid his pants. Then I held up both hands and slowly backed myself toward the door while trying desperately to remember what he did with the keys to the goat. "Whoa, there, motherfucker, what the *hell* do you think you're doing?"

He gave me a perplexed look. "I've found that the act of love-making is greatly facilitated by the removal of clothing."

"You have *got* to be fucking kidding me!"

"What did you think I was bringing you here for, mighty Cassie? You have served the Aesir well, and you deserve the finest reward we can offer!"

He started to undo the shorts, and I cried out, "Stop it!"

"Why have you not removed your clothes?" He sounded genuinely confused.

"Let me put this succinctly." I reached behind my back and put my hand on the doorknob to the front door. I also tried not to hyperventilate. "If you and I were the last two people on Earth, I would gleefully live a life of celibacy rather than even *consider* the possibility of fucking you."

Thor's face fell into a scowl, and he pointed at me with one meaty finger, the other hand keeping his now-unbuttoned cargo shorts from falling down. "You dare to reject the gift of Odin's favorite son?"

As if to punctuate his point, another peal of thunder rang through the night.

"Your definition of 'gift' is way different from mine, chuckles. And if you're his favorite, I'm glad I don't know your brothers." I really hoped my knees weren't knocking together as much as my imagination said they were.

Snarling, Thor clutched the ballpeen hammer that had been dangling from his shorts. "You're just like the rest of them, aren't you? Sif, and Sigyn, and Oor, and Njorun, and that aloof bitch Bast, and haughty shrew Athena. Go, then! Depart my presence, and never darken my door again!"

"Not even a little bit of a problem," I said as I threw open the door and ran down the dirt path, away from the cabin and the goat as fast as my long legs could take me. No fucking way was I staying in there. For a moment, when he grabbed his hammer, I was worried he'd try to use force. I'm fairly strong—years of hauling air tanks around and swimming with them on your back will do *wonders* for your upper-body strength—but I had no confidence in my ability to go one-on-one with someone that big who had thousands of years of godhood backing it up.

By the time I got to Ocean Drive, I'd calmed down enough to start thinking straight—including the fact that I was twenty-five miles from home with no vehicle. I probably had enough of my mad automotive skillz left to hotwire the goat, but that would mean going back to the cabin, which was *not* happening ever.

Whipping out my smartphone, I Googled my way to a nearby

car service. They said they'd have a cab for me in twenty minutes.

Just as I hit end on the phone, I jumped at another peal of thunder, and a lightning strike on one of the trees about forty feet from me. The sizzle of the lightning, the crack of the tree, and the smell of burning wood all served to frighten the holy crap out of me.

Then it started to rain.

Of course.

This was your typical Florida downpour: intense, nasty, and immediately soaked every single thing you were wearing.

Which I was stuck in for twenty minutes. These storms usually didn't last all that long, but there wasn't usually a pissed-off thunder god in the Keys, either. By the time the cab arrived, my *bones* were wet. Then it was another half an hour to the Bottroff House. It didn't take that long to get here from Key West, but livery drivers in Chevy Aveos tend to take a more leisurely pace down the Overseas Highway than thunder gods in sports cars.

I got home at about two a.m., by which time the storm had finally stopped. I debated just going to bed, but I knew that wouldn't work. Besides, I had a sudden need to talk to Ginny, who—based on the death glares she was throwing at the table—had some inkling of what was going to happen. And I, like a moron, hadn't paid any attention, or at least waited until the set was over so I could get a second opinion.

After changing into dry clothes and toweling down, I headed back to Mayor Fred's. My last bra was soaked through—needed to do laundry Saturday, obviously—so I wore the tank top with the built-in support cups. It wasn't the most comfortable thing in the world—its claims to be one size fits all only applies if you have a B-cup or less—but it would do.

I walked into Mayor Fred's just as Bobbi was saying, "This is one our drummer Ginny Blake asked us to do," before diving into the opening riff of Joan Jett's "I Hate Myself for Loving You." I noticed that Loki was sitting at the bar, chatting as usual with Larry St. Joseph, one of the regulars. Hell, at this point, Loki—under the name of Sigurd Jarlsson—was a regular too...

213

As soon as he saw me, Loki gave me a similar death glare to that of Ginny, and motioned for me to come over. All the tables, including my usual one by the ficus, were taken. It *was* Friday night of a holiday weekend, and 1812 was really *on* tonight, so the turnover was slower than usual.

I landsharked through the crowd and squeezed in between Larry and Loki. The latter didn't waste any time. "Ginny told me my cousin came by and left with you."

News travels fast. "Yeah, he did. He said—"

"He wanted to take you on an 'adventure'? That he was taking you to your reward for whatever deed he thought you might have performed?"

"Well, the deed I performed was cleaning up your mess."

Larry just stared at Loki. "What in Sam Hill didja do *this* time, Sig?"

Loki's lips curled into a sneer. "Why does everyone assume that *I* have done something?"

"In this case, you did. Thor was here because of what happened last weekend."

"Unbelievable." Loki shook his head in disapproval, which was just hilarious. "I cannot believe that you simply *went* with him. Did you return to your inn, or did he find a remote location to have his way with you?"

That got me a look from Larry. "Hey, I thought Rance was your young man?"

"We're *not* dating," I said automatically, "and that's not the point."

"Isn't it?" Loki had gone from disapproving to mischievous. "I wonder how Special Agent Demitrijian would feel about your having a tryst with my cousin?"

"First of all, it would hardly be my first 'tryst' since I got here."

"Really?" Larry looked a little revolted.

I glared at him. "Guys who stick their dicks in water elementals and get cursed by them to die when they go to sleep should not throw stones."

Larry angrily grabbed his coffee, muttering, "You don't have to get personal about it, sheesh."

I turned my angry gaze back to Loki. "Secondly, I didn't have a tryst. The minute he took his shirt off, I was out of there. Had to take a cab home in the rain."

Loki smirked. "Yes, when Thor is displeased, it tends to be reflected in the weather."

Now that I'd burned through my outrage, I was starting to get worried. I spent most of my cab ride home wondering about the consequences of my rejection might be. Not that said consequences changed anything, but I wanted to know what to expect.

"So what happens now?" I asked. "What does Thor generally do when women reject him?" Then I had an awful thought. "*Do* women reject him?"

That got Loki to grin widely. "All the time. Did he try the line about how when he rubs his hammer it grows larger?"

Larry just looked at both of us. "Are you kidding me? He *says* that?"

"More than once."

After the Joan Jett song ended, Bobbi said they were taking a break. Once more, a mess of helpful audience members aided her in getting down, but she just sat on the edge of the stage and took in the accolades of just about every person in the bar, while Adina brought her another drink.

Ginny, though, came over to join me, Loki, and Larry at the bar, and she was *still* giving me the death glare.

I cut her off before she could even get her mouth open. "Don't *you* start. Yes, I left with Thor. Yes, he said it was an adventure and all his usual bullshit that, in retrospect, was an obvious line I should've seen through. But no, once he made it clear that his only interest was in fucking the Dís, I got the hell out of there."

"Good." Ginny packed a lot of relief into that one syllable. "He attempted that on me after Loki was imprisoned and before the earth nymphs found him for me."

Loki immediately went back to being outraged. "He *did?*"

"Oh, calm down, I refused him. He tried to convince me that Mjolnir would grow larger if I rubbed it."

Larry actually did a spit-take with his coffee. "Jesus, Mary, and Joseph, he really *did* say that."

Ginny nodded gravely. "The good news, Cassie, is that you're now one of his failed conquests, and he'll probably never even speak to you again."

"Yeah, he gave me a list. Sif, Oor, Njorun, Bast, and Athena. And by the way? It's freaking me out a little that it's not just half the Norse pantheon running around, but we've got Egyptian and Greek gods, too."

Ginny shook her head. "He and Sif were married, actually, but after he slept with some valkyrie or other, she refused to join him in his bed."

Loki chuckled. "I told him that he would regret sleeping with a chooser of the slain. The next day, he laughed at me and said he didn't regret a thing. Then he went home." He sipped his bourbon. "I *did* try to warn him…"

Ihor finally made it over to us. Ginny ordered a bourbon, but I found that all the energy had drained out of me. Plus, my ribs were starting to ache from the stupid tank top. "Look, much as I'd love to hear more stories of Thor crashing and burning with the ladies, I think I need to head home and collapse in a heap. This night was *way* more draining than it should've been. See you guys tomorrow night."

When I got back to the B&B, I was rather surprised to find five people sitting on the front porch, who got up and cheered upon seeing me approach.

"Thank the *Lord!*" De'Andre cried.

Rosita wiped imaginary sweat off her brow. "Thought for *damn* sure we was gonna be stuck on that porch *all* night long."

I put my hands on my hips, screwing a mock-stern expression on my face. "Okay, I remember when I checked you guys in, I gave you a front door key."

Dravon looked at Steve with a dangerously sweet smile on her face. "You wanna tell Cassie 'bout the front door key?"

Steve stared intently at the ground. "I *thought* I put it in my pocket…"

De'Andre was shaking his head. "You b'*lieve* that?"

I couldn't help but notice that Anwan was totally checking me out. I also remembered that the tank top I was wearing, for all its discomfort, looked pretty fucking good on me.

I dug into the pocket of my shorts, which had my keychain.

216

"Lucky for you guys, I come prepared. It's also even luckier that I came home earlier—I'm not usually back here until four."

De'Andre looked at Steve and grinned. "Hope you like sleepin' on the floor, yo."

"Fuck you."

I snorted at Steve's oh-so-mature response as I unlocked the front door.

Then Rosita cuddled up to De'Andre. "That's my job."

"TMI, people." Even as I spoke those words, the other three made gagging noises. I opened the door and bowed with a flourish to let them in. "Your castle awaits. Keep the noise down, as the other three rooms have sleeping people in 'em. I'm going to bed. See you all tomorrow at one." The main house had four rooms upstairs, three of which were occupied by this bunch, and two downstairs. The two cottages had two rooms each, giving us ten altogether, which is just the right number for a B&B with a staff of three (Debbie, the owner; Lisa-Karen, the maid; and me, the Lord High Everything Else).

"Oh, hey, Cass?" Anwan asked as the two couples went inside. "Can you do me a favor? I like to read 'fore I go to bed, but the bulb's out in the lamp on the nightstand."

I blew out a breath. My bed was calling my name very loudly, but—well, I *was* the Lord High Everything Else. "I'll fetch a bulb and bring it up."

Anwan followed the others upstairs. I didn't spend the *entire* time he went up the steps staring at his ass, honest. I went to the storage closet, pulled out a bulb, and then went upstairs. Anwan had left his door ajar, even though I had a master key for all ten rooms.

I pushed the door the rest of the way open. Anwan had taken his shirt and flip-flops off, so he was only wearing his shorts. Remember how nice his arms were? The chest went along *very* nicely with them. And the light from the lamp on the nightstand shone off his bald head.

I grinned. "Thought the bulb was out."

"Yeah, I guess I was wrong." He smiled and moved closer to me. "Sorry 'bout that."

That was twice in one night I totally missed two, in retrospect, horribly transparent attempts to get into my pants.

217

I kicked the door shut behind me, just to make it clear that, this time, I was okay with it.

Suffice it to say that Anwan's ex is a fucking moron. "Too physical," my ass.

And several other of my body parts. Damn.

The one negative about the whole thing was that Anwan was up before dawn. The five of them were taking a boat tour that left at some ungodly hour of the morning (which was any time before noon, as far as I was concerned), so I stumbled in a half-asleep haze to my room in one of the cottages out back. I passed through the kitchen, where Debbie was preparing breakfast, and she just gave me the biggest shit-eating grin in the history of the world. "Somebody had a good night."

"It didn't suck." Then I stopped, thought about it a second, then added, "Although several things *were* sucked. Gotta go collapse."

Anwan was hardly the first tourist I'd had a one-nighter with, and Debbie hadn't minded any of the other times. In fact, more than once she'd encouraged me to get laid more often.

And hey, they weren't flying back to Baltimore until Sunday night, so it might even be a two-nighter. There were a couple of positions we hadn't gotten around to.

I did my usual routine after that: slept until eleven, drank coffee, went to Seaclipse, ran a dive. When I got back from the dive (during which Anwan and I exchanged all kinds of coy looks, to the point that Dravon was wondering what was wrong with us), Noah, the other part-timer, had called in sick and so I had to run his night dive, and then when I got back from *that*, we'd gotten a call from one of the other shops up on Sugarloaf Key that one of their boats had gone missing. The Coast Guard was alerted, of course, but like the Springsteen song says, we take care of our own: we took all three of our boats, *Groucho*, *Chico*, and *Harpo*, out to search. We spent four hours doing that, until the shop called back to say they found it. Turns out a couple of tourists had provided the dive master with some weed laced with— something. Put 'em all to sleep and they drifted. Assholes were lucky they didn't crash on a reef.

The upshot is that I never made it to Mayor Fred's Saturday night, as I was too fried. I didn't even go into the main house to see if Anwan was up for round two, mostly because I knew I wasn't. Hell, I never made it to the stage of taking my clothes off, instead just collapsing on top of my made bed.

Sunday morning, I got a text from Bobbi: "Jana got laid!"

I texted back: "Me, too!"

We quickly arranged to have a late lunch at her place. After my dive, I drove up to Cow Key, where Bobbi was waiting for me on one of the many picnic tables the Milewski family had in their back yard, complete with sandwiches from her parents' store's deli section. Bobbi, who knew me all too well, had gotten me beef salami with mustard and sautéed onions. She was having her usual bologna with mayo on white bread. Yes, really. Apparently being blond-haired and blue-eyed didn't make her quite white enough.

She started talking the second my butt hit the bench. "Okay, on the one hand, I'm dying to find out, like, every single detail—I'm guessing that's why you didn't make it last night?"

"Sadly, no." I told her the quickie version of what happened at Seaclipse. "This was Friday night, after I left."

Bobbi's eyes widened. "Really? Wow."

"Y'see—" I started, but she cut me off, waving her hand back and forth.

"Later, seriously. Jana's been my best friend for twenty years, so she goes first."

I laughed. "Okay, fine."

"So this guy comes in—big guy. Seriously, I've seen bouncers that could fit in this guy's left arm. He spends about half a second hitting on me—"

I snorted. While living on one of the more hedonistic islands on the face of the Earth, Bobbi was asexual. She wasn't interested in sex with anybody, regardless of gender. She usually told men that she was into women and women that she was into men, just to shut them up sooner. We won't even get into the people who wanted to "fix" her...

"—and then he went after Jana. Followed her outside where she was smoking, and then he did it again at the next break. She

219

went off with him. Ginny was kinda pissed, because she didn't help with teardown, but ever since Russ…."

I nodded as Bobbi trailed off. Until Russ, Jana had never not had a boyfriend, but in the months since, she hadn't even evinced an interest in any of the legion of guys who hit on her. Of course, many of them had, like this guy, tried Bobbi first, as she's less scary looking. (They never hit on Ginny. It's like she had goddess mojo or something. I kept meaning to ask her how she did that.)

"Anyhow, this guy was *really* into her. Was telling her about the adventure they'd—"

Oh, fuck. "Did he have short red hair and a thick-ass beard and a hammer on his belt?"

Bobbi choked on her sandwich. "Seriously? You know this guy?"

I put my head in my hands. "Fuck. Ginny was *not* pissed because Jana didn't do teardown." And then I explained to Bobbi about Thor. "I'm kinda surprised Ginny didn't tell you Friday."

"Yeah, well…" Bobbi looked away, and I swear she was blushing.

"What is it?"

"Well, I was a little busy Friday. Everyone was trying to talk to me."

I threw up both hands. "Well, *duh*, woman! You were *en fuego* Friday night."

"God, you really *did* get laid, if you're whipping out the Spanish."

That got me slightly annoyed. "Excuse me?"

"Remember that construction worker over Fourth of July weekend? Next day, you called him '*muy bueno*'."

I had no recollection of this. "Really?"

"And then there was that grad student you spent all of Memorial Day weekend babbling about poetry with. After he flew back to Michigan, you were talking about his *cojones* and—"

"All right, all right!" I really didn't need *every* one-nighter since I moved down here thrown in my face. "Let's get back to Jana. If she went off with Thor…" I trailed off, realizing I had no idea how to finish that sentence. "Fuck, I only know about

220

women who've rejected him. Ginny and Loki didn't tell me a damn thing about anyone he actually stayed with." Then I remembered something Ginny had said. "Okay, no, wait, he was married to one, but she left him when he cheated on her."

Bobbi was rubbing her chin. "Well, wait a minute. Remember what Russ's Mom said? That Jana would never love anyone like she loved Russ again? And since then, she's been as celibate as I am, and I know she hates that. Maybe a god can overcome a water fae's curse?"

I took a thoughtful bite of my sandwich. "Never know." I grinned. "And hey, now I can ask Jana if his hammer really *does* get bigger if you rub it!"

Unfortunately, I didn't make it to Mayor Fred's until much later that night. A boat from the shop on Sugarloaf went missing *again*, and we volunteered to help *again*, and then it turned up *again*, only this time it was the Coast Guard who found it.

My instinct was to drive back to the B&B and collapse, but I noticed two texts on my smartphone. One was from Anwan: "u made the trip thanks for helping me forget bitch"

The other was from Bobbi: "Come to Mayor Fred's. Doesnt matter how late. Trust me."

Thus intrigued, I slammed Rocinante into gear and headed back to the Bottroff House, parking the truck and then walking the rest of the way to Mayor Fred's.

By the time I got there, it was almost four, and Jana was standing outside the bar, puffing away, alongside Larry.

"Hey, Zukav."

"Hey yourself. Guess I missed the show, huh?"

Larry blew smoke into the night air. "They weren't as good as Friday, but they brought the house down anyhow. Bobbi said you had some sort of crisis at Seaclipse?"

I nodded. "Boat went missing from one of the other shops—a shop that may not be in business much longer if this shit keeps up, since that's the second night in a row it's happened." I regarded Jana with significant concern. "You okay?"

"Yeah, I'm good." Jana used her usual Goth studied-indifference tone, which was actually the best possible news, since she'd tended toward defensive and annoyed since Russ and his mother left the island.

"I heard you hooked up last night."

Larry made a face, dropped his cigarette, and stepped on it. "I'm gettin' outta here. G'night." He wandered off down Greene Street to do whatever he did when Mayor Fred's wasn't open and he was guzzling caffeine at the bar so he wouldn't sleep and therefore die.

Jana gave me a look. "'Hooked up'? Seriously?"

"Sorry." And I meant it. I didn't hate that phrase as much as Jana did, but it was close. "I just wanted to get rid of Larry."

She snorted. "I get that. So you wanna know about Thor?"

"Just want to make sure you're all right."

"I'm fine." She shrugged. "I mean, he wasn't exactly what you'd expect from a god, y'know?"

My eyes went wide and a feeling of giddiness came over me. "Really?"

"Oh yeah. He told me his hammer got bigger if I rubbed it—it didn't, and neither did any other part of him."

I burst out laughing, and Jana joined me.

"Seriously," she went on, "he had the technique of a fucking sixteen-year-old who just touched his first boobie. And it was over in half a second." She grinned. "Kinda like lightning."

She finished her cigarette and dropped it on the sidewalk. "He's inside, y'know. Talkin' with Jarlsson, or Loki, or whatever the fuck his name is. Keeps smilin' at me like we're fuckin' soulmates or some shit."

I pointed at the entrance with the big fish over it. "They're still inside? Even *Larry's* left, and he's the last one out, usually."

"Go fig'."

I walked in just as Chet and his white-woman-fuck-buddy-*dujour* left. Ginny was packing her drum stuff, and Bobbi was sitting on the edge of the stage with a pint of beer, her guitar case next to her.

Ihor was cleaning off a table when he saw me, and looked incredibly relieved. "Oh, Cass, thank Christ you're here. You think you can get those two outta here?"

He jerked his thumb toward the bar, where Thor and Loki

were both talking and laughing. The former had very few consonants and the latter was even more braying. They were the only people left in the bar besides Ihor, me, and the band.

I regarded Ihor. "How drunk are they?"

Ihor just shot me a look of disgust and I held up both hands.

I walked over to the bar, and I heard Thor slur, "Then i's settled! We sh'll sojourn to Hollywood an' find these varlets Hemston and Hiddlesworth an' *smite* them!"

Loki swung his arm down as if to pound on the bar, but he missed. Undaunted, he cried out, "Yes! We are in agreement, then!"

I put a hand on each of their shoulders. "Okay, Jay, Silent Bob, it's time to leave."

"Nonsense!" Loki cried. "It's still early!"

"It's four, 'Sigurd.' Even Larry's gone home."

Loki frowned, trying very hard to process this. "Larry's left?"

I nodded.

Loki swung his head to look at Thor. "If Larry's left, then the tavern's definitely closed."

"Bah!" Thor actually succeeded in slamming his hand on the table. "I am th'thunderer, an' I demand more ale!"

"Demand all you want, you're not getting it."

Thor stared at me, as if recognizing me for the first time—which, to be honest, he probably was. "Cassie? What're you doin' here? How dare you talk t'me after you rejected me?"

"As I recall, 'thunderer,' two nights ago, you swore you were going to rip Loki's entrails out and strangle him with them."

Thor almost fell off the bar stool. "*Did I?*"

I nodded again.

Loki pointed at him. "It certainly sounds like something you'd say, cousin."

Thor considered that. "Yes, it does. But whassa point in holdin' grudges, tha's what I say. Come, Cassie, join us f'r a drink!"

"Can't, Thor, the bar's closed. Look, we can—"

"Nonsense!" Thor clambered off the stool, and then fell face first to the floor. I managed to dodge out of the way just in time, and I swear, the entire bar shook when he hit the hardwood.

He didn't move.

I bent down over him just as Loki did the same, and our heads collided. I saw stars as my skull hit his, and I fell backward. Next thing I knew, Ginny and Ihor were on either side of me as I sat on the floor, about a foot from where Thor fell.

"What happened?"

Ginny pointed at Loki, who I now realized was out cold on the floor behind the thunder god. "The immovable object met a very resistible force."

I snorted and clambered to my feet.

Ihor moved to help me, but I was up before he could do anything. He shrugged and, his chivalrous instinct having been stymied by my independent streak, folded his arms and stared at the two unconscious gods on his floor. "What the fuck am I supposed to do with *those* two?"

"I have a few creative suggestions," I said slowly before Ginny cut me off.

"I will take care of them. Thor's 'chariot' has a mind of its own, and it will take us to wherever he's living."

"It's a cabin on Summerland Key."

From the stage where she had just finished packing her synthesizers, Jana added, "It's a shithole!"

It took the combined efforts of me, Ihor, and Ginny to drag Thor to the sidewalk, but Ihor was able to handle Loki alone. By the time the bartender got the trickster out front, the goat had shown up of its own accord and was again idling in front of the bar.

"Really was hoping not to see that car again." I shook my head and grabbed Thor's ankles while Ihor went for one shoulder and Ginny the other. As we strained to pick him up, I said through clenched teeth, "I'm telling you right now, whatever doesn't fit the first time, I'm cutting off!" This time I actually *had* my dive knife with me, so I could back up my claim.

However, we got him into the back, and then tossed Loki on top of him. Ginny then hopped in the driver's seat. Neither Jana nor I actually told her where the cabin was on Summerland, and she didn't seem to have a set of keys, but she somehow guided the goat away.

Whatever. I may have been a Dís, but the gods' problems were *not* mine. Dammit.

Some days I even believed that.

Ihor and I walked back into the bar, and he said, "Want a beer? On the house? Taps're shut down, but I can give you a bottle."

I was a beer snob, and the idea of drinking out of a bottle was not appealing. On the other hand, my father always used to say that if it's free it tastes better. "Yeah."

Ihor went to get me a beer. Bobbi, for some stupid reason, was grinning ear to ear as she sat by the stage.

"What are you so fucking happy about?"

"Well, remember how Thor said he would give you a reward?"

I wondered where she was going with this. "Ye-e-e-eah."

"He succeeded." She looked at Jana, who was hopping off the stage. "With both of you."

"What the unholy *fuck*, Barbara Ann?"

Bobbi glowered at the use of her hated first name—which was why Jana used it—before continuing. "It's simple, Jane Anne."

Jana scowled.

"Thor showing up when he did got Cassie out of the bar, and then led directly to her going back to the Bottroff House early, which led equally directly to her fucking that guy's brains out."

I held up a hand, which Ihor then put a bottle of beer in. "Thanks, Ihor. To be fair, Anwan did a pretty nice job removing my cranial matter via intercourse, too."

"So noted." Bobbi nodded. "But because Cassie so brutally rejected Thor, he came back to the bar and tried for someone else who was around when his Dad died. He struck out with me, but got Jana—who hasn't been intimate with a man in months."

"Not much of a man," Jana muttered.

"More of a man than you've had since Russ, though."

Jana nodded. "Yeah, okay, it was good to be back in the saddle, even if I got thrown in two seconds."

I gave Jana a mock-solemn look. "Careful, Jana—using a rodeo metaphor may get your Goth card revoked."

"We don't have cards, Zukav." Jana then modulated her tone from pissed to amused. "They just cut off our supply of eyeliner for six months."

We all chuckled, and then Ihor clapped his hands. "Okay, enough hilarity, I really wanna close this fucking place."

225

Jana nodded. "I'll go get the van."

Bobbi stared up at me. "Help me up?"

I dashed over to her, setting my beer bottle on a table, and holding out an arm. She grabbed it and used it as a brace to put herself upright. I snatched her crutches and handed them over, and picked up her guitar.

We headed toward the exit. "Thanks, Bobbi. I was really kinda pissed tonight, but you put it all in perspective. And after kicking ass all weekend."

"Hey, s'what friends are for." Bobbi's smile fell. "Now, though, I just want to sleep until Thursday."

Emphatically, I said, "Amen."

Bonus Track:
How *You* Can Prevent
Forest Fires...

Author's note: This story was the very first Cassie Zukav story, printed in *Urban Nightmares*, an anthology of stories based on urban legends that was edited by myself and the late Josepha Sherman in 1997. Jo and I also each did a story for the anthology, and mine dealt with the old saw about scuba divers being scooped up and dumped on forest fires. We include it here in *Ragnarok and Roll* as a historical artifact that only really fits into the continuity of the other Cassie stories with a big hammer (Mjolnir, perhaps?), but was also Cassie's first adventure, long before she knew what she truly was.

How *You* Can Prevent Forest Fires…

"Cassie, *what* are you doing?"

I wanted to ignore the voice, I knew it was my younger sister, and I did not want to talk to her. Or to anyone else, really. But she hadn't gone away when I ignored her any other time in the last eighteen years. So I was pretty sure that wouldn't work this time either.

I looked up to see her standing in the doorway of the bedroom she and I used to share before my twin brother Paul moved out. Her right hand occupied itself by twirling her not-naturally-blonde hair. "Well, gee, Sunni," I said, "I'm checking over the stuff in my dive bag. I'm wearing a bathing suit. It's a beautiful Saturday morning. What do you think I'm doing?"

"You're going diving, aren't you?"

I sighed. "Your grasp of the blindingly obvious remains strong." I turned my back to her, hoping that now she'd go away. Kneeling down next to the big mesh dive bag, I went on checking to make sure it was all there. Wetsuit—check. Fins—both here. Knife—present. Mask, hood, and snorkel—yup. Buoyancy Compensator jacket and regulator—all there. First aid kit—yes. Sunscreen—no. Damn. Have to stop at the drugstore.

"Cassie, you *can't* go diving."

I snarled, but did not look at my sister as I made sure the dive computer had fresh batteries in it. She could insist on staying, but I was damned if I'd give her the satisfaction of looking at her. "Why not?"

In a tone that implied a "Duh!" Sunni replied, "'Cause there

229

are *forest* fires!"

My sister had made a lot of leaps in logic in her life, but none so high, so far, and so graceful as this one. I gave it a 9.2.

Realizing I wouldn't get any peace until she finished whatever loopy train of thought she was on, I turned, put my hands on my hips, and glared at her. "Sunni, what're you talking about?"

"Don't you know how they put out forest fires?"

"With water, generally," I said, throwing her "duh!" right back at her.

"Don't you know how they *get* the water?"

"It can't be that hard. Three-quarters of the world is covered in it, y'know."

"They've got these, y'know, *helicopters* with these really *big* scoops, and they scoop up the water and dump it on the fires."

I suppose it was possible. I guess. All I really know about forest fires was that they were bad and that there'd been too many of them near here lately—both north of us, near L.A., and east of us in New Mexico and Arizona. We hadn't had any fires here in the San Diego vicinity, at least, but that didn't stop us from getting drought warnings.

Sunni wasn't finished. "And every time they do this, they always find some divers in the forest, *burned to a crisp.*"

Make that a 9.5. "Who told you this?" I asked as I zipped the bag up.

"That skanky guy you've been hanging out with—he told me when he came over last week."

"You mean Xcott?"

"Yeah, him. And that ditzy girlfriend of his."

That would be Geena. And yes, his name really was Xcott, which is pronounced the same as Scott; it's just spelled with an X. We're both victims of ex-hippie parents–in fact, that's why my boyfriend Gary introduced us. His parents named him Scott-with-an-X; mine named me and my twin Castor and Pollux (yes, I know that "Castor" was a guy, please don't get me started) and named our younger sister Sunflower.

Xcott was also my mentor in diving. When I first saw that copy of *Ocean Realms* in Gary's dorm lounge, I realized that I just had to become an underwater photographer. See, I've always loved taking pictures, but never found a subject I liked to photograph—until I saw that amazing shot of a sea anemone that was taken in Bonaire. Then I knew what I had to do.

Or, at least, I thought I did. Xcott was the one who told me that I couldn't just go underwater with a camera, I needed to get certified as a diver (Sunni, who thought the whole thing was stupid, said *certifiable* would be a better word) and get a ton of equipment. It still didn't take that long for two reasons: One, we live in La Jolla, California, about six seconds away from the beach. Two, I have very rich, high-powered-lawyer parents. They seem to figure that they've built up a huge karmic debt from spending their "sordid youths" (their words) sticking us with names like Castor, Pollux, and Sunflower. So they will indulge virtually every whim we have. When Paul decided to quit college and wander the roads "looking for America," our parents sent him off with their blessing and a wad of cash. When Sunni decided she just had to have a Jaguar, she got one. And when I realized that I had to be an underwater photographer, which included a big shopping list of equipment, that list was filled.

Xcott showed me all the places to dive in the area, he taught my certification course at the dive shop he co-managed with Geena, and he was my buddy on my first few dives. He also introduced me to Dina Rosengaus, a tall Russian woman who, as it turned out, was the one who took that picture of the anemone in *Ocean Realms*. She showed me all the tricks of underwater photography, and how it differs from the abovewater kind. (Dina also turned me on to a source for a wetsuit that would actually fit. I'm 5'11", and they just don't make wetsuits for amazons. Of course, except for Dina, every female diver I've met was 5'2" and petite, so there probably wasn't much of a demand.)

I moved past Sunni to the bathroom (one of the three upstairs) that doubled as my darkroom.

"*Cassie*, you're not *listening* to me! You *can't* go diving!"

"Sunni, you didn't actually believe him, did you?"

Inevitably, she followed me into the bathroom. "Of *course* I did. He's been diving, like, *forever*, and he *knows* this stuff. You said so yourself."

I had, too—mostly when I first started diving, and Sunni kept asking me thousands of times if this "jerk friend of Gary's" knew what he was doing.

"Well, he was probably pulling your leg," I said as I gave the underwater camera—same as a regular camera, mostly, except for the waterproof casing and the huge strobe light attachment—a once-over.

"I *still* don't think you should go diving until they put that *fire* out."

I once again barreled past Sunni and went back into the bedroom. She followed, not giving up. "Cassie, I—"

"Sunni, look," I said, whirling around and putting on my best I'm-your-older-sister-and-I'm-six-inches-taller-than-you-dammit voice, "I have had a really fucked-up week, okay? I've been completely submerged in that stupid Keats paper, and when I haven't been doing that, I've been taking shit from Liverakos." Dr. Liverakos was the professor to whom I was a teaching assistant at the University of California–San Diego's Revelle College, where I'd been a grad student for a year. "It looks like next week is going to be even worse. So today, I'm finally getting a chance to take a break from all of it, and I'm going diving. Period, end of discussion."

And with that, I turned my back on her, packed away the camera in its bag, hefted it and the dive bag, and for the third time barreled past my sister.

"Okay," Sunni finally said to my back as I went down stairs "But if you get killed, *I get your room!*"

It's really hard to describe how much I love diving. Most non-divers just don't get it. I mean, I tell people I'm a diver, and they nod and say, "Oh, yeah, I've gone snorkeling a few times myself," like that means anything. Saying you know about scuba diving because you've gone snorkeling is like saying you know about skydiving because you've jumped off a low tree branch.

I'll never forget my first real dive. When you train to get certified, you start out in a classroom, then you go into a pool, then finally in open water. The pool diving didn't excite me, and I almost gave it up, but then Xcott took me into the Pacific for the first time.

The freedom is amazing. I mean, yeah, you have to keep track of your bottom time and your air intake and your surface intervals and all that, but after a while you do that as easily as you walk on land. And you don't think about it, and you just enjoy the freedom. You can move any way you want, you can go over things and under them, and the water covers you like the world's biggest flannel blanket.

But the best part is the fish. So many different shapes, sizes— and colors! The colors are just incredible. There's nothing like it on land. And they just love to dart around you and toward you and under you and over you, and I swear some of them actually pose for my photographs. And then there's the kelp forests, which just have to be seen to be believed.

So, of course, the dive that day was incredibly boring—I just saw a few flounder and a bunch of starfish. It just made me crankier. Probably my last chance to dive for at least a couple of weeks, and none of the fish wanted to come out and play. Not even a sea otter to frolic with.

Eventually I'd had enough. I swam up toward the surface, taking a safety stop at about twenty feet below the surface. (Safety stops are three-to-five minute pauses during your ascent to give the body a chance to shed any excess nitrogen that's built up during the dive; you don't always need to, particularly after a dive this short, but I don't like to take chances.) About two minutes into the stop, I saw a quick glint of something that reflected the sunlight. I turned to see a curved piece of metal coming toward me. In a moment of sheer lunacy, I thought it was a scoop. *Oh my god, Sunni was right, I'm gonna get scooped up and dumped on a burning Sequoia....*

Then I came to my senses and actually looked at the thing. It was a hubcap. As it floated slowly downward, I got grumpier— partly because I hated finding crap like that in the ocean, mainly because for a minute there I actually believed Sunni's bullshit story.

Afterward, I angrily tossed the dive bag into the back of my pickup truck, said goodbye to Geena and the other folks at the dive shop, and went home. Things looked up immediately— Sunni's Jag wasn't in the driveway. So she was probably off with her dippy friends pretending to study while really cruising for guys. With Mom and Dad in Las Vegas on business for the weekend, it meant I had our big house to myself.

The pictures I took were all of real dull subjects, so developing them would have depressed me, and the absolute last thing in the world I wanted to do was tackle Keats. So I turned on the computer and checked the scuba diving list on the Internet that Xcott and Geena had spent ages talking me into trying out. I finally give in a month earlier, and also joined a commercial online service that had a scuba section on it, including weekly live chats on Saturdays.

So what's the first message I download? Somebody asking about the helicopters with their scoops that dump water and divers on forest fires. This guy's question resulted in about twenty-five replies within an hour of the original post, all with the same pissed-off tone, all saying, basically, "Don't be stupid."

Except for one guy. His email address was something cutesy like SEALION@whatever-it-was.com. He kept insisting that it was true, that his wife died that way. Nobody paid any attention to him, but, thinking about it, no one ever paid any attention to him, no matter what he said. And he'd posted quite a bit in the past month. I thought that was pretty mean, really. I mean, his wife *died*.

My boyfriend and his suitemates were throwing a party in their dorm for no real reason that night. ("We're seniors," he said, "we're supposed to party." I don't remember ever acting like that when I was a senior.) But he told me it would start at nine, which meant it wouldn't get going until at least ten-thirty, so I figured I could hang out in the scuba chat room.

Within minutes, I was having a great time gabbing with Anna Bronstein, the sysop, and four other people about how hard it was to photograph parrotfish.

Then a guy with the user ID SEA.LION joined the chat.

```
<SEA.LION> Hey there. Are you the same
C.Zukav who's on the scuba list?
```

I blinked, then typed, "Yup, that's me."

<SEA.LION> Cool. I just joined up here. Good
to see a familiar face.

It was the same guy, I realized. The one who said his wife died by being scooped.

But everyone on the list said that was just a joke.

I decided that Mr. Sea Lion had been trying to razz the guy who asked the question on the list, so I didn't bring it up in the chat.

At close to eleven, I finally logged off. SEA.LION hadn't said a lot, and none of what he did say mentioned his wife or scoops. And nobody really responded to the few things he did say. This made me feel better for some reason. I announced that I was heading off to my boyfriend's party, and everyone said goodbye.

We live walking distance from UCSD, which is why I never bothered to get a room on campus. Seemed stupid to give up one-fourth of a huge house for one-half of a dorm room the size of my parents' walk-in closet. So I hoofed it to Revelle College's senior dormitory for the party.

I grabbed a beer from the plastic garbage can by the door that was full of ice and Budweiser cans. I couldn't see Gary. But I did see Xcott. I said hi, told him about my dull dive that morning, then asked him why he told Sunni that dumb story.

He laughed. "Oh, man, I'm real sorry, Cass. But Sunni's, like, so easy, y'know?"

Geena walked up just then. "Who's easy?"

"Cass's sister." After Geena fixed him with a very nasty look Xcott quickly said, "I mean she's like, easy to *tease*. Remember, we got her with the forest fire story?"

That brought a smile to Geena's face. "Oh, yeah, she bought that one with a credit card." (Geena always came up with metaphors that sounded wrong somehow.)

I felt reassured after that. Then I asked, "Hey, you seen Gary?"

Xcott frowned. "Not in the last few minutes."

I wandered around for a while, but no sign of Gary. His roommate, Mike, was acting like an asshole in the middle of the room. Half a beer, and Mike was completely plastered. The other four guys who lived in the suite were nowhere to be found—probably off at someone else's party.

Finally, I gave up and went into the bathroom.

That's where I found Gary. He was liplocked with some bimbo. Neither her hair color nor her chest were the ones she was born with.

I stood there with my mouth hanging open. I couldn't actually say anything, but I just kept standing there. They didn't even notice me for something like five minutes. Then Gary came up for air and saw me standing there.

"Oh, uh, hi Cass. How you doin'?" He sounded very drunk. "Didn't hear y'come in. Oh, sorry, this's Bambi. Bambi, this's my friend, Cassie. Sheeza grad student."

Bambi. Her fucking name was Bambi. My boyfriend was making out in the bathroom of his suite with a woman named after a fucking cartoon character, and his reaction is to introduce me to her! As his "friend."

"You goddamn pissant pus-eating slime-caked insectoid Neanderthalic fucking *shithead*!"

Then I threw my beer can at him.

My memory is hazy on what happened next. I think I yelled at him a little. He acted all innocent. Bambi looked confused (probably still trying to figure out what Neanderthalic meant).

Then I stormed out. I think I knocked Mike on his ass when he got in my way. (It's easy when you're 5'11" and really pissed.)

I don't actually remember walking home, but I must've. The next clear memory I have is logging on.

Sure enough, the scuba chat was still going on. However, the only two people in the room were SEA.LION and Anna the sysop. This scrolled by just after I came into the chat room:

```
<SEA.LION> They finally found her in the
forest. Right there in the *middle* of the
forest. In full scuba gear. I mean, how else
did she get there?
```

Oh God.

I didn't type anything until Anna prompted me:

<A.Bronstein (Anna)> Hey there, Cass. How
was the party?

Thank you Anna, for changing the subject. "Lousy." I typed.
"My boyfriend is the scum of the earth."

We went on for a while about how men are pigs. Mr. Sea Lion
didn't say a word until he finally left the room without even saying goodbye. Some others joined the chat, at which point Anna,
good sysop that she was, steered the topic back onto diving stuff.

When I left, I checked the email on my UCSD account. There
were four. One was from Gary, time-stamped from before the
party, which I deleted without reading. Two were from the scuba
list. The last was from the Sea Lion. "Sorry for leaving so suddenly," he said. "I just wanted to warn you to be careful. With all
the fires over in your neck of the woods, diving might be risky."

I don't know what possessed me, but I actually replied to this. I
decided to play dumb, and ask what possible connection there
could be between diving and forest fires.

After I sent it, I regretted it, but it was too late.

Maybe he'd ignore it.

I went down to the kitchen, yanked open the freezer, and was
relieved to find that Sunni hadn't touched my tub of chocolate
chip cookie dough ice cream. I put a depressing Nick Cave album on the CD player, ate ice cream, and tried to come up with
imaginative ways to kill Gary.

I didn't get a reply to my e-mail to Mr. Sea Lion for two days,
but when I did, it was a doozy.

I'd spent Sunday holed up in my room with Keats. Sunni tried
talking to me at one point, but I gave her a real nasty look, and
she stayed away from me for the rest of the day. I spent Monday
on campus, helping Liverakos, and being surly to anyone who
came within ten feet of me.

Monday night, I logged on and found a pile of scuba list e-
mail, another e-mail from Gary (I didn't delete it—yet—but I
didn't read it, either), and one from the Sea Lion.

He wasn't kidding. He hadn't been pulling anyone's leg. His
wife really was found in full scuba gear in the middle of a forest
fire that had been put out in Canada somewhere.

The e-mail he sent went on for several pages. It was into all kinds of specific detail—where his wife was found, where she'd been seen last, stuff like that—most of which I glossed over.

My first thought was: *It's true. It's all true.*

My second thought was: *Get a grip, stupid. You don't know who this guy is. You don't even know his real name.*

He's probably just a psycho. There are lots of them on the net.

I closed the file and read the rest of the stuff from the list. It was a typical day's worth of messages: Lucienne had just gotten back from the Cayman Islands and posted the beginning of her trip report; Greg's dive computer turned out to be a lemon, and he posted full brand information so people could avoid it; Glenn and Brandy asked for hotel recommendations in Key West, to which half a dozen people had replied; and the schmuck calling himself "The Regulator" kept the flamewar about solo diving going for another day. All typical, ordinary, normal diving talk. No scoops. No charred corpses in forests.

Then the phone rang. We have a dedicated modem line, so the call didn't kick me offline, but it took me a minutes to locate the cordless—I barely made it before the machine kicked in. "Hello?"

"Cass, it's Geena. You seen Xcott today?"

"Uh, no, why?"

"'Cause I haven't seen him since noon, that's why. His gear's all gone, though."

I sighed. "Geena, are all the boats still there?"

"Uh, I think so—lemme check."

I heard Geena put the phone down, and I put my head in my hands. She didn't even think to check the boats. Worse, if Xcott's not around, she's supposed to be managing the dive shop, and she doesn't know if all the boats are accounted for?

"Well, the boats are all there," Geena said when she got back to the phone, "but Manfred just told me that Xcott had been talking about doing a beach dive. So maybe that's where he is. Sorry to've bothered you, Cass."

"Hey, no big deal. Hey, did you read Lucienne's trip report yet?"

From there, we spent half an hour doing scuba gossip. Geena

was still pretty worried about Xcott, since he obviously went off somewhere without telling her. I thought at first that that was pretty mean—what if something happened to him? But then, I didn't always tell Sunni or my parents where I was going all the time. Hell half the time, they'd only know I was gone because the truck wasn't in the driveway.

By the time we got off the phone, it was almost ten. Liverakos had some kind of family thing Tuesday, so I had to handle his sophomore lit class by myself—and it started at eight-thirty. So I got undressed and climbed into bed.

At one, the phone rang. I'd kept the cordless in my room so it woke me up. "Mfginer?" I said, the closest I could come to, "Why the hell're you calling me at this hour?"

"Cass, it's Geena!" She sounded completely nuts—the way Sunni sounded when she broke a nail. "Xcott *still* hasn't come back! Marty and Nic said they saw him do a beach dive at six, and he hasn't come back yet. We gotta find him—can you get down to the shop?"

"Uh—"

"And bring your dive light!" And then she hung up.

I stared at the phone for a while, not sure that this wasn't all part of a dream.

After a minute, I realized that it wasn't, and that I'd never hear the end of it if I didn't go down to the shop. Besides which, I'd never get back to sleep.

I clambered out of bed, put on a bathing suit, started to go downstairs, remembered I'd need my gear, went back upstairs, grabbed the dive bag, started down again, remembered Geena asking me to bring the dive light, went back up again, rummaged through my closet, found the light, put it in the bag, then went down a third time.

The television sounded from the living room. I went in to find my father channel surfing, various bits of paperwork all over the floor around him. He did this when he had to stay up late working—take occasional TV breaks.

"Where you going, hon?" he asked hitting the "mute" button on the remote.

"Dive shop," I said, and realized that I sounded like the walk-

239

ing dead. I was not in any shape to dive, much less search for someone who probably had already finished his dive and gone home and didn't bother to call Geena. Or maybe he was seeing another woman. It's all the rage these days. Maybe he and Gary had a contest to see who could cheat on their girlfriends more successfully. Or maybe Nic and Marty saw someone else on the beach. Why wasn't I in bed like a sensible person?

"Isn't it a little, uh—late for that?"

"Some kinda crisis. Gotta go help."

My father frowned. "Well, okay, but be careful. And remember, it is a school night."

I nodded and started to leave. My father gave me a final concerned look, then demuted the TV.

"*—fires are now under control. One body was found in what was left of an oak tree, apparently wearing some kind of r—*"

"*—nd, there can be only one. May it be Du—*"

Suddenly, I was wide awake. "Go back!"

"What?" my father asked.

"Go back to that news thing on the fires!"

He flipped the channel. "*—e'll have more on the latest fire to hit Southern California in a little while. Up next, Headline Sports.*"

Then it cut to a commercial.

"What was it he said?" I asked. "The body was wearing what?"

"I'm not really sure. Why?"

"Did he say 'rubber'?"

"I don't think so. Cassie, are you okay?"

I shook my head. This was insane. "Never mind, it's nothing. Really."

Of course, it was nothing. That was just a story. A myth. It didn't really happen. How the hell would they get the scoops onto the helicopters anyhow? It was crazy.

I went out to the driveway, tossed my dive bag into the bad of the truck, got in and pulled out.

"*They've got these, y'know, helicopters with these really big scoops, and they scoop up the water and dump it on the fires.*"

"*Cass's sister, I mean she's, like, easy to tease. Remember we got her with the forest fire story?*"

"*Oh yeah, she bought that one with a credit card.*"

"They finally found her in the forest, Right there in the middle of the forest. In full scuba gear. I mean, how else did she get there?"

"One body was found in what was left of an oak tree..."

No, it was stupid. Xcott was probably off drinking somewhere. He had not been dumped on a forest fire.

I pulled into the dive shop parking lot. Several other regulars had shown up and were piling into one of the shop boats. Geena looked the most worried, but everyone seemed kinda nervous. That's when it hit me that Xcott could still be lying dead underwater somewhere. And the cops wouldn't be any help—he hadn't been missing long enough. Just because he hadn't been scooped didn't mean he wasn't in trouble.

So a bunch of us went out in the boat. One guy who's name I couldn't remember was fiddling with the tuner on a radio.

"—orest fires continue to rage—"

Then the guitar riff from some Eric Clapton song or other came on. "There we go," he said. "Always better to dive with classic rock."

We each took an area where we would look for Xcott. When we got to my location, I got onto the platform, held my mask and regulator to my face, and started to stop forward.

"Uh, Cassie?"

I turned back toward the radio fiddler. "What?"

"You may want to put your fins on first."

Great. I can't even remember to put the stupid fins on. As everyone laughed at me, I got off the platform, put on my fins, and then stepped off the platform into the ocean.

I felt like I was being smothered. Tonight, it wasn't a flannel blanket, it was a pillow someone had shoved onto my head. I turned the dive light on and started looking.

Every time the light shone off something metal, I panicked, thinking I was going to get scooped. At one point, I almost lost my regulator, which would not have been a good thing. Then I'd drown and everyone'd be searching for me. Then Gary could feel guilty. Might even be worth it for that.

Christ, Cass, get a grip!

I didn't find him. That's probably because he wasn't there to be found. This whole thing was a waste of time that was just keeping me from getting a good night's sleep. If Xcott did turn up alive, I'd probably kill him.

We each agreed to search for an hour. After I'd been down for forty-five minutes, I headed back up for the surface, giving myself time for a safety stop.

As I trod water twenty feet under the surface, the water started churning. I looked up, pointing the light upward. Between that and the almost-full moon, I could make out some kind of shape right above the water.

I squinted, trying to figure out what the shape was.

After a minute, I realized that it was a helicopter. Panic started bubbling in me—the water churned more as the 'copter moved closer to the water—

—and then it pulled away. The water grew calm again.

If I hadn't been wearing a wetsuit, I would've have put my head in my hands. The 'copter was probably there for some legit reason. Maybe Geena had a friend with access to one and had asked him or her to help look for Xcott.

Whatever it was, it didn't have a scoop and wasn't about to dump me on a forest fire. This was the last time I dive when I'm half-asleep.

Five minutes had passed, so I prepared to swim back up to the surface.

That's when the tentacle grabbed my foot.

I looked quickly down and saw a massive thing that was all scales and teeth. It started pulling me closer. Three days worrying about a scoop, and I get attacked by some kind of crazy sea monster!

My regulator came loose as I started to scream…

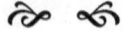

242

Keith R.A. DeCandido is the author of some fifty novels, covering various and sundry universes both his own and other people's. His work in media fiction—prose and comics based on TV shows, movies, comics, and games—earned him a Lifetime Achievement Award from the International Association of Media Tie-in Writers in 2009, which means he never needs to achieve anything ever again. His most recent work ranges from the *Leverage* novel *The Zoo Job* to the "Precinct" series of high fantasy police procedurals (*Dragon Precinct, Unicorn Precinct, Goblin Precinct, Gryphon Precinct*, and the short-story collection *Tales from Dragon Precinct*, as well as upcoming comic books and audios) to the comic book miniseries *The Fallen* (written with Ænder Steven Harris) to the *SCPD* series of cop novels set in a city filled with superheroes (*The Case of the Claw* and *Avenging Amethyst*) to *Star Trek: The Klingon Art of War.*

He's contributed to several shared worlds: Jonathan Maberry's *V-Wars* (the story "The Ballad of Big Charlie"), Steven Savile's *Viral* (the novella *-30-*), and Aaron Rosenberg & David Niall Wilson's *Tales from the Scattered Earth* (the novel *Guilt in Innocence*), and his recent short fiction has appeared in *Apocalypse 13, Bad-Ass Faeries: It's Elemental, Defending the Future 5: Best-Laid Plans, Dragon's Lure, More Tales of Zorro, Star Trek: Seven Deadly Sins*, and *Tales from the House Band Volumes 1 & 2.*

Keith is also an editor, having put together many anthologies and supervised many a book line; a musician, the percussionist with the parody band Boogie Knights (you can hear him on their CDs *Many a Sleepless Knight* and *Wasted Days and Wasted Knights*); a black belt in *Kenshikai* karate; a longtime fan of the New York Yankees (he co-edited *In the Dugout: Yankeres 2013* for Lindy's Sports with Cecilia M. Tan); and a veteran podcaster, contributing to *The Chronic Rift*, doing his own podcast *Dead Kitchen Radio*, and doing voices for the audio dramas *HG World*, *Gypsy Cove*, *The Dome*, and more.

Find out less at his cheerfully retro web site:
DeCandido.net
which is a gateway to his blog, his Facebook page,
his Twitter feed, and tons and tons and tons more:

kradical.livejournal.com
www.facebook.com/kradec
@KRADeC on Twitter

Follow Cassie Zukav on Twitter:

@CassieZukav

www.ingramcontent.com/pod-product-compliance
Lightning Source LLC
Chambersburg PA
CBHW020204270626
47157CB00028B/1125